Thank you Pam, for allowing me to use (The Honeymoon Cottage).
Also to Lynda and Colin, co-inventors of The Pithing Puffer.
Not forgetting Anne and Malcolm Gray, Bev and Pete Carter, Irene,
Pip's Nickertut, and Adizian the Mighty Atom, Magnus, Mary, and the
gang in Sweden. I am sure that if your houses could talk, they would
only say nice things about you.

Tomas Stone

One of the founders of the famous Bayswater Road Art Exhibition, London born Artist and Stage Hypnotist, Tomas Stone, lived for over thirty six years in Luton. Now retired, he lives with his wife Pamela, in the beautiful town of Beaminster in Dorset.

Tomas has written both **Bony Willy the Naked Viking** and **Long John Silver's Magical Bicycle Bell.** This is his third published novel. To those whose eyes travel the pages, he has one word to say, (enjoy).

Also by Tomas Stone:

Bony Willy the Naked Viking

ISBN: 978-1-84944-006-6

Long John's Magical Bicycle Bell

ISBN: 978-1-84944-017-2

ISBN: 978-1-84944-043-1

British Library Cataloguing in Publication Data.
A catalogue record for this book is available from the British Library.

Published by UKUnpublished

UKUnpublished
.co.uk

www.ukunpublished.co.uk
info@ukunpublished.co.uk

Whoever Said Houses Can't Talk.

###

A whimsical fantasy.

Houses are inanimate. They show no signs of consciousness or life, therefore they lack the qualities of human beings.

The houses in Piddle Close however are unique. They are able to take note of everything that their tenants say and do and they have the ability to talk to each other.

If your house could talk, would it be gossiping about you?

Whoever Said Houses Can't Talk

By

Tomas Stone

Prologue

Burnbury

Situated some six miles from Melderton-on-Sea, the ancient town of Burnbury stands like an undiscovered island in a sea of green fields. Like sleeping beauty, time seems to have passed it by. The town boasts one church, one cemetery filled to overflowing, five shops one of which is an undertaker's, two public houses, and a population of three thousand two hundred.

Once there had been four pubs. For year after year, the thirsty drinkers of Burnbury had willingly poured drink after drink down their throats in a determined effort to support them. Bravely, on behalf of the pubs, they had suffered headaches and hangovers to keep them open, but 'The Star' and 'The Jumping Cricket' had been running at a loss for too long. With their minds set only on profit, the brewers decided that the time had come to close them down.

The two publicans both agreed that before they shut their doors for the last time, they would each throw a party. With free drinks for all of their regulars, and to hell with closing time, the partygoers had managed to drink both pubs practically dry.

A quick lick of paint plus some interior refurbishment soon changed the two ancient public houses into sought after domestic residences.

The painted signs still swinging and creaking in the wind outside, remind ex-customers of what they have lost, they also tell strangers to the town, that the two houses they enviously admire were once 'The Star' and 'The Jumping Cricket'.

During the summer, 'The Red Lion' and 'The Owl and Duck' become busy near the seaside watering holes, filled with tourists sampling the local brew as they enjoy the simple pleasures of country life.

The thatched roofed 'Red Lion' with its oak beamed ceilings, and inglenook fireplaces, simply oozes old-world charm.

Strangers to the pub cannot fail to notice Mr Bones the skeleton sitting at the end of the public bar, with his bony fingers wrapped around a pint of best bitter and a sandwich on a plate in front of him. Placed upon the stool by Malcolm the landlord when he took over the tenancy, Mr Bones has become a popular macabre attraction for holidaymakers who visit the pub. Often, he receives mail from them when they return home, telling him how much they had enjoyed his company and enquiring about his health. For the time being Mr Bones seems content to sit at the bar with his fresh sandwich and pint gazing sightlessly back at the past. Malcolm however has big plans for the skeleton's future, he dreams that one day Mr Bones will be able to hold an intelligent conversation with anyone who wants to speak to him. To achieve his dream, when he isn't working behind the bar, Malcolm can be found studying books and manuals in his search for the information that will show him how he can hide a miniature speaker in a skeletons head and animate his jaw.

Mr Bones doesn't always sit at the bar. Sometimes on cold winter evenings, he sits in the inglenook with some of the regulars. With a permanent grin on his face and a pint in his hand, he sits silently listening to their conversations. His expression always remains the same, even when their words get heated.

Most of the winter fireside regulars, are looking forward to the day when the speaker has been successfully installed in his skull and his mouth moves in synchronization with Malcolm's words when he speaks into a throat microphone. Then, instead of being a silent observer, the skeleton will be able to add his own words to their discussions.

Most of the townsfolk have lived all of their lives in Burnbury, and they know every house in every street. Eight years ago a developer built nine pairs of semidetached properties on a vacant plot of land. When they were finished, the council decided to name the small residential road after its developer Mr Arthur Piddle, so they called it Piddle Close.

###CHAPTER ONE###

July

Number 1 Piddle Close had been silent since the sun went down. As it started to peep over the horizon the next morning, the house gave a sigh.

'What's the matter with you?' mumbled Number 2. 'You haven't spoken a single word to any of the houses in the close all night. Are you feeling depressed or something?'

'I'm not depressed. It's a bit more than that.' The house sighed again. 'I'm distressed.'

'You shouldn't let things get you down. You're far too young to be distressed, that only happens to old houses, you're practically a new build.'

'It is nice of you to say that, but I wouldn't exactly call myself a new build, I'm nearly eight years old.'

'I already know how old you are, you're the same age as me. We're semidetached; I'm your conjoined twin.'

'It's my new tenants; they are really getting on my nerves. They've only lived in me for a couple of months and I'm frightened that if they remove any more of my inner walls I'm going to collapse.'

4

Number 2 sounded puzzled. 'Why have they taken walls down?'

Number 1 snorted a thick cloud of obnoxious looking smoke out of her chimney. 'They wanted an open plan kitchen and a see through lounge. I haven't a clue where they lived before they moved here, but wherever it was I should think the ruin of their old house was glad to see the back of them when they left.'

'This close has really come down in its quality of residents since we were first erected. In the old days, even if tenants moved in without much furniture, they always used proper furniture vans.'

'Your right,' agreed Number 1. 'Did you see what the family living in me used?'

'No, unfortunately I missed it.' Number 2 sounded annoyed. 'I was asleep at the time and none of the other houses thought to wake me.'

'I'm glad that you didn't see it, but, all of the other houses in the close did. I felt really embarrassed when two adults, three snotty nosed kids, four cats, a budgerigar and two dogs, turned up at half-past two in the morning with all their furniture packed inside an old ice-cream van.' Number One paused for breath. 'When the van pulled into the close, there was so much smoke coming out of its exhaust it looked like it was dragging a big black cloud along. And the noise it made when it came to a shuddering halt in the gutter in front of me, succeeded in waking most of the residents in the close.'

'I must have been extra tired that night,' said Number 2 lazily. 'I didn't hear a thing. Were they *really* that noisy?'

'The dogs were barking loud enough to wake the dead, and as soon as the children got out of the van they started kicking an empty coke can around. As you already know, it's normally as quiet as a graveyard around here at half-past two in the morning, even a whisper can sound like a shout and the people who were moving into me, haven't yet learnt how to whisper.'

'Except Friday nights,' said Number 2. 'It's never as quiet as a graveyard around here on a Friday night.'

Number 1 tutted impatiently. 'Shall I continue, or do you want to have a debate about Friday nights?'

'I quite like Friday nights,' murmured Number 3. 'I think they're exciting. Especially when some of the residents in the close come home from the pubs shouting and singing, and then someone says something out of place and they all end up having an argument. That was a good one last week when Mr Peacock at Number 7 threw half a brick at his wife, luckily she saw it coming and ducked, then, it went flying through their neighbours window.'

'You won't think it's so good if it ever happens to you,' mumbled the house with the boarded downstairs front window.

'You would think they'd appreciate a nice house and take good care of me.' Number 1 craftily steered the conversation back to the subject of her new tenants. 'But the family living under my roof seem to get their kicks out of pulling me apart.'

'I put it down to drink and drugs,' said Number 2. 'And you've also been very unlucky. How many families have you housed so far?'

'Seven. That's a family a year for every year of my life.'

'No it isn't,' said Number 19, the only detached house in the close. - *Privately built on a large plot of land two years ago, it stood out like a white daisy in a field of poppies.* - 'You just told him that you are nearly eight.'

'I am nearly eight, but not quite, so it's a family a year for every year of my life so far, so there.' Number 1, didn't like Number 19 very much, she thought she was rather pompous and stuck up.

'How many times have you been trashed?' asked Number 2.

'Seven. I've been trashed by every family that's ever lived in me.'

'It's like I said,' grunted Number 2. 'You've been very unlucky.'

'And I don't think my luck is about to change with the lot that's living in me now, unless it is for the worse. I really hate kids and they have two sons and a daughter. The daughter's three years old coming on four and she hasn't been potty trained yet. The boys are nine and thirteen. The thirteen year old is an unruly shaven-headed monster called Damien. I wouldn't be at all surprised if he's got three 666's tattooed on the top of his head and cloven hoofs inside his shoes.'

Number 4 decided to get into the conversation. 'What's the nine year old like?'

'His name is Stuart, but I call him Vincent. His mother and father are very proud of him; they believe he has the talent to be a great artist when he grows up. I suppose that's why they have allowed him to paint pictures on all of the walls that they have left standing. I call him Vincent because he seems to have a passion for painting sunflowers, but I think he's taken the art of painting that particular flower a bit further than Van Gough ever did, unless he also painted a gigantic four by three metre blue one on his bedroom ceiling.'

'It must have been really hard work for a nine year old to paint a large picture like that on a ceiling,' said Number 4. 'How long did he take to do it?'

'He was at the top of a stepladder for about three and a half hours, before he got bored and packed up.'

'I've never heard of a blue sunflower before. What does it look like?'

'Blooming awful, but his mother thinks it's the best thing he has ever painted.'

'What about the father?'

'He prefers the black one in the toilet.'

'Do you believe he has artistic talent?'

'I won't answer that question if you don't mind. You know that I don't like to swear.'

'Why did he paint it on his bedroom ceiling?' asked **Number 3**. 'Was it because he had run out of walls?'

Number 1 blew another cloud of soot out of her chimney. 'Practically every inch of space on my walls is covered with his paintings. There are matchstick men going up the stairs, there's a knight fighting a dragon on the loft trapdoor, and there's a picture of a two-headed parrot on the patio door. He has even painted a portrait of his mother inside the toilet pan, but *hopefully* that will be washed away, when someone *finally* gets round to pulling the chain.'

###CHAPTER TWO###

Number 2 coughed to get Number 1's attention. 'What on earth is that dreadful smell coming out of your windows and back door?'

'I was hoping, that you wouldn't notice it.' **Number 1 sounded embarrassed.**

Number 2 sniffed and coughed again. 'I wish I hadn't, it's really quite vile. What is it?'

'Priscilla wet her knickers during the night and her mother dried them in the tumble dryer.'

'Didn't she think to wash them first?'

'She might have, but if she did, she didn't bother to do it.'

'If it smells as bad as this on the outside, what must it be like in the room where the tumble dryer is?'

'Don't ask, but I reckon that room is going to smell like a Victorian public house toilet for weeks.'

'I doubt if Victorian public house toilets smelt any worse than public house toilets do today,' **shouted Number 19 from across the street.**

'They *did* you know,' **Number 2 shouted back.** 'They didn't have the disinfectants and deodorizers that we have today.'

'Have you any idea what your family will be up to today?' **asked Number 3.** 'Do you think it will be something worth watching?'

'It isn't my family, said **Number 1 indignantly.** 'I haven't got a family. Houses don't have families. The Kreamer's are the family living under my roof, but they definitely aren't my family.'

'You have got a family,' said **number 2.** 'You've got me. I'm your conjoined twin.'

'That's a different kind of thing. Every house in the close has a conjoined twin, but that isn't family in the true sense of the word.'

'Not me,' said **Number 19 arrogantly.** 'I'm detached. I haven't got a conjoined twin.'

'Do you think it be something worth watching?' **Number 3 asked again.**

'Oh yes, it will be worth watching all right, but unfortunately we won't be able to see it.'

'Why won't we?' **Number 3 sounded disappointed.**

'They're all going out for the day. The little darling's father is taking them on a trip to the Zoo. I heard them planning it last night.'

Number 19 gave a little cheer. 'My owners will be pleased to see them leave. When they go out, it's usually nice and peaceful in the close'

'But it won't be peaceful will it? If your owners decide to have a slanging match, like they did last week.'

'Are the Kreamer's going in the ice cream van?' asked **Number 2.**

'Of course they are. Didn't you hear the racket he made getting it ready?'

'They won't get very far in that old van,' said **Number 4 gleefully.** 'Last night, just before bedtime, I saw young Damien stick a rather large banana up the exhaust.'

'I hope his father finds it and takes it out,' whispered **Number 1.** 'I really want them to get to the Zoo. Who knows? With a bit of luck, he might decide to leave his little monsters there and bring three chimpanzees back instead.'

'The van doesn't look very hygienic does it?' said **Number 19** pompously. 'He won't be trying to sell ice creams when he gets there, will he?'

'He told his wife that he had taken a good day's wages at a cricket match yesterday, so he intends to take the whole day off and walk around the Zoo with her and the kids.'

Number 19 sounded like she was beginning to enjoy herself. 'Cricket fans can't have much in the way of brains if they are happy to sit in the sun all day watching someone throw a ball at a bat, but even they must have a bit of grey matter, so why did they actually spend good money buying ice creams from a dirty scruffy looking individual like him?'

'I wonder if he's licensed to sell ice creams?' shouted **Number 15**.

'I suppose he had a license once, when the van was new,' said **Number 14**. 'That however would have been a long time ago. I doubt if he has got one now.'

'It doesn't seem right, does it?' said **Number 2**. 'Whilst he and his brood are walking around the zoo pulling faces at monkeys and teasing the lions, most of his yesterday customers could be doubled up in bed with stomach pains.'

'This is going to be fun,' **Number 19** sounded excited. 'They are all getting into the van. I wonder what will happen when he tries to start it.'

All of the houses in the close stood silently watching; eagerly waiting to see what would happen.

'Doesn't the father know a lot of swear words,' said **Number 3**.

When a few minutes later, the family climbed despondently out of the van.

'He knows quite a few,' grunted Number 1. 'But Damien knows a lot more than him, and he delivers them with more venom.'

Mr Kreamer looked puzzled. 'I can't think what it can be,' he said scratching his head. 'The van was behaving perfectly yesterday.'

Stuart pulled several different coloured chalks from his pocket. Parking his bum in the middle of the road, he started to draw a huge multi coloured sunflower. Three-year-old Priscilla stood sucking her thumb watching the masterpiece take shape. Then, she started to cry.

'What's up with Priscilla?' Mrs Kreamer shouted from inside the house.

Stuart quickly moved his chalks away from a growing puddle. 'She's gone and wet herself again,' he shouted in reply.

'Be a darling Stuart, will you take her knickers off and bring them into me so that I can put them in the tumble dryer.'

'Here we go again,' mumbled Number 2. 'As soon as that tumble dryer starts working, my twin is going to smell like a Victorian public house toilet.'

As Mrs Kreamer pushed Priscilla's wet knickers into the tumble dryer, Damien walked out of the front door carrying two bananas.

'What are you doing with *two* bananas?' asked his dad. 'You're not that hungry are you?'

'Don't be silly,' Damien mumbled under his breath. 'I don't intend to eat them. I'm going to stick them up a couple of exhaust pipes.'

'Will we be going to the zoo today or not?' shouted Mrs Kreamer from the doorway.'

Dennis Kreamer scratched his head with an oily hand. 'It doesn't look like it,' he replied.

Mrs Kreamer shrugged her shoulders and walked back inside. 'If that's the case, I'm going to set up a picnic in the garden for the kids.'

'Don't do anything for me,' Dennis shouted back. 'I haven't got time to eat. I've got to find out what's wrong with this blasted van; it was working like a dream last night.'

Damien glanced slyly over his shoulder, when he was sure that his father wasn't looking in his direction, he rammed a banana in the exhaust of the car standing outside Number 19. He was half way back to his house when he stopped. With a devilish grin, he turned and walked back to the car. When he walked away again, there were two bananas blocking the exhaust.

'My owners won't be very happy if they can't start their car, when they want to go out later,' moaned Number 19.

'Your owners are never happy,' snapped Number 1. 'But today, with two large bananas stuck up their cars exhaust, they will really have something to be miserable about.'

Mr Kreamer wiped his lips with the back of his hand smearing thick black grease across his mouth, then, he looked down at Damien's empty hands. 'You greedy little pig, have you eaten those bananas already?'

Damien grinned up at his dad. 'If we're not going to the zoo, I think I'll have a lay down on my bed and read a comic.'

###CHAPTER THREE###

August

The last two weeks of July had been the hottest ever recorded in Dorset, and according to the weather forecasters, August was set to continue the same.

'Morning Number 2,' said Number 3 mournfully. 'How are you standing up to this heat?'

'The mortar between my ridge tiles has turned to dust, apart from that I think it's great. I like to feel a bit of heat on my roof; it beats rain and snow any day.'

Number 3 sighed wearily. 'I don't know how much more I can take in my loft, with the sun beating down relentlessly hour after hour and day after day, it's hotter than an oven up there.'

'It's the same for all of us you know,' grunted Number 4 unsympathetically. 'You're not the only one this heat is affecting, just look around and you will see that none of us are standing in the shade.'

'It's worse for me,' Number 3 sighed again. 'I doubt if you, or any of the other houses in the close, have got their attics lined with tinfoil.'

'Why has your tenant lined your attic with tinfoil?' asked Number 2 curiously.

'My tenant didn't do it, it was his son Percy. I think he has turned into a mad gardener. He has about thirty pot plants in the loft and he keeps eight one hundred watt light bulbs burning all day and night. I dread to think how much their electric bill would be, if his dad didn't fiddle the meter.'

'No wonder you're feeling hot, eight one hundred watt light bulbs give out a lot of heat, especially if they're burning twenty four seven.'

'You know what he is doing, don't you?' Number 4 said knowingly. 'If he's lined the attic with tin foil and growing pot plants under electric light, then he's growing happy weed.'

'I can't understand why they call it happy weed,' said Number 1. 'Have you seen the state of some of the people who smoke it?'

'I've noticed that there's been a strange, sickly, sweet smell around here lately,' Number 2, whispered to Number 3. 'I wasn't sure if it was coming from you, or Number 1.'

'Last month you said that Number 1 smelt like a Victorian public house toilet, do you think that I smell as bad as that?'

Number 2 had a bit of a soft spot for Number 3. He found her more attractive than the other female houses in the close, mainly because she was the only one with a ground floor bay window. 'Of course you don't,' he said reassuringly. 'You smell more *sweet* than sickly, besides, you can't help it if one of your idiot tenants is growing cannabis up in your roof space and smoking it in your lounge. I wonder if his parents know what's going on above their heads.'

'Of course they know. That's why his father fixed the electric meter.'

'Do you think they smoke the wacky baccy as well?'

'They're smoking it all the time, and his mother uses it when she's baking biscuits. She says it gives them a flavour that's unique.'

'That figures,' said Number 2. 'The three of them always seem to be soppy, but happy.'

Number 4 tutted gravely. 'This close seems to be going down hill fast. First it was an unhygienic ice cream seller, and now we've got a drug baron.'

'That's not fair,' said Number 3 protectively. 'You can't really call him a baron. I don't think he sells any of it.'

'How many plants did you say he's got up in the attic?'

'Thirty.'

'If he's got thirty plants, then he must be selling some of it on. They would all have to be chain-smoking for twenty four hours a day, to get through that many leaves.'

'Don't forget the cooking.' Number 4 was really enjoying himself; he hadn't had as much fun since Mr Peacock at Number 7 threw half a brick at his wife and it went through the window at Number 8. 'His mother would use a lot of leaves if she's making biscuits.'

Number 3 decided to come clean. 'He's got another twenty two plants growing in the greenhouse at the bottom of the garden. He calls it his nursery.'

Number 4 did some quick arithmetic. 'That's fifty two cannabis plants,' he gasped. 'He can't be growing that many for his own use, he must be dealing.'

'How often does he water them?' asked Number 1. 'Fifty two plants will drink an awful lot of water.'

'He fits the hose on the cold tap in the bath and runs it up to the loft every morning and night, then, he strips down to his boxer shorts and goes up and drenches them with water.'

Number 5 suddenly showed a bit of interest. 'Why does he strip down to his boxers? Is he kinky as well as an addict?'

'Your cavities must be really thick if you don't know why he strips off,' rasped Number 1. 'With eight one hundred watt bulbs burning day and night, it must be as hot as hell up there.'

'I feel really sorry for you Number 3,' **said Number 6 softly.** 'With all that water slopping about in your loft, it can't be doing your bedroom ceilings any good. Are they water marked yet?'

'They've gone way beyond being marked. The one in his parent's bedroom came down on them the other night whilst they were asleep.'

'The poor things,' **Number 6 sounded genuinely concerned.** 'It must have scared them half to death.'

'They didn't know it had happened until they woke the next morning and found their bed covered in plasterboard.'

'Had they been smoking the happy weed before they retired for the night?'

'No more than they usually do, but they did drink a few small double whiskies, and they were more than just a bit tipsy when they climbed up the wooden hill to bed.'

Number 2's letterbox rattled slightly as he tried to muffle his laughter.

'What are you laughing at?' asked Number 3 indignantly.

'It stuck me as funny. The two old folk went to bed plastered, and after a good night's sleep they woke up in the same condition.'

'It's nothing to laugh at,' said **Number 1.** 'I know how it feels. I haven't had any of my ceilings come down, but mine have ghastly pictures painted on them. And so many of my walls have been taken away, I'm just a shell of what I used to be.'

'You know whose to blame don't you?' **said Number 19.** 'It's the people living in the Council houses, and they are all claiming benefit I suppose. If they had to find the money to pay their own rent then maybe they would treat you with a bit more respect. I count myself lucky that I am not a Council house property like all of you. Mr and Mrs Wyatt-Jones bought me for cash, which makes me privately owned.'

'Hey! You just watch what you're saying.' Number 7 shouted angrily. 'Most of the houses in this close *are* private. Only six belong to the Council, and they haven't any reason to be ashamed. They were built as strong as you were. Unfortunately, we couldn't do anything about it when you were being erected. If we had been able to choose what kind of property we would have liked standing in the close with us, your foundations would never have been laid.'

Number 19, didn't have anything else to say for the rest of the day.

###CHAPTER FOUR###

Dennis Kreamer walked to the back of his van and examined the exhaust. Satisfied that there were no foreign bodies stuck up the pipe he got to his feet. 'I'm going to the football ground today,' he shouted to his wife. 'They are playing at home so there should be a good crowd. Who knows? I might even be able to make a decent day's wages.'

'Are you ready for it Number 2?' said Number 1.

Number 2 yawned sleepily. 'Why did you have to wake me?' he snapped irritably. 'I was having a lovely dream.'

'I was trying to do you a favour. I wouldn't have bothered, if I had known that you were going to be testy. I thought you would like to know that my tenant is about to start his ice cream van.'

Number 2 was suddenly wide-awake. 'Thank's,' he said. 'I'm really grateful that you woke me. If he had started the van whilst I was asleep, the explosions from that blasted exhaust would have shaken my roof tiles and one or two might have fallen off. Now that I know he's going to start that monstrous thing, I'll be able to brace myself against the shaking and they shouldn't get disturbed.'

'What about the odious smoke that comes out of the back and creates a fog in the close?' asked Number 1. 'How do you combat that?'

'I swallow it.' Number 2 replied. 'Like the rest of you.'

Percy Grant picked up a plastic bag that had been standing on a table at the foot of the stairs and opened the front door. 'I won't be a minute mum,' he shouted towards the kitchen. 'I'm just popping out to have a word with Dennis Kreamer.'

'Alright darling,' a voice replied. 'I'll have another batch of nice tasty biscuits ready by the time you get back.'

'Where's he going Number 3?' asked Number 4.

'Where's who going?'

'Your young green fingered tenant.'

'Oh, you mean the drug baron. He's just told his mother that he's going to have a word with the ice cream man.'

'He will have to hurry if he wants to catch him; he's just about to turn the corner.'

Slamming the door behind him, Percy ran into the cloud of dark grey smoke coming out of the back of the van. Then, the roaring engine stopped and the smoke drifted away.

Dennis Kreamer turned in the drivers seat slide the window open and poked his head outside. 'It's a good job you caught me before I left the close. Once I'm on a straight road this little old van really starts to move. In a minute or two I would have been out of sight.'

'You were out of sight before you started moving,' Percy said with a grin. 'Your van pumps out so much carbon, it's invisible to anyone standing at the other side of the road.'

Kreamer sat coughing for several seconds. 'You're exaggerating,' he said. 'It's not as bad as that.' Then, he started coughing again.

'Where are you off to?' asked Percy.

'I'm going to the football stadium. There's an important match today, so there's sure to be a good crowd.'

Percy held the bag up for Kreamer to see. 'I've got some of my mum's specials in here; do you want to take them?'

'Are they as good as the last batch?'

'Judging from the state she was in when she was cooking them, I would say that they are even better.'

Kreamer pulled the bag through the window and laid it on the seat beside him. 'What's your mother like at ordinary cooking?' he asked.

'Percy shrugged his shoulders. 'How would I know? She never does any.'

Kreamer glanced at his watch. 'I'll have to be on my way, I want to get parked as near to the Stadium as I can. There's nothing I like better than watching my regulars licking a ninety nine and munching a tasty biscuit, while they are queuing to get in.'

Percy nodded down at the bag lying next to Kreamer. 'Once your punters have got one or two of those little darlings inside them, they'll come out of the stadium at the end of the match as happy as Harry and singing their heads off, even if their team has been beaten by eight or nine goals.'

Kreamer shook his head doubtfully. 'Your specials may be good,' he said, 'but they're not that good.'

Number 19 had been in a particularly nasty mood all morning. As she watched Percy swagger nonchalantly back to his house, she shouted across the road. 'You mark my words Number 3. When it gets out that Percy Grant and his parents are farming cannabis in your loft and back garden, you're going to get raided by the police.'

'Do you really think so?' said **Number 3** nervously. 'Can you tell me what happens when they raid a drug pusher's house?'

'I've never actually seen a police raid myself. As you already know, I'm the newest house in the close and there hasn't been enough trouble to merit a raid since I've been standing here. But I saw one in a programme on the television a couple of days ago.'

'Now I suppose you're going to boast about your tenant's new digital giant flat screen television,' snapped **Number 6** jealously.

'Actually, I wasn't going to mention *our* new television.' **Number 19** had put on the voice that irritated all of the other houses in the close. 'But I can tell from the tone of your voice that you must have seen it arrive.'

Number 6 liked nothing better than a good row, and he was clever enough to know that if he kept sniping at Number 19 he would end up having one. 'That's right I saw it arrive, and no doubt I will see the police when they arrive to arrest your tenant's for buying stolen goods.'

In her anger, Number 19 dropped her posh voice. 'If you are inferring that our new television fell off the back of a lorry, then you are wrong. If you really must know, it cost over £1500 and my owners bought it in a proper shop.'

'Will someone tell me what will happen if the police raid me?' shouted Number 3.

'The police are really crafty devils,' said Number 19. 'They usually arrive at about five thirty in the morning when everyone is tucked up in bed fast asleep. When they decide to raid you, we will all be aroused early one morning by the sound of police cars arriving in the close. Three or four cars will pull up outside your front door and about a dozen specialist officers dressed in riot gear and armed with battering rams will jump out run up the path and bash your front door down. Then, they will all belt up the stairs and arrest young Percy and his mum and dad. It will all be over before the old folk have time to put their false teeth back in their mouths. After they have been handcuffed, they will take them to the police station and hold them for questioning.'

'What about the drugs in the attic and garden. What will the police do about them?'

'Your guess is as good as mine. Before they got to that part in the program I was watching, Mr Wyatt-Jones said he wanted to see the news and turned to another channel. As far as I know, any substances that they find are supposed to be taken away to be analyzed. However, I wouldn't be at all surprised if the police take all of the plants back to the nick and share them amongst the other officers. You can't tell me that they don't puff on a bit of wacky-baccy themselves now and again.'

'Don't you go worrying about your front door,' said **Number 7**. 'The police will have to replace it if they break it down, and they will make good any other damage they do as well.'

'But if I get raided by the police, I'm going to lose my good reputation,' said **Number 3 unhappily**. 'People will come from miles around to point at me, and they will call me the drug-house.'

'I wouldn't worry about that if I was you,' said **Number 9**. 'A little bit of notoriety won't do you any harm. Growing a few cannabis plants up in the attic seems to be a minor offence these days. Now if your tenant was running a brothel that would really be serious. The police don't like people who run brothels. Besides they haven't raided you yet, and for all we know they may never find out that your tenants are drug farmers. If I were you, I wouldn't take any notice of Number 19. She's only jealous because she can't get high on exhaled cannabis smoke every night like you.'

'What's a brothel?' asked **Number 3 naively**.

'You don't know much do you?' interrupted **Number One**. 'Everyone knows that a brothel is a place where you can buy broth.'

###CHAPTER FIVE###

September

'Your green beard is quite becoming these days.' Number 5, was referring to the ivy growing up the sides and over the top of Number 6's porch.

'Thank you,' said Number 6. 'It's nice of you to say so. I'm proud of the way it's coming along, it's got a lot thicker these last few weeks, do you think it needs a trim?'

'It needs is a good wash if you ask me.' Number 19 shouted spitefully. 'It's looking more black than green these days.'

'It's Kreamer's fault that it's as dirty as it is. If his old van didn't puff out that obnoxious smoke every time he started it up, my beard would be shiny and healthy looking. It will look smart again, when a good soaking of rain wash's out the soot.'

'It's never going to look smart, even if it rains from now until doomsday,' snapped Number 19. 'And it makes you look a lot older than you really are.'

'You're only saying that because you're jealous that you haven't got one,' said Number 5 protectively.

'My owners have got more sense than to make me grow a beard; they want me to look attractive.'

'They haven't succeeded so far have they?' countered Number 5. 'I haven't seen any passers-by look at you twice like they look at him.'

'I wouldn't want one anyway. Ivy's no good for our brickwork it eats into the mortar.'

'It's got its good side,' Number 6 mumbled under his breath. 'It keeps my porch warm in the winter.'

'What's the matter with you lately Number 19?' asked Number 8 angrily. 'Your always picking on someone, take my advice and cool it. If you're not careful, all of the other houses in the close will send you to Coventry.'

'I wish you could send me to Coventry,' Number 19 replied snobbishly. 'They have classier houses up there. That's where Lady Godiva used to live.'

Number 9 thought the time had come to change the subject. 'I would like you all to know that from today I am going to drop the number part of my name. Number 9 makes me feel like I am a criminal in prison. In future, I would like all of the houses in the close to refer to me as Nine.'

'That's a good idea,' said Number 6. 'Addressing a house as Number this and that does sound a bit impersonal, and it is quite a mouthful. It will be easier and friendlier just calling you Nine. In fact I like the idea so much, I think I will join you.'

Number 1 rattled her letterbox several times in quick succession to get the attention of every house in the close. 'I think we should all vote to see if we would like to drop the Number bit or not.'

'A vote would be democratic,' said Nine. 'So all of you who are in agreement to drop the number prefix and be called by your name, rattle your letterboxes, then, I will count to see who's in agreement.'

Eighteen out of the nineteen houses rattled their letterboxes simultaneously. In response to the rattling, most of the front doors in the close were pulled open. Seconds later, they were closed again, by people wearing puzzled frowns.

'You were the only one who didn't vote.' Nine said to Number 19.

'That's because I'm not a number any longer.' Number 19 replied pompously. 'If you look at the plaque beside my front door you will see that my owners have given me a real name. I am now called Dunroaming.'

'That's a stupid name for a house,' said Five. 'Houses are always stationary, so why did they call you Dunroaming when you've never been anywhere?'

'Mobile homes aren't always stationary,' said Eighteen. *Most of the houses in the close thought that he was a bit thick, but they never told him so.* 'If Number 19 was a mobile home, then, she could be called Dunroaming.'

'But she isn't mobile, is she? She's static like us. What's more, she's arrogant, overbearing, and unfortunately standing in our close. Personally, I don't care what name her owner's have decided to call her. As far as I'm concerned, she is always going to be Number 19.'

'I've had a plaque beside my door with my name spelt on it for years,' said Seven. 'Haven't any of you ever noticed?'

'It isn't a real name like mine,' said Dunroaming. 'It's only your number spelt in capital letters.'

'It is my name.' Seven said adamantly. 'And I can prove it. My tenant's son is called Steven, if you cross out the t it leaves Seven, so if Steven is a boys name then so is Seven.'

'But you're not a male,' said Dunroaming. 'You're female like me. Every house in the country knows that even numbers are male and odd numbers are female. So if you're an odd number, then, you must be female.'

'Blimey,' said Seven. 'If you've got it right, then it's scary, really scary. All of my life I've been standing between two males, and I didn't even know it.'

'You would have known that you were female, if I had been standing next to you, instead of six or eight,' said Two licentiously.

'Have you noticed that the tilers have arrived at Eighteen to replace the tiles that were broken by a rocket last November?' whispered Nine to Ten.

'I should think every house in the close knows the tilers are here by now,' Ten replied. 'The way Eighteen keeps going on about it, anyone would think they're going to replace his whole roof.'

'It does seem to have gone to his *head* a bit.' Nine replied humorously.'

'He won't be so full of himself next week, when he sees the workmen replacing my old front door with a brand new double glazed PVC unit.' boasted Twelve.

Thirteen sounded envious. 'You lucky thing, are you really going to have a new front door?'

Twelve seemed to grow with pride. 'I heard my tenant ordering it on the phone last week.'

'The tilers won't be replacing my tiles today after all,' said Eighteen sadly. 'When they arrived at half past two, I heard one of them tell Mr Curtis my tenant that they were sorry they were late but they had to finish an urgent job before they could come here, but he wasn't to worry because replacing a few broken tiles would only take about an hour. They had only been up on the roof a few minutes when they came down again. "We've been sent the wrong tiles," one of them said. "But don't worry, we haven't taken the broken ones off yet, so if it rains during the night it won't get in, and if it's all right with you we'll leave the ladders where they are, they are quite secure, it will save us wasting time putting them up again in the morning." '

'Hey Eighteen,' Dunroaming shouted to get his attention. 'Have you seen what's climbing up the ladder that the tilers left standing against your wall?'

'Is it a burglar?'

'Of course it isn't a burglar, why would a burglar want to climb a ladder that only takes him to the roof? He would have to remove some tiles before he could gain an entry.'

'If it isn't a burglar, then, what is it?'

'It's a cat.'

Young Samantha Pettigrew, who lived at Number 4, had been standing at the back door for several minutes, calling 'Mr Tom! Mr Tom! Mr Tom! I wonder where he's gone?' she said, closing the door. 'Usually when I'm dishing up his dinner, he's running around my feet trying to trip me up.'

Samantha's father reluctantly dragged his eyes from the television when she walked into the front room. 'Have you seen Mr Tom?' she asked.

'He was sitting on the settee about half an hour ago when I came in to turn the television on. I think he knows that I don't like cats very much, so he got up and walked out. Have you looked in your bedroom? Maybe he went upstairs to have a kip on your bed.'

'I'm worried,' she said. 'It isn't like him to go missing at dinner time. I've been calling him at the back door for ages, and I've searched in all of his favourite hiding places, but I can't find him anywhere.'

'I know where he is.' Her brother's voice came up from the carpet where he was playing with some plastic toy soldiers. 'He's a prisoner of war.' Samantha looked down her nose at Jack. 'Just get on with your game,' she snapped irritably.

Her father's eyes were back on the television watching the football. 'It's your mother's fault; she should have had him seen to months ago. He's probably wandered off for a night on the tiles.'

Mum gave Dad a look that would have turned milk sour. 'That's right, blame me,' she snapped. 'Just because I thought it would be cruel to have him doctored.'

'You didn't think it was cruel when you made me have a vasectomy.'

Some ten minutes later Samantha came back into the room looking worried. 'I've found Mr Tom,' she said.

'Have you dear?' Her mother glanced up from her ironing. 'That's good. Where was he?'

Samantha looked like she was about to burst into tears. 'He's up on the roof at Number 18. It's getting dark and he can't get down.'

'No he isn't.' Jack's voice came up from the carpet again. 'He's a prisoner of war.'

'I see Number 19's owners are peeping from behind their curtains practicing their own special kind of neighbourhood watch.' said Five, to Six. 'I wonder what they are nosing at this time.'

'They seem to be staring up at Eighteen's roof.'

'I can't see why they would want to do that, the workers went home ages ago and they won't be back again until tomorrow.'

'I suppose they're looking at the cat that's walking along the ridge towards the chimney.'

'How on earth did a cat manage to get up on the roof?'

'It must have climbed up the workmen's ladder.'

'I hope all of the other houses are watching this,' said Six, gleefully. 'It looks like it's going to be fun.'

Keith Pettigrew, Samantha's father, kept both eyes on the football match. 'I can't do anything about Mr Tom just yet,' he said. 'I'm watching an

29

important game. How did he get up on the roof anyway?'

'He must have climbed up the ladder that the tilers left leaning against the house.'

'There's nothing I can do if he's up on Mr Curtis' roof. You'll have to go and ask him if he'll climb up and get your crazy cat down.'

Samantha started to cry.

'Alright!' her father shouted irritably pushing himself out of his comfortable chair. 'If you won't do it, then I suppose I'll have to ask him if he'll rescue your cat.'

Tim Curtis and Keith Pettigrew stood at the bottom of the ladder looking up at the cat meowing on the roof. 'I'm not going to climb that ladder,' said Tim. 'Even if you offered to pay me, I wouldn't be able to do it, I'm afraid of heights.'

'So am I,' whispered Keith. 'And it's a long way to climb. Perhaps we should call the fire brigade.'

'I should think you would have to pay if you called them out just to rescue a cat.'

A crafty smile spread across Keith's face. 'I think you'd better conquer your fear of heights and go up and get him if you don't want to pay the firemen for getting him down, after all, he is up on your roof.'

With a look of fear in his eyes, Tim Curtis backed hastily away. 'Not blooming likely,' he said. 'You can't con me into climbing that ladder when it's your cat.'

Keith stepped back from the ladder. 'Mr Tom seems quite comfortable except for his meowing and cats are always doing that, so maybe we should leave him up there until the tilers come back tomorrow.'

'Mr Tom isn't comfortable and he's not meowing, the poor thing's crying. Please Dad,' pleaded Samantha. 'Go up and get him down. He's sitting on the chimney stack really terrified.'

'I'm terrified too,' snapped her father. 'And I haven't even started climbing the ladder yet.'

'Why do Tom cats always climb trees, walls and roofs, when they go looking for mates,' said Mr Curtis. 'I wonder if they can see more she cats when they are up high.'

Smiling grimly, Keith took his first step up the ladder. 'Maybe, I'll know the answer when I'm sitting up there with him.'

'I think your tenant is awfully brave climbing that ladder to rescue his daughter's cat.' Six's green beard rustled when he spoke.

Four didn't sound at all impressed. 'It isn't bravery that's making him climb up to the roof, its desperation. He's anxious to get the cat down as quick as he can so that he can get back to the football match.'

Some ten minutes later with the light fading fast, Keith had managed to climb eight rungs of the ladder. 'I'm beginning to feel sick,' he shouted down to his wife. 'And I'm afraid to look up.'

'You'll be alright,' his wife shouted encouragingly from the safety of the ground. 'It doesn't matter if you don't look up. But, whatever you do, *don't* look down.'

Keith's face blanched, when he foolishly ignored his wife's advice and took a quick look at the ground. 'I've gone dizzy now,' he whimpered.

Jack came running from the house. 'You'll never guess what's happened Dad,' he shouted.

Keith looked down at the ground again, and shuddered. 'Sometimes I find it hard to believe that you are my son,' he said through chattering teeth. 'Here am I hanging on for dear life half way up a ladder and you want me to start playing guessing games.'

'Alright then,' said Jack sulkily. 'I won't tell you that your team has just scored a goal.'

Keith eased himself off the ladder and spread himself flat on the roof. 'I can't go any further,' he shouted down. 'My legs are shaking like jelly.'

'You'll be alright in a minute.' His wife yelled encouragingly up the ladder. 'Just take a short rest. You've probably got a touch of vertigo.'

As he slowly inched his way up the roof on his belly, Keith shouted down to Samantha. 'When I get my hands on your cat, I'm going to wring its neck.'

'There's not much point in trying to save him, if you intend to kill

31

him.' She shouted back.

'You be careful up there,' Jim Curtis said anxiously. 'Remember that cats are supposed to have nine lives, and you have only got one.' Then, as if it were an afterthought, he added. 'And try not to break any tiles.'

'It won't matter if I break one or two will it?' Keith snarled sarcastically. 'The tilers will be able to replace them tomorrow.'

Jacks mother grasped his hand firmly in hers and gave it a squeeze. 'I never thought I would ever say this,' she whispered, with a look of pride. 'I think your father is a real hero going up on to that roof to rescue Mr Tom.'

'He's more of a dope than a hero,' said Jack. 'I've already told him that Mr Tom is a prisoner of war.'

Urged on by the crowd that had gathered below. Keith nervously stood up. Then, like a drunken tightrope walker, he made his way along the ridge of the roof. With the knuckles of his left hand standing out white against the red bricks, he took a limpet like hold on the chimneystack and slowly reached up for the cat. Ignoring the beckoning hand, the ginger menace jumped on to Keith's shoulder and ran down his back to the roof. Then, with its tail held high in the air it ran along the ridge and down the tiles. For some time, the cat stood posing at the top of the ladder as if acknowledging the gathered crowds applause. With a quick look back at Keith, it nonchalantly walked down the rungs and jumped into Samantha's awaiting arms. 'This isn't Mr Tom,' she shouted, holding up the cat for her dad to see.

'Of course it's him,' her dad replied. 'I'd know that blasted creature anywhere.'

'If it is Mr Tom, then he's gone and got himself pregnant.'

As if in a trance Keith stared down in disbelief, and then he started to sway back and forth. 'Will someone ring the fire brigade?' he yelled, flinging his arms desperately around the chimneystack. 'And tell them that it's *urgent*.'

'It doesn't matter about ringing the fire brigade Dad,' Jack shouted back. 'The cat's found its own way down.'

'Stuff the cat.' Keith screamed hysterically. 'Do as I say and ring the fire brigade, I'm the one who needs rescuing now.'

'I must have aged at least five years during the time I was stuck up on that roof,' moaned Keith, as Jim Curtis and a laughing fire fighter helped the jelly-legged hero into his kitchen.

'Sit down love and make yourself comfortable,' his wife said warmly. 'I've just made you a nice hot cup of tea.'

Lifting the cup shakily towards his mouth, Keith succeeded in spilling most of the sweet strong beverage before it got to his lips. 'Look at the state of me,' he mumbled holding out a trembling hand. 'I climbed to the top of that blooming roof and we still don't know what's happened to Mr Tom.'

Jack's war game had moved from the lounge into the kitchen. With a long loud sigh, he got up from the floor. 'I've already told you,' he said. 'He's a prisoner of war.' Walking to the laundry basket, he lifted the lid and pulled out Mr Tom.

The strained look vanished from Keith's face when he glanced at the clock on the kitchen wall. 'I wasn't on that roof as long as I thought,' he said, breaking into a smile. 'I should be able to catch the last ten minutes of the match.'

Jack, Samantha, and their mum, followed Keith into the lounge, where they found him with an incredulous look on his face staring at an empty space in the corner of the room.

The two children watched their mother's hero fall from grace when she snapped. 'While you was up on that roof showing off, somebody sneaked into our house and walked off with the television, so it doesn't look like you will be seeing the end of the match after all.'

Keith glared down hatefully at Mr Tom. 'Just look at that blasted cat,' he snarled. 'He's sitting in my armchair licking its backside.'

'Someone has stolen the Pettigrew's television,' whispered Twelve to Eleven.

'Go on,' said Eleven. 'Have you any idea who took it?'

'Don't pretend you didn't see him take it. You're always looking up and down the close. You must have seen the thief walking away with it in his arms.'

33

'Honest.' said Eleven. 'I didn't see a thing. I was busy watching that brave man trying to rescue his daughter's cat.'

'You might not have seen him carrying it away, but you will know who took it, when he brings it through your door. It was stolen by one of your squatters, the little fat one.'

'Will one of you come and give me a hand.' Smithy shouted through the small boarded up window in the back door at Number 11.

Bob turned the key and pulled it open. 'Where did you get that?' he grunted, as Smithy struggled through the opening carrying a television.

'I got it from the man who was stuck up on the roof.'

'Did he give it to you?' asked Eric.

'Of course he didn't. You know that people never give us anything. Besides, how could he have given it to me if he was up on the roof? I sneaked into his house and pinched it while everyone was out in the street watching him doing his balancing act on the tiles.'

'Does it work?' asked Eric excitedly. 'I haven't seen television for ages.'

'Of course it works. Do you think I'm daft? I wouldn't have pinched it if it didn't work. As a matter of fact there was a football match showing on the screen, when I took it.'

'Was there any drink in the house?' asked Bob.

Smithy laid the television on the floor and plugged it into a socket on the wall. 'There might have been. I didn't hang around long enough to find out.'

'A bottle or two of booze would have been more use to us.'

'But this is a television. We haven't got a television have we?'

'You're right,' said Bob. 'We haven't got a television. And do you know why we haven't got one?'

Smithy shook his head.

'We haven't got a television because we are living in a squat, and the people who own it aren't too happy that we are living here without their permission. That's why they have had the gas and electricity disconnected. I don't know if you've noticed it or not but televisions don't work very well without electricity running through them.'

Smithy took a couple of steps back to admire his latest acquisition. 'Personally I don't care if it doesn't work; it makes a nice piece of furniture.'

###CHAPTER SIX###

At 4 a.m on Saturday morning, distant singing disturbed the still night air.

'I think it's about time my tenant learnt a new song.' said Seven with a sigh.

'I blame the blooming government,' grunted Eight.

'Be fair. You can't blame the government because my tenant sings badly and he only knows one song.'

'I'm not bothered about his singing, although it is loud and awful.' Eight said irritably. 'What I'm trying to say is he wouldn't be out boozing all of the time if the government hadn't brought in 24 hour drinking.'

'I don't like to say this, but you've got it wrong,' said Seven. 'My tenant isn't out boozing all of the time. He comes home every evening at 9 o'clock for his dinner. However, I believe that the main reason he staggers back from the pub is to collect some of the compensation money he received after they amputated his leg. Once he's filled his belly with food and his wallet with money, he staggers back to the pub again for the late night session, which usually lasts until this time in the morning.'

'If he's in the pub for most of the day and night, when does he sleep?' asked Eight.

'He doesn't sleep at all; at least that's what he tells his wife. The pain in his amputated leg keeps him awake. The reason he drinks, is because he can't sleep.'

'That's stupid,' grunted Six. 'How can he get a pain in a leg that he hasn't got?'

Two decided the time had come to air some of his knowledge. 'It can happen, and sometimes it does,' he said. 'Lots of people get pains in limbs that they have lost. They are called phantom pains.'

'Mr Peacock used to be a heavy drinker before he lost his leg,' said Eight. 'In fact I heard that he lost his leg because of drink. Is that true?'

'In a way, I suppose it is.' chuckled Seven. 'A surgeon had to amputate it after he got knocked down by a brewer's lorry.'

'My tenant Mrs Kreamer had a phantom pregnancy once,' whispered One. 'But they mainly happen to cats and dogs. For six months, she kept moaning at her husband accusing him of not being careful. Then, one morning, after a bad night, she woke up and found that her belly had returned to normal. She was alright after that.'

'I bet you wish that Damien, Stuart, and Priscilla had been phantom pregnancies instead of the real thing,' said Two.

One, thought for a moment, then she said. 'A phantom is something apparently unpleasant or horrific that has no material form. That description fits Damien, Stuart, and Priscilla, to a tee, except for one thing, the state of me since they've moved in is enough to prove that they definitely *do* have material form.'

'Talking of your tenants,' Dunroaming shouted across the close. 'Will Mr Kreamer be selling ice creams at the Hospital fete today?'

'I wouldn't be surprised if he does,' said One. 'Why do you want to know?'

'Fourteen's tenant Jenny is a nurse and she works at the Hospital. If Kreamer is going to sell ice creams, then, she will probably be working overtime tonight trying to cope with the influx of patients brought in with suspected food poisoning.'

Jenny could hardly believe her eyes when she lowered them to check the numbers on the ticket. She lifted them to the stage again to admire the magnificent price that she had won in the Hospital Fete Draw. Of course, she would have preferred one of the four main prizes, but never having won anything in her life before; she reasoned that the booby prize was better than nothing was at all.

'Aren't you the lucky one?' Her best friend whispered enviously. 'I wouldn't mind winning a dishy man as my personal slave for a day.'

Jenny smiled at her friend. 'Unfortunately, he's only allowed to do domestic and light housework and he's only mine from sunrise to sunset. I'm sure I would enjoy him more if there were no restrictions and he was going to be with me from sunset to sunrise.'

The draw organizer winked mischievously at Jenny when she gave him her name and address. 'Most of the nurses at the hospital are going to envy you tomorrow morning when Doctor Goodheart arrives at your house. Judging from the disappointed looks on their faces, they were all hoping to win him.'

On Saturday evening, with pen and paper in hand Jenny walked around the house writing a list of the jobs for her slave to do.

As the first rays of Sunday mornings sunshine forced their way into Jenny's kitchen through the slates in the blinds, they found her sitting fully dressed at the table sipping coffee awaiting the arrival of Doctor Goodheart.

'Your tenant was up early this morning wasn't she?' Dunroaming shouted to Fourteen.

'She's often up early,' Fourteen mumbled gruffly. 'As you already know she's a nurse, and nurses have to work shifts.'

Dunroaming lowered her voice to almost a whisper. 'But she isn't working today is she? Have you any idea what she is up to, she usually lies in bed on her day off.'

Fourteen sucked some air in through his front door keyhole and expelled it out of his chimney in the form of a sigh. 'You must have good eyesight, if you can see into her bedroom from where you are standing.'

Dunroaming sounded embarrassed. 'I can't exactly see into her room, and even if I could, I wouldn't look. I believe that people should be allowed their privacy.'

'If you can't see into her room, then how do you know that she usually lies in on her day off?'

'I heard her telling Mrs Braithwaite at Fifteen that she likes to lay in when she's not working.'

'*Get off of me you messy thing,*' shouted Three, when one of Mr Speedwell's racing pigeons landed on her roof. Then, in a softer voice, she said. 'Do you know what Fourteen, this must be the nosiest close in the world, every time a light is switched on all of the houses want to know why.'

Jenny was already beginning to regret winning her prize. With her slave, arriving at seven she had been obliged to leave her bed three hours earlier than she normally would on her day off.

'Hey Fourteen,' shouted Dunroaming. 'Who's that handsome man walking up the path to your front door is he your tenant's boy friend?'

'I don't know, and if I did I wouldn't tell you, but I'm sure you'll find out soon or later.'

The knock on the door brought Jenny quickly to her feet; it also caused her to spill hot coffee down the front of her dress. 'I won't be a minute,' she shouted, as she ran upstairs to change.

Five minutes later, when she opened the door, her slave for the day was standing with a sheepish grin on his face and a lion-head knocker in his hand.

'It must have been loose,' he explained apologetically. 'When I lifted it to knock again, it came away in my hand.'

I've a feeling this is going to be one of those days, thought Jenny, as she pulled the work list from her pocket and wrote-(Fix broken front door knocker).

Doctor Goodheart took off his jacket hung it up on a hook behind the door and rolled up his sleeves. 'Have you had breakfast yet?' he asked with a smile.

Jenny shook her head.

With courteous charm, that was more befitting a butler than a doctor, he said. 'Would you like me to prepare it for you?'

'Thank you,' Jenny replied. 'Coffee, toast and marmalade, and a couple of three minute eggs would be nice.'

'If you will point me in the direction of the kitchen, then, I will get started.'

With the sounds of pots, pans, and crockery ringing in her ears, Jenny retired to a comfortable armchair in the lounge. Her eyes had travelled over several pages of her book when the sound of the smoke alarm, and the smell of burning, dragged her out of her seat into the kitchen.

'Your tenant's visitor must be really hot stuff to set the smoke alarm ringing,' shouted Dunroaming.

'You're really curious to know what's going on aren't you.' Fourteen shouted back. 'Personally, I find you quite objectionable. You are also fanciful, nosey, and a bore, and if you think that I am going to tell you my tenant's business, then, you are also a bit of a twit. What's happening inside me is her business, not yours.'

'There's no need to worry' Doctor Goodheart shouted reassuringly, as he removed the batteries from the smoke detector. 'You can go back to your book. I've burnt a couple of slices of toast, but everything is under control.'

Ten minutes later, he walked into the lounge carrying a tray. Then, with an apologetic smile, he served Jenny the sorriest looking breakfast she had ever seen. 'I'm sorry you've had to wait so long,' he said. 'I had a bit of trouble cooking the eggs; they kept exploding when I put them in the microwave. And then I remembered that my mother told me, that the best way to cook an egg is to boil it in a saucepan.'

As Jenny drank weak lukewarm coffee, and dipped burnt toast into runny half-cooked eggs, she promised herself that she would never buy a Lucky-Draw-Ticket again.

'Did you enjoy it?' asked her slave, as he took the tray away.

'Thank you, it was lovely,' she lied, almost choking on her words.

As the day progressed, the list of the good doctor's catastrophes grew longer with each job he tackled. First, it had been the doorknocker, then a revolting inedible breakfast, most of which was now hiding in a plastic bag under the settee in her lounge. The washing up had been no problem, until he started drying the dishes. Before he had finished, one eggcup, a saucer and a plate, had found new homes in the rubbish bin. To Jenny's eyes the egg-splattered microwave, that had taken him the best part of an hour to clean, was still dirty.

'Forget the laundry,' said Jenny. When Doctor Goodheart told her that he had never used a washing machine, but he was sure that he would be able to master it if he tried. 'Don't bother,' said Jenny with a sigh. 'It will give me something to do tomorrow.'

'But I want to do it,' he insisted, as he loaded the machine. 'I've got to learn sometime, and it isn't much use having a slave for the day if you don't make him do the jobs that you've put on the list.' The fact that he had never laundered clothes before became dramatically apparent when the machine came to a halt at the end of its program. 'It looks like some of the colours have run a bit,' he said, as he unloaded whites that had become pinks and woollen jumpers that had shrunk to half their size.

For the next hour, Jenny's slave polished the mahogany dining room suite. When he had finished, it smelt marvellous but looked awful.

'I don't think much of that polish,' he said, handing Jenny an almost empty can of air freshener. 'I'm sure that the table didn't have a white bloom on it when I started.'

Good or bad, everything comes to an end eventually. With a weary smile, Jenny screwed the slaves work list into a paper ball and opened the door.

Doctor Goodheart nodded at the front of the door. 'I haven't finished yet. There is still one job left to do. Before I leave, I'm going to fix your faulty door knocker.'

It wasn't faulty until you arrived, thought Jenny.

Released from bondage, Jenny's ex-slave walked down the garden path towards the setting sun.

At the gate, he turned looked at Jenny and smiled. 'When I arrived this morning I was feeling a bit apprehensive, domestic work has never been my forte, but thanks to your patience and understanding, I have actually enjoyed slaving for you. In fact the whole experience has been so rewarding, I am thinking of putting myself forward as a prize again next year.'

For several seconds the lion-head knocker trembled in its housing when Jenny closed the door, then, it fell to the ground.

'How did you enjoy being a slave-master?' asked Jenny's friend at the other end of the phone.

Jenny grinned. 'The doctor did his best, and I can honestly say that he tackled every job I gave him with a Goodheart. But if the slaves of yesteryear were as useful as mine, then, that must have been one of the reasons why they abolished slavery.'

###CHAPTER SEVEN###

October

'You'll have to speak a bit louder Two, if you want us to hear what you are saying.' shouted Ten.

'I wasn't speaking. I was counting how many layabouts we've got living in this close.'

'Great minds think alike. I did the same thing last week. How many did you make it?'

'Seven, it would have been eight if I had counted Mr Pringle, but I gave him the benefit of doubt because of his bad back.'

'He hasn't got a bad back,' snorted Eighteen. 'He's just a good actor. I've seen him doing press-ups in the back garden.'

'Who are your seven layabouts?' asked Ten. 'Like you, I didn't count Mr Pringle, but I only made it six.'

'There's Percy Grant the drug baron at Three. He's so good at lying around he could give lessons. And there's Mr Dingle at Five.'

'Hang on a minute,' said Five, 'that's my tenant you're talking about, how can you call him a layabout, he's a hard worker?'

'You must be joking, Six interrupted with a laugh. 'Your tenant hasn't done a days work since he came to live in the close.'

43

'We've got to be fair about this,' **said Eight**. 'Some people work harder dodging work than they would if they actually did some, and Mr Dingle at Five, has actually built a successful career out of not working.'

'Six's tenant Mr Speedwell the pigeon man. Is number three on my list of layabouts,' **continued Two**.

'I agree with you on that,' **said Six enthusiastically**. 'He's always telling his wife that he hasn't got the time to go out to work, he's too busy breeding and racing his pigeons.'

'Does he ever beat any of them?' **asked Nine naively**.

'Of course he does,' **giggled Seven**. 'With a name like Speedwell, it's expected of him.'

'Then there are the three stinking squatters living at Eleven,' **said Two**. 'I don't think they've ever worked in their lives, nor are they ever likely to, as long as they can find an empty house and get their hands on a bottle of cheap sherry.'

'That makes six layabouts,' **said Ten**. 'You made it seven. So who's the other one?'

'I don't suppose you will thank me for saying this,' **said Two**. 'It's the hippy type fellow who lives in you.'

'He would work if he could,' **said Ten**. 'But he's too highly qualified to find the right sort of job around here. All of the local businesses are too small to employ a full time inventor.'

'Is he really an inventor?' **Dunroaming asked excitedly**. 'What has he invented?'

'No one seems to know,' **said Nine**. 'But judging from the amount of old junk he's dumped on the path outside Ten, it certainly isn't a waste disposal unit.'

'It may look like junk to you, but, it isn't,' said Ten protectively. 'It's material that he needs for his ongoing invention and, when it's finished, he'll be recognized as the genius he is.'

'Who told you that he's a genius?' asked Dunroaming.

'Nobody actually told me,' Ten replied sheepishly. 'It's something that I overheard him saying to his partner.'

'Did he happen to tell her what he's inventing?'

Ten lowered his voice to a whisper. 'He said that he's working on an environmental friendly machine that will convert all kinds of rubbish into a gas that will be used to fuel cars.'

'Isn't that strange,' said Nine. 'Last night was the first time I had ever heard the word environmental, and now I've heard it again today.

'That's interesting,' said Ten. 'It's a long word isn't it? Do you know what it means?'

'I haven't a clue, but I heard my tenant say to his wife. "I've just about had enough of that lazy so called inventor who's living next door. He has turned his house into a rubbish tip. There is so much junk piled up in the rooms his family has hardly any space left to live in. That house is a health Inspectors nightmare. I have decided to report him to the Environmental Health." '

'How did he find out about the rubbish stored in my rooms?'

'The three squatters living at Eleven told him. They said that there's rubbish piled up to the ceiling in every room including the bathroom and stairs.'

'That's a case of pot calling the kettle black, if there ever was one,' snorted Eleven. 'Since those three have been living in me, they've succeeded in turning most of my rooms into a blooming used bottle bank.'

'What about the loft?' asked Three. 'Has the inventor put any of his junk up there? There is usually plenty of space in the attic. As you already know, I've got thirty cannabis plants growing in mine.'

Ten gave a disheartened sigh. 'Up in the loft is where he started, and when the ceiling joists started to bend under the weight, he worked his way down.'

'What sort of rubbish is it?'

'You name it, and he's got it. There must be at least two thousand books, and there are several thousand newspapers, brochures, magazines and comics piled up high on the stairs, there is a bike without any wheels hanging from the banisters, and a shop window dummy wearing a corset standing on the landing. He's got five old gas lamps that once lit a London Street, which he says are worth hundreds of pounds laying on the floor of the bathroom, and there's a room full of weight lifting equipment that's far too heavy for him to lift.'

'If it's too heavy for him to lift, then, how did he manage to get it into the house?' **asked Eleven.**

'He asked your blooming squatters to give him a hand; that's how they found out about the junk stored in my rooms.'

'He must have regretted asking them to help carry heavy equipment,' **giggled Eleven.** 'They don't usually lift anything heavier than a bottle. How did he pay them? They wouldn't have done it for nothing you know.'

'He gave them a couple of empty whisky casks.'

'It must have been more than that. My squatter's wouldn't have been daft enough to take two empty whisky casks as payment for carrying heavy weight lifting equipment,' **said Eleven, with a touch of pride.**

'The inventor told them that over the years the wooden casks had become impregnated with the whisky they had been holding, and if they were to pour about a litre of water into each cask the water would become whisky within a month or two, as long as they remembered to roll them around for several minutes every day.'

Eleven sighed gloomily. 'I wish the inventor hadn't given them whisky casks. When they drink whisky, they want to fight everyone in sight. Now if it had been sherry casks, that would be a different story, especially if they originally contained cheap sherry, that stuff has a different affect on them, it makes them happy, giggly, and sleepy.'

'I don't know why you've allowed them to squat in you for so long,' said Twelve. 'Why haven't you forced them to leave like you did the last lot?'

'I was hoping that I wouldn't have to do the haunted house bit again. Having to make my floorboards and stairs creak, and slamming doors every night is a bit wearing; besides, it isn't really my style. It took me so long to drive those two squatters out the last time, I ended up thinking that I really was haunted. Anyway, Smithy, Eric, and Bob, aren't easily frightened. They've lived with all sorts of imaginary mind-blowing creatures for too long to be afraid of any noises that I could conjure up. Besides, the last time I pretended to be haunted, it ruined my reputation. For miles around, I became known as the haunted house.'

'It's better to be called a haunted house than a slum,' said Four wisely.

'I reckon the inventor must have a mental disorder to have collected so much junk,' said Nine. 'Surely he doesn't intend to burn it all in the machine that will turn waste into gas.

'Don't be stupid,' said Ten. 'He can't burn it all. Some of it's metal and metal doesn't burn.'

'What does he want the metal for?'

'He told his partner that the bicycle, the shop window dummy, and the five old gas lamps are some of the components he will need when he builds his environmentally friendly gas producing machine'

'He must be nuttier than a bag of peanuts, if he thinks he's could possibly build a machine that will be able to turn rubbish into a gas that will fuel cars, using an old bicycle without wheels, a shop window display dummy, and five old gas lamps.'

'That isn't the only materials he'll be using. There is that heavy weightlifting equipment, which he intends to use as counterbalance weights, whatever that means. And there's that old car that's standing on my front path, and several sheets of corrugated iron that are stacked in the back garden.'

'Has his partner seen the plans for this wonderful machine?' asked Nine sceptically.

'He hasn't drawn up any plans. He said plans could be stolen, so he's filed them away in his head.'

'I think your tenant is in urgent need of a brain doctor,' said Nine.

Thirteen whispered softly to Twelve so that the other houses couldn't hear. 'Talking of Doctors, was that the House Doctor's van that I saw parked in the road outside you yesterday afternoon? Aren't you well?'

'I'm afraid it was.' Twelve whispered in reply.'

'You haven't got rats, have you? I really hate rats.'

'No, it isn't anything as bad as that. In fact, I didn't even know there was anything wrong with me until the doctor went up into the attic and examined my rafters. When he came down shaking his head, he told my tenant that the roof joists are badly infested with woodworm.'

'That explains the scratching noises I've heard coming from your loft recently. I was beginning to think that your tenant might be housing a few illegal immigrants.'

'As far as I'm concerned, the woodworm living in my joists didn't get in legally. So in a way I suppose you were right.'

'What's going to happen now?'

'The House Doctors are coming back in a day or two to fix it.'

'Is it contagious?' asked Thirteen nervously. 'Do you think I will catch it as well?'

'I certainly hope not, but if you do, don't worry. I heard the doctor say he can put it right, but he will have to replace a few of my joists.'

'So you've got to have an operation. Bits and pieces cut out and all that.'

'That's right,' said Twelve bleakly. 'It will only be a small one, but the operation would be complicated if I was infested with deathwatch beetle.'

Even though they had been talking in whispers, Fourteen, had heard every word they said. 'Your tenants will have to move out for several days, if you are going to be fumigated,' he said loud enough for several of the other houses to hear.

'They didn't say anything about being fumigated,' Twelve sounded frightened. 'I have never heard that word before what does it mean?'

'It means that they are going to get rid of your nasty illegal immigrant woodworm infestation by using chemicals, fumes, and smoke. After the doctors have finished, your loft is going to look vile, smell vile, and you'll feel violently sick. And that isn't all; you'll have a hacking cough and such a throbbing headache you won't feel like talking to any of us for a couple of weeks.'

'I know how that feels,' said One sympathetically. 'It happens to me

49

three or four times a day when Mrs Kreamer puts Priscilla's wet knickers in the tumble dryer.'

'Will you please stop talking about woodworm,' said Ten. 'It makes me feel itchy, like I've got fleas.'

'I wouldn't be at all surprised if you have,' said Dunroaming who hadn't had much to say for a few days. 'With the amount of rubbish the Inventor has dumped inside and outside of you, I reckon you must be running alive with all sorts of things including fleas.'

'I wish it was you who was going to be fumigated instead of Twelve,' said One nastily. 'I'm sure most of the houses in the close would really appreciate it, if you were silent for two or three weeks.'

'If I am running alive it won't be for much longer,' said Ten under his breath. 'According to Nine, the Health Inspector should be paying my tenants a visit in a day or two.'

###CHAPTER EIGHT###

Most of the tenants in Leyland Close bought their milk at the supermarket in town. Mr and Mrs Wyatt-Jones at Dunroaming however preferred having their milk delivered straight to the door. The electric milk float that carried their daily two bottles of semi-skimmed was practically silent, but Samuel Sprocket the farmer and milkman who opened the gate and ran up the path with the two bottles clanking together in one hand wasn't silent, he had never been silent in his life.

'Why do your owners have to be different to everyone else in the close?' Eight shouted across the road to Dunroaming. 'They should have some consideration and buy their milk at the supermarket instead of Sprocket's farm. I am sure he clangs those two bottles together purposely, just because he has to get up early every morning to do his deliveries. I suppose he thinks that everyone in the close should get up early as well.'

'It's nothing to do with you where my owners get their milk, and it's not their fault if Sprocket makes a noise delivering it.'

'They could ask him to make less noise.'

'They've already asked him, and he told them that if they didn't like it they could always buy their milk somewhere else.'

How many times will I have to tell you to get off, before you'll take any notice?' Three shouted up at the pigeons roosting on her roof. 'This isn't your house, you live at Six, so why don't you all go and mess on his tiles?'

'You can shout at them for as long and as loud as you like,' said Fourteen. 'They won't take any notice. Pigeons are a bit thick, besides they can't hear you, and they don't *all* belong to Mr Speedwell you know.'

'It isn't much use being able to talk, is it?' said Three grouchily, 'if houses are the only ones who can hear what we say.'

'Even if the pigeons could hear you shouting at them, I doubt if they would leave.'

'My roof isn't any different from the others around here, so why do all of the pigeons for miles around have to make it their meeting place?'

'They like to feel the warmth under their feet,' said Four. 'If you didn't have all of those lights burning in your loft day and night, I doubt if many pigeons would land on it. As for saying, your roof isn't any different from the others around here, if you could see it, then, you would know that it is. There must be hundreds of birds roosting and messing on your nice warm tiles every night and come morning when they fly away, your roof looks like it has been whitewashed and feathered.'

'I don't care what you say,' said Three stubbornly. 'It isn't my roof that attracts the birds; it's the amount of seed Six's tenant throws to his racing pigeons every morning. They're so fat it's a wonder they ever get off the ground to take part in any races.'

Tom Dingle looked up from digging his garden when he heard someone clearing their throat just above his head.

'Good morning Tom,' his next-door neighbour was peering at him over the garden fence. Clearing his throat again, he said. 'Are you going to Exeter today?'

'It's Monday isn't it? I always go to Exeter on a Monday; I've been doing it for years. Why do you want to know?'

'I was wondering if you would mind doing me a *favour* when you get there.'

Having been on the losing end of some of the favour's that he had granted him in the past, the word put him on his guard. Tom sighed loudly hoping that it would put him off, but it seemed to have the opposite effect.

As if he had read his mind, Mr Speedwell gave him a disarming smile. 'There's no need to worry Tom,' he said. 'It won't cost you anything, just a few minutes of your spare time.'

Tom was about to say, 'I don't seem to have any spare time whenever I go to Exeter,' but before he could open his mouth, Mr Speedwell disappeared behind the fence.

He reappeared a few minutes later, holding a wicker basket above his head. 'I've got four young pigeons in this basket ready for their first long-distance flight. I was hoping that if I asked you nicely, you would take them to Exeter with you and release them when you get there.'

Tom wasn't going to let Speedwell think he was easy, so he pretended to give the matter a bit of thought. He waited until the look on Speedwell's face told him that the basket was getting heavy, then, he said. 'What time do you want me to release them?'

Speedwell broke into a broad grin. 'If you can let them go dead on 12 o'clock, they should be back in the loft again by half past.'

Tom looked at him doubtfully. 'Do you expect them to fly from Exeter to here in 30 minutes? That will take a bit of doing. They would have to fly at over a mile a minute for 35 miles.'

His neighbour gave him a condescending smile. 'Racing pigeons fly at about 60 miles an hour and 35miles will be just a sprint to these little beauties. Once they have some experience behind them, they will think nothing of flying hundreds of miles. And these pigeons will travel in a straight line, so they shouldn't have to fly much more than 30 miles.'

Later, in an Exeter car park, Tom lifted the pigeon basket from the boot and carried it to the bonnet of his car. Looking at his watch he waited until both hands were touching 12, then, he opened the lid.

Several small feathers floated to the ground as the four birds lifted themselves from the basket and took to the sky. With both hands, fanned open on his brow Tom followed their flight until they had become tiny dots in the sky. Suddenly the lead bird banked and turned. As if playing following the leader, the others followed suit. Tom's look of surprise became a smile as he watched them grow larger. After circling the car several times, one by one they returned to the basket. His smile turned into a chuckle, when he remembered what his neighbour had said. 'Thirty miles is just a sprint to these little beauties. When they are fully trained, they will think nothing of flying hundreds of miles.'

As Tom closed the lid on the pigeons, they looked up at him as if to say, 'Of course we know the way home, but thirty five miles is an awful long way.'

He released the birds again at 1 o'clock, and 2 o'clock, each time with the same result. Before climbing into his car for the homeward journey, Tom decided to give the pigeons one more chance. They looked up at him sleepily when he opened the basket. 'Let's see if you can beat me home,' he said. This time however, they didn't even bother to fly out.

It was almost 4 o'clock before he stopped the car within sight of his house. This time, he opened the basket whilst it was still in the boot and shook it hard, as the last bird lifted itself wearily into the sky he slammed the lid shut.

Like four flying darts, they headed straight for home. For several seconds Tom held his breath expecting to see them turn. A deep sigh of relief left his lips, when he saw them descend.

'Hey Six,' shouted Three, when four tired looking pigeons landed on her roof. 'It looks like your tenants racers have finally made it back from Exeter.'

'Mr Speedwell doesn't look too happy does he?' said Five. 'He's standing in the garden waving his fist at them.'

'I can understand why he's doing that,' Four said, with a chuckle. 'If Mr Dingle released them at 12 o'clock like he promised, they've taken five hours to fly thirty five miles.'

'I think he's lucky to get them back at all,' grunted Three. 'He feeds them far too much. The four that are up there now are the fattest of the lot; in fact, it's a wonder that they didn't all have heart attacks before they got halfway home. I get frightened every time they land on my roof; they're so heavy they could break my tiles.'

'You know why he keeps feeding them don't you?' said Six, as Mr Speedwell scattered seed on the ground. 'It's because your roof is so comfortable under their feet, it's the only way he can tempt them down.'

For almost half an hour Tom sat watching the sky darken as the sun sank behind the roof of his house. Then he drove home.

As he was lifting the empty basket from the boot, he heard the sound of his neighbour hurrying towards him. 'Here's your basket, Don,' he said. 'Did the pigeons arrive back OK?'

Don's smile didn't quite disguise his puzzled frown. 'Yes, thanks Tom. They all arrived back safely. Just for the record, what time did you release them?'

'They were heading for home dead on 12 o'clock.' He was going to add, and they were in the air again at 1 o'clock, and 2 o'clock, but he didn't. Instead, he said. 'What time did they get back?'

Tom expected him to say. 'They arrived just a few minutes ago.'

'They were all back in the loft by half past 12,' he said proudly, 'which means they covered the distance in exactly 30 minutes, just like I said they would.'

###CHAPTER NINE###

Halloween

'My Owners have been dreading Halloween since the Kreamer's moved into the close,' Dunroaming shouted across the road to Four, who was one of the few houses left in the close that she could still speak to. 'And now it's here.'

'They'll be knocking on your door before the evening is over,' Four replied solemnly. 'I saw Damien, Stuart, and Priscilla go out about an hour ago dressed as ghouls carrying pumpkins with candles burning inside.'

Sucking air in through her chimney pot, Dunroaming nervously took a deep breath.

Sitting in the dark in front of the fire, Mr and Mrs Wyatt Jones moved back in alarm when a shower of soot fell down the chimney.

'Remind me to call a chimney sweep tomorrow,' Mr Wyatt Jones whispered to his wife.

'Why are you whispering dear?' she asked. 'We've got all of the windows and doors shut and the lights are off. I should think that if the little darlings opposite come knocking at our door tricking or treating they will think that we've gone out for the night.'

Mr Wyatt Jones shook his head. 'They won't let us get off that easy,' he said pessimistically. 'You wait and see. If they think that we have gone out, they will tip flour through our letterbox and bombard our front door with over ripe tomatoes and rotten eggs. And the chances are that they'll be back again early tomorrow morning to tell us that they came tricking or treating and we weren't in, so we owe them a treat for last night.'

###CHAPTER TEN###

November 5th

'I don't suppose your looking forward to tonight, are you Eighteen?'

'Of course I'm not,' Eighteen replied angrily. 'Nor should you be Seventeen. November the Fifth is the most dangerous night of the year, with all those bonfires and smoke polluting the atmosphere, it is also environmentally unfriendly. Personally I think they should ban Guy Fawkes Day celebrations.'

'You might think November the Fifth is the most dangerous, but I think Halloween is more frightening.' Seventeen's involuntary shiver caused most of her doors to slam shut. 'All of those ghosts and goalies walking around knocking on doors saying trick or treat give me the willies.'

'It isn't ghosts and goalies,' laughed Eighteen. 'It's ghosts and ghouls. A goalie is a footballer.' Eighteen became serious again. 'I really do think it's about time they got around to banning November the Fifth, not only is it dangerous when those rockets hit your roof and break the tiles, it hurts. And I should know several of mine were broken last year.'

'You poor thing,' said Sixteen, sympathetically. 'And you had to stand with that injury for ten months before your tenants got round to healing it with new ones.'

'Ten months was a long time to wait,' said Eight. 'Fortunately I was luckier than you; I only had to put up with a broken downstairs front window for about five weeks before it was repaired.'

'It was only replaced that quick, because Mr Peacock who broke it had to pay for a new sheet of glass.' Eighteen shouted in reply. 'If your tenants had had to pay for the job to be done themselves, you would still be waiting now.'

'I wouldn't,' Eight shouted back rancorously. 'My tenants insurance covers them against breakages and that sort of thing. I don't suppose your tenants have any insurance, so they had to save up to get your roof repaired. That's why you had to stand injured for so long.'

'Will you two stop bickering?' Seventeen snapped angrily. 'Before tonight is over one or two of us are probably going to end up with injuries, especially if that Damien gets his hands on any fireworks.'

'Let's hope that he doesn't,' said Eighteen. 'If he does, he will probably do more damage than Guy Fawkes ever did.'

'Guy Fawkes didn't do any damage at all,' said Eight. 'If you knew your history, you would know that he got caught before he could blow up the Houses of Parliament.'

'I'm really concerned about the bonfire that my tenant's have built in the gravelled car park next to me,' said One. 'It's enormous!' You mark my words, when they set fire to that there's going to be trouble.'

'It isn't as big as it would have been if Damien hadn't set it alight last week,' said Two. 'So we should be thanking him for that, I suppose.'

'I'd like to know where they got all the wood to build it,' said Three.

'That isn't hard to figure out,' mumbled Dunroaming. 'That wooden shed probably came from the allotments a couple of streets away, and those fence panels from some poor old lady's back garden, and I saw the inventor give them several bags of books and magazines.'

'Did he really?' said Ten. 'I thought my loft felt a bit lighter, but give him a day or two and he will have replaced the things that he gave to be burnt.'

'Has he started building his environmentally friendly machine that will turn rubbish into car fuel yet?' asked Thirteen.

'Of course he hasn't,' snorted Ten. 'If he had, he wouldn't have given any of his precious rubbish away, but the day when he starts building it is getting nearer. The other day he told his partner, that he has managed to get his hands on the crucial part that he's been looking for.'

'I wonder what the crucial part is.'

'We'll find out soon enough. It's being delivered next week.'

Damien looked up at the sky as he walked towards the gravelled car park. 'It's getting dark dad,' he said impatiently. 'Can I light the fire?'

'You come back here this minute Damien,' his mother screamed. 'It's only two o'clock, we aren't going to light the fire until your grand-dad gets here at seven. Besides, you had your turn at lighting the fire last week. Now be a good boy and go and see if you can find some more wood, but *please* don't go cutting down trees like you did last year.'

'I've got a better idea,' said his dad. 'He can come with me to Mrs Braithwaite's at Number 15, she's just told me on the phone that she's got an old armchair that she wants to get rid of, I told her that it would be worth a fiver.'

His wife gave him an incredulous look. 'You're not going to pay five pounds for an old armchair are you?'

Kreamer pointed at his face. 'What's the colour of this?' he asked. 'Is it green? She's going to pay me a fiver to take it off her hands.'

On the way to Fifteen, Kreamer stopped at the Grant's to enlist Percy's help. The pale skinned twenty two year old seemed to be on a high when he answered the door in his wet boxer shorts. 'I hope it won't take long,' he said. 'I haven't finished watering my pot plants yet.'

Mrs Braithwaite gave Kreamer a cold smile and a five-pound note, then, she glared at Damien, and blushed when she noticed that Percy was standing in wet skin clinging boxers. 'Did he drag you out of the bath to help carry my armchair?' she asked with a coy smile.

'Percy is always dressed like this,' said Kreamer. 'He's a hot blooded young man who likes lounging around indoors practically naked.'

Mrs Braithwaite stared down at Percy's lower half. 'I think you can rule out the word practically, his pants are clinging to him like a second skin.' With her eyes still on Percy, she said, in a trembling voice. 'Would you like a cup of tea?'

'No thank you,' Kreamer replied. 'It isn't the warmest of afternoons and if we stand around drinking tea Percy might catch cold. If you will just show us where the armchair is, we'll pick it up and be on our way.'

Mrs Braithwaite's eyes strayed down to Percy's waist again. 'Are you going to the bonfire tonight young man?' she asked.

Percy hitched up his boxers and gave her a cheeky wink. 'I wouldn't miss it for the world, Mrs Braithwaite.'

With another quick glance at the reason why she was suddenly feeling so hot, the flushed woman whispered. 'If you are going to be dressed like that, I might even pop over myself for an hour or two.'

Kreamer fingered the fiver in his pocket. 'It's a family and friends affair really,' he said. 'But, seeing as you've contributed the armchair that Guy Fawkes will be sitting on, you can come along as a guest.'

'Hang on a minute,' said Kreamer, as they were carrying the large armchair up the close towards the car park. 'This chair is too good to go on the fire; I think I'll swap it for one of mine.'

The filthy threadbare armchair that Kreamer and Percy carried ceremoniously out of Number 1 had definitely seen better days. With Damien following closely behind them grinning like a demented Cheshire cat they made their way to the car park. Kreamer frowned as they lowered the bulky armchair to the ground in front of a smartly dressed Guy Fawkes sitting with its back against the bonfire. 'Who made the guy, Damien?' He asked, eyeing the effigy suspiciously.

Damien stuck a roman candle in each of the guy's hands and a rocket in the top of its head. 'I did dad,' he said proudly.

'That's a nice suit he's wearing, it looks a bit like the black suit that I keep especially for funerals, where did you get it?'

'I bought it at the charity shop.' Damien replied, crossing his fingers behind his back. 'When I asked the lady if she had an old suit that I could use to make a guy, she sold me this one for a £1.'

'It looks too good to be burnt. I wish you had shown it to me before you stuffed it.'

Granddad arrived in the close dead on seven carrying two large boxes of fireworks and a sack of King Edward potatoes. 'Right,' he said, taking control of the evening. 'Give me a minute to get my hands on a drink, and then I'll light the fire.'

Half an hour and three drinks later, Granddad lit the fire. Unfortunately, during the operation he managed to burn the tips of three fingers. As the flames started to eat their way into the paper and wood, he hurried back into the kitchen at Number 1 mouthing several swear words that Damien had never heard before whilst sucking his injured digits and a badly scorched thumb. A few minutes later, he returned to the fire carrying his fourth beer and the sack of King Edwards.

Mrs Kreamer looked at the potatoes distastefully. 'I hope you're going to wash those before you put them in the fire.'

'There's no need to do that,' granddad replied. 'The heat of the fire will kill any germs and I'm going to wrap them in tinfoil.'

With a pint of beer in one hand and a half eaten burnt jacket potato in the other, Mrs Kreamer moved closer to her husband beside the fire. 'That suit looks smarter on the guy than it ever did on you,' she said with a grin. 'And he's a darn sight better looking.'

Mr Kreamer looked at the fire eating its way up Guy Fawkes legs, then; lifting his beer to his lips, he took a long swig. 'That's as well as maybe, but his looks aren't going to last for much longer.' Then, he moved away to have a few quick sharp words with Damien. 'You little liar,' he shouted angrily. 'You didn't get the guy's suit from the charity shop. It's the one that I kept especially for funerals.'

'Stand back everyone,' shouted granddad with an air of importance. 'I'm going to start lighting the fireworks now.'

'Whatever you do, don't let my Dennis light any,' pleaded Mrs Kreamer. 'He might take the instructions literally, and he doesn't do much work as it is.'

Granddad studied the firework in his hand. 'I see what you mean,' he said with a husky laugh. 'It says, (LIGHT THE BLUE TOUCH PAPER AND RETIRE IMMEDIATELY).'

'Fire! Fire! Fire!' shouted Thirteen, hysterically. 'Can't any of you hear me shouting that I'm on fire?'

'Of course we can hear you,' said Eight. 'You're shouting loud enough for the houses in the next street to hear. I'm sorry, but, there's nothing we can do about it.'

'What about your smoke alarms?' asked Twelve sympathetically. 'Aren't they working?'

'Of course they're not,' coughed Thirteen. 'If they were, they would be ringing by now. The bed in my upstairs front room has been burning for several minutes.'

'Calm down,' said Eight. 'Somebody's sure to notice that there's smoke coming out of your window soon, and when they do they will phone for the fire brigade.'

'You're being optimistic aren't you?' Dunroaming said gruffly. 'Nobody's going to notice that Thirteen's on fire, they're all busy looking at the fireworks.'

'My tenant's a fireman,' Nine said casually. 'If he was at home, he would have noticed that you're on fire, he's been specially trained to notice things like that and the fire brigade would be on its way by now.'

Twelve coughed several times when some of Thirteen's smoke drifted through one of his open windows. 'It seems to me that firemen are like policemen,' he said huskily. 'They're never around when you want them.'

'My tenant's only human you know,' Nine replied angrily. 'He can't be in two places at the same time.'

'Where has he gone?' asked Dunroaming inquisitively.

'Where nearly every fireman goes on the Fifth of November, you dumb house. He's out somewhere, fighting a fire.'

'Was anyone in bed when your fire started,' asked Eleven, sounding more like an investigative reporter than a house.

'Only the idiot who woke up for a quick smoke and fell back to sleep again with the cigarette still alight in his hand. Any second now you'll see him come running out, stark naked, and shouting Fire!'

'What about your others tenants?'

'Don't worry about them,' Thirteen answered miserably. 'They won't be naked, but you can bet that they'll be following close behind. There isn't anyone amongst my tenants who is brave enough to stay and tackle the fire.'

'Look!' shouted Five. 'The drug baron living at Three is dragging a hose along to Thirteen. It looks like he is going to fight the fire.'

'Mr Kreamer the ice cream man is pulling a hose along as well,' shouted Six excitedly. 'That's what I like about this close they all pull together in an emergency. They had that kind of community spirit during the Second World War when incendiary bombs were falling on London. Only in those days they used to put them out with things called stirrup pumps.'

'How do you know that?' asked Five sceptically. 'You're only eight years old; the Second World War was years and years ago.'

'I'm lucky enough to be able to watch a lot of television and there was a programme on about the London blitz a couple of weeks ago.'

'I glad I wasn't around in those days, said Eight. 'It sounds like it was worse than bonfire night.'

'Your dead right,' said Six dramatically. 'In those days if a rocket hit your roof, it didn't just break a few tiles, it flattened the whole street.'

'Maybe the inventor who lives in Ten has designed a gadget that will put out my fire,' coughed Thirteen.

'You'll be lucky if he has,' Dunroaming mumbled dryly. 'The only thing that man has ever invented is the story that he's an inventor.'

Stripped down to his boxer shorts, Percy Grant stood at the bottom of the stairs in Number 13 with his hose pointing up. 'Right,' he said, talking to the end of his hose. 'I've never had you turned up to full pressure before, so let's see what you can do.' With a quick flick of his wrist, he turned the nozzle. For several seconds he stood waiting for the water to come spouting out, but nothing happened. Then, he remembered that he hadn't turned the tap on. Whilst he ran back to his house to turn it on, Dennis Kreamer went from door to door asking the tenants if they would bring their garden hoses to help fight the fire at Number 13.

'I'd like to help, but I can't,' said Mr Pringle at Number 17.

'Why not?' asked Kreamer angrily.

'I've got a bad back, and I haven't got a hosepipe.'

Swearing under his breath, Mr Kreamer went next door to Number 18. 'He won't be able to help you either,' Mr Pringle shouted from his doorstep.

'How do you know?' Kreamer shouted back, as he waited for the door to open.

'He hasn't got a hosepipe either, and he's taken his son to the firework display at the recreation ground.'

Kreamer grunted, then, stiffening an index finger, he waved it at Pringle.

'You know what you can do with that don't you?' Pringle shouted with sneer. 'You can stick it up your vans exhaust pipe, it could do with a damn good clean.'

By the time Percy got back to his hosepipe, he could hear fire engine sirens in the distance. 'I was hoping that I would be able to put it out before they got here,' he said, giving Kreamer a disappointed look.

'At least you tried,' the ice cream man replied. 'Which is more than can be said for anyone else in the close?'

'Was it started by your bonfire?' asked Percy.

'I suppose that's what everyone in the close is thinking.' Kreamer pointed at three young men standing in the middle of the road. 'But the idiot, who went to sleep with a lighted cigarette in his hand and woke up with his bed on fire, knows different.'

Percy glanced at the three young men. 'Which one was it?'

Kreamer nodded his head. 'The bloke who's standing stark naked talking to Mrs Braithwaite.'

Everyone in the close with the exception of Damien was now standing outside Thirteen watching the fire. Damien however, was lurking behind the ice cream van with a devilish look in his eyes and a long thin rocket in his hand.

'I'm sure your Damien is up to something,' Dunroaming shouted across to One.

'If you have to talk to me at all,' One shouted back. 'Would you please tell me something that I don't already know? Of course, he is up to something, he's always up to something, and if you don't mind, he isn't *my* Damien. He's my tenant's child.'

'Can you see him?' asked Dunroaming. 'Or is he hidden from your view?'

'He's hidden from my view,' One replied with a sigh of relief. 'And the longer it stays that way the happier I shall be.'

'You wouldn't be very happy if you knew what he's doing. But you're going to find out soon.'

'He isn't sticking a banana up the exhaust again is he?'

'No, he's more ambitious this time.'

'You wouldn't believe that a child with a name like Damien could be such a monster would you.'

'I must admit, Damien is a nice name.'

'The name might sound nice, but as every house in the close knows the boys a monster.'

'You know why he's such a monster don't you? It's because of way they spelt the name when he was christened.'

'How do you make that out? Why does the spelling matter?'

'There are two ways of spelling the name. If it's spelt D-a-m-i-a-n it means Saint, but, if it's D-a-m-i-e-n, it means the son of Satan.'

'How do you know that?' **asked One.**

'My owners were arguing about the name the other day, Mr Wyatt Jones said it meant Saint, but his wife disagreed. To settle the argument, they looked it up in their expensive book of names, and as usual, Mrs Wyatt Jones was right.'

'Didn't I say he's a monster?' **said One.** 'His name is spelt D-a-m-i-e-n, so if he's the son of Satan, then, he must be a monster.'

'Did they pick your name out of their expensive book of names Dunroaming?' **asked Four.** 'If they did, then, it doesn't sound like the book was worth the money.'

Damien peered from behind the van and looked at the crowd of spectators watching the firefighters. 'If I run really fast, I should be in amongst the crowd before it goes off,' he mumbled as he rammed the rocket up the vans exhaust. Then, bending into a sprinting position he touched the blue paper with a piece of glowing wood and started to run. The excited

67

crowd watching the firefighters failed to notice the fast moving youngster heading towards them. 'It should have gone off by now,' he mumbled, as he quickly make his way into their midst. 'Maybe it's gone out.' He was about to weave his way back out of the crowd, when the bottom of the van exploding in a kaleidoscope of colour.

For some time Damien's father stood staring at the burning van in dumbstruck disbelief. Then, with an ear-splitting explosion, and what sounded like a dying sigh, the body of the van collapsed. Suddenly finding his voice, Dennis shouted accusingly. 'Where's Damien?'

'I'm right here beside you dad,' his son replied, establishing his alibi.

Dragging their hoses behind them, Dennis Kreamer, and Percy, closely followed by Damien, hurried back up the road to tackle the fire that was now blazing in the remains of the ice cream van.

The houses in the close had plenty to talk about for the next few days. The main topic of course, was the fire at Thirteen. They always ended up however discussing Damien's latest escapade, which had brought about the destruction of the thing that they hated most of all, the black cloud pulling environmentally unfriendly ice cream van.

'Hey One.' Dunroaming shouted across the close. 'Has Damien's granddad gone home yet?'

'Of course he has, he left the next day. They asked him to stay on for a bit longer, but he said that he had to get back to the old peoples home. He has his eye on a lady who has just moved in, and there are a few dirty old reprobates at the home with the same idea as him. He said, that if he were to stay away for another day they wouldn't think twice about trying to get their feet under her table. Before he left, he took Mr Kreamer to one side. "I couldn't stay any longer even if I wanted to," he said. "I don't know what it is that your wife puts in the tumble-dryer, but whatever is, the smell it produces whenever she switches it on, makes me feel violently sick." '

'Did you notice that strange necklace he was wearing around his neck?' asked Dunroaming. 'I couldn't see it very well, but it looked like a small leather pouch hanging on a thick gold chain.'

'You don't miss much do you, but for once you've got it right.'

'It's intriguing isn't it? I wonder what he keeps in the pouch.'

'Maybe it's an extra set of false teeth,' said Two. 'It's always handy having another set hanging around, in case the set you're wearing fall out and break.'

'That couldn't happen,' said One. 'I've never heard of anyone's false teeth falling out. Anyway, Damien's granddad doesn't have false teeth. When he was crunching his way through a half-cooked baked potato last night, I heard him boasting to Mrs Braithwaite that he had his own teeth.'

'If he has false teeth, they would be his own. He would have had to pay the dentist for fitting them, wouldn't he?'

'I know what's in the pouch.' said One, importantly.

'How do you know that?' asked Four.

'Unlike Dunroaming, I don't just look, I listen as well. I heard him telling Damien how he got the necklace and what's in the leather pouch last night. It's a real good story, but telling stories makes me tired, so that's all I'm going to tell you for today. If you want to hear the rest, then, I'll tell it tomorrow morning. When it's nice and quiet.'

At six o'clock the next morning, Two said to One. 'I haven't slept a wink all night worrying about Damien's granddad. Are you going to tell us what he's got in that leather pouch?'

'Of course I am. I told you that I would yesterday, didn't I? Now if you are all standing comfortable, then, I will begin. Damien had been staring at his granddad's necklace for some time.

'Why are you wearing a necklace Granddad?' he asked. 'And what have you got in the leather pouch?'

His Granddad stroked the pouch loving. 'I've been wearing this round my neck since I was sixteen and I've lost count of the amount of people who have asked what is in the pouch.' He continued stroking the leather with a far away look in his eyes. 'In all that time I've only ever dared to tell story of how it came into my possession to a few trustworthy relatives. You are my grandson, so I suppose I should be able to trust you. In 1962 when I was sixteen, like most teenagers I yearned to see the world and have an adventurous life. The only way I could possible achieve such a dream without any money, was to join the Merchant Navy. My first voyage as cabin boy was on a rusty old cargo vessel. The ship had become becalmed somewhere off the coast of Africa. For almost twenty-four hours, the ship had been floating motionless in a sea as flat as a road that stretched in all directions as far as my eyes could see.

"This isn't a good sign," the ships cook said gravely. "It's the lull before the storm. I've been in situations like this several times. Once we were becalmed for two days, then, the mother of all storms came at us from out of nowhere."

I looked at the sea nervously, then, I said. We will be all right, won't we?

Cookie nodded his head. "Of course we will. If there is going to be a storm, I'm sure it will only be a small one."

Two hours later, in the middle of the day, the sky suddenly became as dark as night and thick, dark, clouds, enveloped the ship.

"Here it comes," Cookie said prophetically.

Then, with a frightening roar a gigantic wave the likes of which I had never seen before crashed down on us. The wave that followed seemed larger that the first, it continued that way for several hours, whipped up by the howling gale, giant waves ceaselessly battered the ship. Five of us were sheltering in the gallery when it happened. As if she knew that she was about to die the ships creaking hull seemed to scream aloud. Then, as if it had been sliced with a giant cleaver, the ship broke in half.'

'What happened then granddad?' asked Damien. His granddad shook his head to dispel the memories of the storm. 'luckily, I was thrown into the sea.' He said. 'There were two lifeboats on the ship and a wooden raft, which in normal circumstances would have been sufficient for a crew of twelve, but these weren't normal circumstances. The ship had gone down so fast we didn't have time to launch the boats. Luckily, the raft had broken free before the ship went under. I could see it bobbing up and down in the water fifty or so metres in front of me. I will remember that swim to the raft until the day I die. Several times, I thought I wouldn't be able to make it, but when you are afraid, you find hidden strength. The last thing I remember before passing out from sheer exhaustion was somebody pulled me aboard the raft. I don't know how long I was unconscious, but it must have been for quite sometime. When I came around, the storm had abated. The only visible evidence that there had ever been one was a thick black cloud on the horizon. There were only two others on the raft. Robert, a lad who was roughly the same age as me, and Charlie, whose body told me that he was a lot older. Robert offered me a drink of water. "Drink it slowly," he said. "And try not spill any, it's too precious to waste. This raft isn't equipped with much in the way of emergency provisions. There are about two gallons of drinking water and a few tins of food, and we don't know how long it will be before we are rescued, that's if we ever are," he said, pessimistically. Have you seen any other survivors, I asked. Robert shook his head. "The ship went down so fast it must have dragged the rest of the crew with it. Charlie and I thought everyone must have perished until we saw you swimming towards us. I don't suppose any of us would have made it to the raft in a sea like that if we hadn't been good swimmers."

For ten days we drifted on the open raft under a baking sun, for four those days we were without drinking water. The only respite we got from the sun was at night when it sank on the horizon. Then, it was so cold we had to cuddle together to keep warm. On the eleventh morning, I was the first one to awake. I was surprised to find that during the night the raft had washed up on a beach. As I was waking Robert and Charlie, I noticed several black men moving cautiously down the beach towards us. We've got company, I said trying to sound casual.

"They don't look like they are going to be friendly company," gasped Charlie in alarm. "They are all carrying spears, maybe they are cannibals."

Glaring at us fiercely, they raised their spears and waved them menacingly. The tallest of the men who seemed to be their leader, moved towards us and tapped me on the shoulder with his spear. "You will all come with us," he said in perfect English. "Our King is waiting to greet you"

The King looked at us glumly. "I'm afraid I have bad news," he said. "We have searched our coastline. It seems that you are the only survivors of the ship that went down in the storm." Then, his face broke into a smile. "I am sure that you will be pleased to know." His smile grew broader. "With the changing of the tide tomorrow, all three of you could be leaving my Kingdom very rich men."

The King rose from his diamond-studied throne and walked to several wicker baskets. Waving a finger down at one of the baskets, he said to Charlie. "Open it please."

When Charlie lifted the lid, we all stared down at the contents in open-eyed amazement. The basket contained hundreds of sparking diamonds.

The King pointed nonchalantly at the other baskets. "Were you to lift those lids, you would find that they also contain precious stones."

Robert turned and stared at the King, in disbelief. "I can't believe it," he said. "You have got seven baskets of diamonds and they are standing unguarded. Aren't you afraid they will get stolen?"

The King shook his head and laughed. "Who would want to steal the fabled treasure of King Solomon? My subjects have no use for diamonds, and if they were to take them where would they go? The cruel sea sometimes allows survivors of shipwrecks to be cast ashore, but it is always too rough to allow my people to leave."

The King must have noticed the look of alarm in our eyes. "Do not worry my friends, I know of a secret undercurrent that will carry a boat away from here and out to sea. Tomorrow you could be on that boat with your pockets filled with many precious stones like these."

As we stood trickling diamonds through our fingers, King Solomon walked to a table and picked up three small wicker baskets. Then, walking to the door, he said. "If you will kindly follow me, I will show you the place where diamonds such as these are waiting to be picked up, and the next people to pick them up could be you."

Greed must have been showing in our eyes, as we obediently followed him outside. We came to a halt at the edge of a gigantic lake. Pointing over the large expanse of water to an island, King Solomon said. "It must have been good fortune that brought you to my country on my birthday."

Charlie looked at me and whispered. "He must be cuckoo, if he thinks being shipwrecked is good fortune, it was the worse time of my life."

King Solomon must have heard his whispered words. "I didn't mean that you were fortunate to have been shipwrecked that must have been a very traumatic experience. You were fortunate however to have been washed on the beach where you were found, and Lady Luck must have been smiling at you to have brought you here on my birthday. Every year to celebrate the event, it is our custom to choose three of our best swimmers, these young men each have one of these wicker baskets fastened around their neck, and then with the lid of the basket open they swim to diamond island. Once they are there, they can take from the beach as many pebbles as they feel they can safely carry back in the baskets." A wide grin appeared on his face, when he said. "This year as my honoured guests, if you wish to attempt the dangerous swim, the privilege will be yours. However, I must warn you, that once you have closed the lid on the basket it will lock and you will not be able to open it again until you are back here. Not every stone that you pick up from the beach will be a diamond, but as you have already seen from my treasure, those who have attempted the swim in the past have returned with more diamonds than stones. It is the custom that I take half of what is brought back, the other half belongs to the swimmer."

As I entered the water, I felt an undercurrent tugging at my body. That is when I realized that the swim to the island would be no easy task. By the time I set foot on dry land again, every bone in my body was aching.

The others had already started gathering stones. Only take a few. I said. Remember that the basket will lock as soon as you close the lid and

if you take too many; their weight will pull you under on the return journey. Foolishly, they disregarded my advice. Whilst they were hurriedly
filling their baskets with the largest stones, they could find. I was pad-
ding mine with bird feathers. My companions were already on their way
back when I picked up two egg shaped pebbles. One for me and one for
King Solomon I thought, as I carefully laid them on the feathers and
closed the lid.

The return journey was a nightmare. One after the other I saw my
two companions dragged under the water by the burden that greed had
placed around their necks.

Finally, I managed to make it back to the beach. As I lay gasping
like an exhausted fish, the King removed the box from around my neck
and unlocked it. He seemed surprised to see that I had filled it with
feathers, then, he smiled. "You were wise," he said. "Feathers, are more
buoyant than diamonds." Then, picking up the two stones, he held one
in each hand. "You brought these back; so the choice is yours, which one
would you like to keep for yourself?" I was so exhausted I could barely
lift my hand. The one in the right, I said. Then, I fell into a deep sleep.'

Damien's grandfather raised a hand and touched the leather pouch.
'When I awoke I was lying in a small canoe out on the open sea with
enough food and water to last a few days. Around my neck was this
chain and leather pouch. When I opened it, I found a note and one of the
egg-shaped opaque stones that I had taken from the beach. When I read
the note, it said. The Royal Jeweller has tested the stone that you gave to
me and found it worthless. With luck, yours may have more value. I trust
that your canoe will carry you to friendly seas. Solomon.'

'Did you have your stone tested.' Damien asked excitedly.

Granddad shook his head. 'I didn't dare. After all, that I had been
through to get it, the disappointment if it had turned out to be just an ordinary stone would have been too much. Ever since that day, I have been
wearing it around my neck. One day when I am gone, it will belong to
your father. Knowing how much he likes money, I reckon he will have it
tested, on the day that he gets it.'

Granddad gave Damien a wink. 'Then, you will know if it's a diamond, and you will also know the end of the story.'

'Come on,' said Two. 'I don't believe Damien's granddad told him a Cock and Bull story like that. You made it all up.'

'Maybe I did and maybe I didn't, I'll leave it up to you to decide, but you must admit it was a good story.'

'I could make up a better story than that,' Dunroaming boasted arrogantly. 'And it would be more believable.'

'Right!' snapped One. 'I've had enough. You are always saying how clever you are; now I'm going to give you a chance prove it. Let's see if you really are capable of making up a story of your own.'

Dunroaming was beginning to regret what she had said. She had never made up a story of her own in the two years that she had been erected, she wasn't even sure that she knew how to begin. 'You will have to give me a week or two,' she said, playing for time. 'I can't just pick a story out of the air just like that; I've got to wait for a spark of inspiration. After all you wouldn't want to hear a trashy story, would you?'

'I'll give you until this time tomorrow, if you haven't made up a story by then, we will all know that you are never going to.'

Exactly twenty-four hours later, One said to Dunroaming. 'Come on then, we are all waiting to hear your story.'

'You don't think that I've been able to make one up do you?' said Dunroaming. 'Well you're wrong, because I have. My story is about a house, or a cottage to be exact, and it's titled.

The honeymoon cottage.

,

'Come on then,' said One. 'We're all waiting.'

Dunroaming cleared her throat. 'Jill gazed up into Jim's soft blue eyes, 'Oh darling,' she sighed, reaching up to kiss him, 'It's absolutely perfect; it's even more beautiful than it looked in the brochure.'

Jim grinned ruefully as he inserted the key in the front door. 'I can't deny that it's beautiful, but it isn't Venice is it? That's where I really wanted to take you for our honeymoon.'

Jill looked at him lovingly and kissed him again. 'I'm sure we'll make it to Venice one day, but at the moment I can't think of anywhere I would rather be. It's so romantic staying in a cottage that is only rented to honeymoon couples.'

Jim gathered his bride in his arms toed the door open and carried her across the threshold.

With her arms linked around his neck, he carried her into the lounge. 'Look!' She gasped excitedly, pointing to a small table by the window. 'Someone has left us huge bouquet of flowers and a bottle of champagne.'

Jim picked up the card that had been standing against the champagne and handed it to Jill. 'It's from the letting agents. It say's, the management and staff congratulate you on your wedding and take this opportunity to welcome you to Honeymoon Cottage.'

Jim gently lowered Jill onto the settee. 'How thoughtful of them,' he said. 'And they have even left the television switched on to make us feel at home.'

Jill looked at Jim coyly. 'This is our honeymoon darling; I don't think we will be watching television.'

Leaving their cases unpacked in the luxurious bedroom, with their arms entwined around each other's waists the newly-weds strolled in the beautifully kept garden which ran down to the cliff top overlooking the sea.

The week at the cottage had been idyllic. The days had simply flown by. With a sad sigh, Jill reluctantly closed the lid on her suitcase.

'I've booked a table by the window at The Tavern on the Cliff,' said

Jim, his words breaking into her thoughts. 'We must make the most of our last night here.'

The sky outside the cottage was moonless and dark. The kind of night that merited a torch. However, when you are young, in love, and only have eyes for each other, a torch is the last thing that you think of.

'Stop walking, before it's too late,' said a soft voice. 'You are going too close to the edge of the cliff.'

Jim gave Jill a puzzled look. 'Did you say something darling?'

Jill shook her head and returned Jim's puzzled look, then, they both heard someone shout. 'If you walk any further, you are both going to fall.' A ghostlike figure of a young woman loomed up in front of them. 'Please stop,' she pleaded. 'If you continue walking you will both end up down there on the rocks.'

For several seconds they both stood motionless with their arms wrapped around each other protectively, their eyes following the direction of the pointing finger.

A gentle gust of wind changed the shape of the phantom figure into a white misty cloud, which slowly drifted away over the edge of the cliff that the finger had revealed.

Now aware of the danger that lay just a few metres from their feet, Jim and Jill backed cautiously away.

The man from the letting agents called at the cottage the following morning to collect the keys. 'I hope you enjoyed your honeymoon.' He said, with a cheeky grin.

Jill glanced nervously at Jim, before she replied. 'Yes thank you. It was wonderful, except for last night.' Then, with a tremor in her voice, she told him about the incident on the cliff.

The grin had disappeared from the young man's face long before she had finished her story.

'If you two had fallen over the cliff,' he said. 'It would have been history repeating itself. If you talk to the locals, they will tell you the story of a young couple who thirty years ago were staying at this cottage on their honeymoon. On their last night at the cottage they went out for a stroll along the cliff, unfortunately they failed to see the edge and fell over. The next day they were found on the rocks below and according to the legend they were still holding hands.'

Ron and Jody were sitting on the settee watching television. Drawing Jody closer to him, Ron said. 'You never cease to amaze me darling, for thirty years we've been hiding the fact of our existence from others, yet to save the lives of Jill and Jim, you went ahead and materialized.'

Jody gave her husband a loving smile. 'I had to do it, there wasn't any choice. Sharing our lovely cottage with honeymoon couples every week is bad enough. Can you imagine what it would be like, having to live here for the rest of eternity, with another couple of ghosts?' '

'Well ?' Said Dunroaming. 'What did you think of it?'

One didn't answer.

'It was a bit scary,' said Three. 'But I thought it was good. Even if it does stop me from sleeping tonight.'

'We could make it a regular thing,' said Two. 'One has already told us the story she made up, and so has Dunroaming. Between now and next week I will try and think of one as well, then it will be Three's turn and so on until we've been all around the close.'

'My story wasn't made up,' One shouted angrily. 'Damien's granddad really did tell him the story that I told you.'

As it happened, Two was better at thinking up stories that he thought he would be. The next morning he announced to the close that he had been awake all night working on his story and now he was ready to tell it.

'You don't hang around do you?' said Three.

'Quiet the contrary,' quipped Two. 'It's because I'm hanging around in this close that I got the time to create my story. Now if you are all ready I'm going to get on with it, because my memory isn't very good, and in an hour or two from now it will have disappeared from my mind. The title of my story is, Yvonne's masterpiece.

The voluntary worker, who had just spent the best part of two hours creating the tableau of a smock-dressed artist standing at his easel painting, rewarded herself with a satisfied smile as she climbed from the hot, shop window. 'Come now,' she said, to the carefully posed fibreglass mannequin. 'Let's see you smile, you should be used to spending most of your life alone in the window. At least this time you shouldn't get bored, I've given you something to do. I want you to ignore all of the people passing by and paint me a nice picture. I'm not expecting a masterpiece, after all this is the first time you've ever had a paint brush Sellotaped to your hand.'

Yvonne's quick glimpse at the display as she jogged past the charity shop window aroused her curiosity enough to bring her daily run to a halt. Turning quickly she retraced her steps to the window. Years of cheeseparing had taught her to recognize bargains when she saw them. A close inspection of the price tickets attached to the artistic paraphernalia on display caused her feet to start moving again. This time, they carried her into the shop.

Yvonne could hardly believe her luck, at £40, the canvasses, brushes, and paints, were a bargain. 'I don't need the easel,' she said. 'I already have two, in my studio at home.'

The woman who had erected the tableau shook her head. 'I can't do that. I'm under strict instructions from the lady who brought them in; everything has to go in a single sale. So if you want the paints, brushes, and canvases, then you will have to take the easel as well.'

Some ten minutes later, having enriched the charity shop by £40, Yvonne stumbled out of the shop carrying the easel, several new canvases, dozens of brushes, the artist's smock, and a wooden box filled to the brim with an assortment of oil paints.

Outside the shop, she stopped to re-adjust her load and grinned up at the now naked fibreglass display model. Stripped of smock and the tools of his trade, the dummy stared fixedly ahead still posed in the position of an artist with a four inch strip of Sellotape dangling from the fingers of the hand that the window dresser had fixed at shoulder height.

Yvonne stared at the wooden easel curiously, as she adjusted it to a comfortable working position. Why had she bothered to dismantle the easel she had been using for years to erect the one she had just purchased. After all, they were identical, except for a few paint stains, and why had she suddenly decided that the time had come to change her style?

Strangely, the new brush felt familiarly comfortable in her hand. As she touched the virgin canvas with her first paint-laden stroke, the tips of her fingers tingled with excitement.

For over a week, the rising sun had called her from her bed to work on the canvas. Throughout the day, inspiration had forced her to keep painting, until pangs of hunger, and fading light, told her it was time to stop working and clean her brushes.

Standing with a brush poised in her hand, a satisfied smile started to grow on Yvonne's face as she gazed at the completed painting.

With a contented sigh, she lowered the brush to the right hand corner of the canvas and signed it. Then, laying her palette on top of the open tubes of paint littering the table, she stepped back from the easel to admire her work. **'I know that artists should never be satisfied with their creations,'** she said, running her eyes over the finished picture. **'But I'm convinced that this one is good enough for any Gallery.'**

When Yvonne had first started out along the hard lonely road of the artist, she had had aspirations of showing her paintings in the posh West-End Galleries. Although she had chased her dream with all the determination of one who really believed in herself, she had not yet had the satisfaction of seeing her work exhibited on the easels of a prestigious salon. Deep down inside she still believed that one day she would achieve her goal and find worldwide recognition.

When she had first brought her charity shop purchases home, she hadn't bothered to sort through the paints. Anxious to get on with the picture that was already taking shape in her mind, she had only used the colours that came easily to hand.

With the painting completed, she could now afford time to rummage through the oils. As she sorted through the contents of the upturned box, her paint-stained fingers uncovered a gold wristwatch. Carrying it to the window, she studied it carefully. Ornamental chase work on the casing, told her that it had value. A business card stapled to the side of the box, gave her an address.

Yvonne could see that the woman who answered the door was grieving; embarrassment brought a pink flush to her face, when she held up the watch. 'I'm sorry to disturb you,' she said, the blush deepening. 'I believe this belongs to you.'

Recognition wiped the sadness from the woman's eyes. 'How kind and honest of you to return it,' she said with a smile. 'It was my husband's most treasured possession. Where on earth did you find it?'

'It was lying amongst the tubes at the bottom of a box of paints that I bought in a charity shop, along with an easel, canvases and brushes.'

Tears welled in the woman's eyes. 'They were my husband's. I gave them to the shop to sell. He must have put the watch in the box before starting on his last painting.' She dabbed her tears away with a handkerchief. 'It was one of his little idiosyncrasies; he never wore the watch whilst he was working. He was afraid that if he did, it might turn him into a clock-watcher. He always believed that artists should never allow their creative minds to be influence by the passing of time.' Her face broke into a smile again. 'Would you like to see some of his work?'

Paintings lined the walls of the lounge. Yvonne recognized several as pictures that she had seen hanging at past Royal Academy Summer Exhibitions. Her eyes showed her surprise.

The woman seemed pleased at her guest's reaction. 'Are you familiar with his work?'

'He was my favourite artist. I've been an admirer of his talent for years.'

Attracted by the paintings, Yvonne ventured further into the room.

The woman walked to an unfinished picture hanging above the fireplace and stroked the frame lovingly. 'This is my husband's last work.' Then, she looked down at the watch and sighed. 'Unfortunately he passed away before he could finish it.'

Yvonne stared at the unfinished painting in disbelief. At the halfway stage, the picture on her easel had been identical to the one they were now looking at. Unable to believe her eyes she stood on tiptoe for a closer look. There was no doubt about it, the subject, and the brush strokes, even the colours had been the same.

Back in her studio, Yvonne ran her eyes over her masterpiece. She had been right. Although her painting was now finished, at the halfway stage it had been identical to the one in the woman's lounge.

Expecting to see her signature, Yvonne glanced down at the bottom right hand corner. What she saw caused her mouth to drop open in surprise.

Although she had not been aware of it at the time of signing, she had credited the painting to the artist whose wife had donated the paints.

Yvonne thought about showing the completed painting to the grieving widow. 'I can't do that,' she mumbled, as she reluctantly stored it away in the cupboard under the stairs. '**If she ever sets her eyes on it, she will accuse me of plagiarism. I would never be able to convince her that the artistic spirit of her dead husband lives on, in the brushes and paints that I bought at the charity shop.' '**

Three was the first to speak. 'Did Yvonne buy the paints and brushes at the charity shop down in the town?'

'There weren't any paints and brushes.' Two answered with a sigh. 'My story's fictitious.'

'You could say that she bought them down at the shop in town. It would add a touch of realism.'

'If you want realism, then, put some into your own story when you write it.' Two snapped angrily.

###CHAPTER ELEVEN###

November 28th

Percy Grant ran an eye of appraisal over Kreamer's new burger van. 'I thought you were going to buy another ice cream van?'

'I was,' Kreamer replied. 'But with this, I've got the best of both worlds. I can sell burgers in the winter and ice creams in the summer.'

'And you can sell my mothers delicious biscuits whenever they are available.' Percy added with a grin.

'By the way,' said Kreamer. 'How is the biscuit situation?'

'Now that you've got your new van, Mum is going to restart production tonight. By tomorrow morning, there should be enough stock to last the weekend.'

'I'm going to work really hard during the winter,' Kreamer said earnestly. 'I've got to make up for the money that I've lost since my old van went up in smoke. Do you think you will be able to keep me supplied?'

'I haven't been selling since the fire either. I should think I've enough cannabis stored away to supply you and the whole of Copenhagen, if they were to ask.'

'That's what I wanted to hear,' said Kreamer. 'I'm expecting business to be manic. It's the first day of December in two days time and I intend to cut myself a nice slice of the Christmas trade.'

'I could package them for you if you like,' said Percy eagerly. 'I could put a dozen biscuits in a box with nice Christmassy printing on the lid. Something like, (Granny Grant's biscuits melt in the mouth.) On the side of the box, we could print, supplied solely to Kreamer's burger and ice cream van. But before we can get into that kind of production, I shall have to find new premises to grow my plants,' *Percy was getting carried away by his dream* 'my loft and back garden won't be big enough.'

'I bet your mum would do a backward somersault with delight if that ever happened,' said Kreamer. 'I should think she's getting really fed up with the bedroom ceiling coming down on top of her every other month.'

'She's not bothered about it now,' Percy replied with a grin. 'She told me the other morning that she quite likes sleeping *under* the bed.'

Kreamer shook his head and started to walk away, then, he stopped. 'If we ever get round to selling boxed biscuits with our trade name printed on them, we'll be in the big time. And when we get nicked by the police, we will end up doing big time.'

'I've finished writing my story,' said Three. 'I got the idea when I thought about the plants that Percy is growing up in my loft.'

'It isn't about a drug baron is it?' Asked Four.

'No, it hasn't anything to do with drugs. It's about a horticulturist. Would you like to hear it?'

'What's a horticulturist?' Asked Five. 'I've never heard that word before.'

'You'll find out as I progress through the story. Now can I get on with it?'

'It's not much use telling a story about a horticulturist, if we don't know what you're talking about.' Mumbled Six, he had never heard the word before either.

Three sighed. 'The Dictionary definition of horticulture is the art or science of cultivating gardens.'

'So it's about a gardener,' said Three. 'Why didn't you say so in the first place? You won't impress us with fancy words you know.'

'Can I start now?' asked **Three** impatiently. 'All stories should have a title, mine is called. Say it with flowers.

Percy had to smile when he read the words on the banner strung across the entrance of the Garden Centre car park.

ADAM WELCOMES YOU TO THE GARDEN OF EDEN. THE HOME OF HEAVENLY FLOWERS.

Part of the printed greeting became verbal, when he passed through the automatic doors. 'Welcome to the Garden of Eden,' said the man in the white coat.

'You must be Adam,' Percy replied with a grin.

'Sorry.' The man replied seriously. 'Adam won't be greeting any visitor's today. Unfortunately he has been rushed to the hospital.' Then, shaking Percy's hand warmly he added. 'I'm his brother James.'

'I hope it isn't anything serious,' said Percy.

'It's going to spoil his good looks, but it's his own fault, he wouldn't listen to me when I warned him. If he had, it would never have happened. Are you interested in crossbred flowers?' He asked as if trying to change the subject. 'If you are.' He waved his hand around proudly. 'Then, you've come to the right place to find them. All of the hybridized plants you will see growing here are the results of my brother's work. Once I have shown you around the gardens and you've seen pansies crossed with stocks, roses with hydrangea and the hundreds of other flowers that he has created, you will be so captivated by them I am sure you will want to return time and again.' '

'Here you go again,' said **Five**. 'Spouting fancy words that we've never heard before. What does hybridized mean?'

'You'll be telling your story soon,' **Three** snapped angrily. 'I bet you won't like it if I keep interrupting you.'

'You won't have to. I won't be trying to confuse you with long words that you won't understand, because I don't know any.'

'Don't take any notice of Five,' said Dunroaming. 'The rest of us are enjoying your story, and the only reason she doesn't know any long words is because she's ignorant.'

'Ignorant?' Shouted Five. 'Did you say that I'm ignorant? Maybe I should be offended, but I don't know the meaning of that word.'

Three decided to continue her story.

'As they toured the nursery Percy's eyes were dazzled by the kaleidoscope of colour.

Percy pointed towards an attractive looking flower standing in a pot on the floor of a small greenhouse. 'What combination of plants did he use to create that one?'

James didn't answer his question; instead, he cupped a hand under his elbow and guided him away.

'This place, and everything in it, is absolutely amazing.' Percy gasped in astonishment. 'How did it all begin?'

'With a surname like Eden, it was inevitable that my parents should name their first born son Adam. No doubt if he had been born a girl, they would have named her Eve. Almost as soon as he could walk, Adam spent most of the day digging in the garden with a toy fork and spade. By the time he reached the age of eight, his green-fingered efforts had convinced our family that when he grew up he would be a horticulturalist. I had always thought that Adam was a bit strange, he didn't play football or cricket like other boys he was only interested in hybridizing flowers. Off course, my parents idolized him. They believed he was a genius and no doubt, they were right. When they both passed away several years ago, they stipulated in their wills that the money raised from their estate would be used to purchase a Garden Centre, which would be owned jointly by Adam and me. They also stated that Adam should be allowed to continue his experiments. Of course, not all of the flowers turned out to be a success. He did have his failures. These he always incinerated as soon as he recognized them as such. Had he not done so they might have contaminated other plants. When my brother first told me he intended to cross an Antirrhinum with a Venus flytrap, I told him it wouldn't work, and if it did, it would be so ugly no one would want to buy it. As usual, he ignored my advice and went ahead with his experiment. Even though he couldn't get it right, he stubbornly persevered. After four years of frustration and disappointment, he finally succeeded in growing a flower, which is different from any other I have ever seen. It's that beautiful plant that you saw locked in the greenhouse. When he showed me the bloom for the first time this morning, I had to take back all that I had said. Not only had he successfully crossed a Snapdragon with a Venus flytrap, it was something to behold, its beauty left me breathless. I had no doubts that once it was on the market, it would make us a fortune. Now my brother is in hospital and my dreams of riches have disappeared. Later today, I shall be carrying the plant that put him in hospital to the incinerator where it will be destroyed.'

Percy seemed confused. 'Why are you going to destroy it? You've just told me that its beauty left you breathless?'

'There's no way we can sell such a plant to the general public.'

'Why can't you? What's wrong with it?'

'We've just discovered that it's vicious.'

'Vicious?' Percy said with a laugh. 'How can a flower be vicious?'

James gave him a serious look. 'Believe me that plant is really dangerous, it has put my brother in hospital.'

'How did it manage to do that?'

'When he showed it to me, I said. It's beautiful; does it smell as nice as it looks? My brother shrugged his shoulders. "How do I know?" he said. "The bud has only just opened, I haven't smelt it yet." Then, when he bent to sniff its fragrance, the flower suddenly raised its head opened its mouth and bit off the end of his nose.' '

###CHAPTER TWELVE###

December 1st

Sixteen sounded puzzled when he said. 'What's the matter Five, you've been staring across the close at me for most of the morning.'

'I was wondering why the curtains have been closed in your front room, they have never been drawn before. Have your tenants got something in the front room that they don't want their neighbours to see?'

'If you keep looking at the front door, you will see Mrs Woodward come out in a minute or two, then, she will hang a wreath above the knocker.'

'Why is she going to hang a wreath on the front door? It isn't Christmas yet, is it?'

Sixteen didn't answer.

'Have you suddenly gone deaf?' shouted Five. 'Why is your tenant's wife going to hang a wreath on the front door?'

'The wreath is to let people know that someone in the house has died.'

'Who is it?' Five shouted again, this time a little louder. 'And how did it happen?'

'Hush!' said Sixteen. 'Don't shout; show a bit of respect for the dead.'

'If the person is dead, then he or she can't hear me, and even if the dead person was alive he or she wouldn't be able to hear me, in fact no one but houses can hear me, so why does it matter if I shout?'

'Apart from some of the residents shouting and rowing occasionally this happens to be a nice quiet close, and we want to keep it that way. That's why we don't want you to shout.'

'Which of your tenants has died?' asked Eight softly.

'It's Mr Woodward.'

'How did he die?' Seven asked curiously.

'He was pulling a wardrobe down the stairs, then, he gave a long drawn out groan and grasped the left side of his chest. Seconds later, he came sliding down the stairs with the wardrobe on top of him. When his grandson Jim, who was the only other person in the house at the time, heard the groan and the noise of the wardrobe sliding down the stairs, he ran to see what had happened. If it had been a light clothes cupboard, instead of the heaviest part of a beautiful hand crafted mahogany bedroom suite, maybe Jim would have been able to lift it off his granddad. Of course, it would have lighter if the old boy had thought to remove the coffin before single-handedly attempting to drag the wardrobe downstairs.'

'Why one earth was there a coffin in the wardrobe?' asked Nine, who, like most of the other houses in the close, sensed that the story Sixteen was about to tell would be worth hearing.'

'I'll be coming to that in a minute,' Sixteen said with a sigh. 'Can I continue now? Because Jim wasn't strong enough to lift the wardrobe on his own he had to waste valuable minutes running next door for help.'

'Those minutes must have seemed like an eternity to poor Mr

Woodward.' **Eight said sympathetically.**

'When Mr Pringle and Mr Curtis, Seventeen and Eighteen's tenants lifted the wardrobe off Mr Woodward, he smiled up at Jim. 'Will you take a look at my coffin and let me know if it's still intact?' he mumbled feebly. Jim opened the wardrobe door and looked inside. 'I **can't see any damage granddad,'** he said. Mr Woodward sighed with relief. **'It's not often a person is killed by their own coffin,'** he said with a laugh, and then he died.'

'It couldn't have done my tenant's bad back any good, lifting a mahogany wardrobe with a coffin in it,' **said Seventeen.** 'But, why was Mr Woodward pulling it downstairs?'

'Your tenant hasn't got a bad back,' **mumbled Sixteen.** 'He only pretends that he has so that he can claim a disability allowance.'

Sixteen was beginning to feel important, all of the houses in the close actually wanted to hear what he had to say. 'Mrs Woodward is the one to blame for what happened her husband would still be alive today if she hadn't thrown him and the coffin out of their bedroom.'

'She didn't throw him out literally did she?' **asked Twelve in surprise.**

Sixteen, tutted angrily at the interruption. 'Of course she didn't, but I'm sure she would have been capable of doing so, if she had tried.'

'What was a coffin doing in the wardrobe?' **asked Nine again.**

Sixteen was really enjoying being the centre of attraction. 'If you'll just keep quiet for a bit longer, I'll tell you. Mr Woodward started making the coffin just after he got married and Mrs Woodward wasn't too happy when he told her what he intended to do.

'It's morbid,' she said. 'You're in the prime of your life, so why do you want to make your own coffin?'

'It's my new hobby,' he replied. 'Everyone should have a hobby.'

'If you want to do something in your spare time,' she said angrily. 'Why don't you knock up a garden shed, or something useful like that? They must be cheaper to make than a coffin, and you can always sell them. We could do with some extra cash.'

Mr Woodward snorted indignantly. 'I'm a skilled joiner, anyone with a hammer and a saw can build a shed. It takes an experienced man to make a coffin. Besides, I won't be able to get anything cheaper than the coffin I'm going to make; it isn't going to cost me a penny. I'm going to use bits of hardwood that were left over from jobs I've completed at work.' '

'How do you know all this?' asked Fourteen.

'Like One said to Four two or three. weeks ago. "I don't just look, I listen as well." As a matter of fact, I heard Mrs Woodward telling her two grandsons the story yesterday.'

'What happened after he told her he was going to make the coffin out pieces of scrap wood,' asked Four, who simply loved hearing gossip.

'They had a bit of a row but she left him to it. Nine months after Mr Woodward had carried the first small piece of oak into his backyard workshop, he laid down his French polish rag and stepped back to admire the finished product. Then, he called his wife and showed her what he had made.'

'Did his wife like the coffin when he showed it to her?' asked Ten.

'No, she hated it, and they had a terrific row when she found that he had used her wedding dress to line the inside.

'You should have asked me if you could have it,' she yelled at the top of her voice. 'I was going to use that dress to make a christening gown for our first child.'

It didn't help matters when he handed her the bodice and sleeves.

'I don't know what you're making all the fuss about,' he said. 'A baby is only small and there's plenty left.'

The next day, ignoring his wife's protests, he proudly dragged the scrap wood coffin through the kitchen and up the stairs to their bedroom.

'Where are you going to put it?' she asked.

'It's going in there, with my clothes,' he said, pointing at his wardrobe. 'Then you won't have to see it again until it's needed.'

Mrs Woodward didn't like the idea one little bit. 'I really hate it,' she screamed. 'And I'm going to see it every time I open your blooming wardrobe door.'

Mr Woodward gave her a hurt look. 'It's a pity you feel that way,' he said. 'I've managed to save several nice pieces of mahogany, oak, and bird's-eye maple from being thrown on the furnace. I was going to start making your coffin next.'

'What were you going to line it with?' she snarled. 'I only had *one* wedding dress.'

Mr Woodward walked to a drawer and pulled out a shirt wrapped in cellophane. 'I was going to use the shirt that I wore when we got married,' he replied.'

'Hang on a minute,' said Four sceptically. 'How could he have carried a small piece of oak into his backyard workshop, you haven't got a backyard, you've got a garden and a very small shed, and there's no way you can call that shed a workshop?'

'I knew you lot wouldn't let me tell the story without interruptions,' Sixteen said with a sigh. 'Mr Woodward made his coffin thirty five years before he came to live in me; he brought it with him when he moved in eight years ago. I can still see the stained looks on the removal men's faces as they struggled with it up the stairs. Mr Woodward waited until they stood it against the bedroom wall, then; he opened it up and showed them what was inside.'

'What did the removal men say when they saw the coffin?' asked Four.

They stood staring at it in disbelief for a couple of minutes, then, one of them swore, and the other one said. 'You'll have to pay us extra mate, we were contracted to remove furniture, not carry coffins.'

Forty-three years later, Mrs Woodward shouted. 'I've had enough. Your blooming coffin has fallen on me once to often. If you insist on keeping it in the wardrobe, then you and that monstrosity will have to move out.'

Poor Mr Woodward stared at his wife in disbelief. 'It's been in my wardrobe for over forty years,' he said. 'Why have you suddenly decided that I've got to move it?'

Mrs Woodward sat on the bed and stared at the wardrobe. 'I'm sick to death of living with a coffin in the bedroom, I haven't had a decent nights sleep since you put it there.'

Mr Woodward looked at his coffin and sighed. 'Where can we go?' he asked, as if the coffin was a person. 'We've only got two bedrooms and our grandsons are using the other whilst their parents are in Australia on business.'

Mrs Woodward gave him a cold hard glare. 'You could put the coffin in the shed at the bottom of the garden.'

'I couldn't put it in there that shed is damp and cold, and damp would ruin the varnish.'

'If you're not going to put it in your shed, then you will both have to move downstairs into the front room.' '

'What happened then?' asked Seventeen.

Sixteen's letterbox flapped gently when he sighed. 'Poor Mr Woodward stubbornly started inching the wardrobe towards the door, so his wife put on her coat and went out for a walk. That was the last time she saw him alive. I'm sure that if she had known that he would be daft enough to try and drag the wardrobe down the stairs on his own, she would never have thrown him out of the bedroom.'

'You poor thing,' said Seventeen sympathetically. 'Your stairs must have taken a dreadful bashing when the coffin carrying wardrobe slid down.'

Sixteen lapped up the sympathy. 'I was pretty lucky really; there were only a few scratches on the wall and three broken balusters.'

'Did it feel creepy having a coffin in one of your bedrooms?' asked Fifteen.

'Why should it?' Sixteen replied. 'The coffin was made of wood and the wardrobe was made of wood, and when you come to think of it there's an awful lot of wood in all of us, and we're not creepy, are we?'

'I was once,' said Eleven proudly. 'Remember when I pretended to be haunted to get rid of my tenants? I was really creepy then.'

'We're not talking about the time you had to get rid of your tenants,' said Fifteen rudely. 'What we want to know is. If Sixteen didn't feel creepy having a coffin in one of his bedrooms, then, why did his tenant's wife keep moaning about it?'

'I think she was entitled to moan,' said Sixteen, in defence of his tenant. 'Nearly all of her married life she had had to live with a coffin in the wardrobe, and every time she opened the doors the ghastly thing fell on her.'

Mr Wakeman the undertaker didn't like the idea of burying Mr Woodward in his homemade coffin. 'Coffins should look like they've been made to last forever,' he said pompously. 'And usually they are crafted out of one type of wood, not several like this.'

Jim's macabre moneymaking idea came to him when we went into the front room to see his granddad laid out in his coffin. 'He certainly made a good job of this,' he said to his brother John, running a dirty finger over the patchwork coffin's highly polished surface. 'But he should have stuck this down a bit better.' His fingers disappeared inside the white silk lining. 'It's coming away here.'

'Maybe he left it like that on purpose,' said John, 'so that he could hide his spare money inside.'

Jim gazed admiringly at his granddads handiwork. 'Don't talk daft,' he said. 'He didn't have any spare money. He wouldn't have made this coffin out of bits and pieces if he had?'

At least Jim had the decency to wait until they were out of the room before he told John what he intended to do. 'My friend Dave's cat got knocked down and killed last night. I'm going to tell him that he can give his pet a proper funeral and the service that goes with it if he wants to, I will put it in granddad's coffin for fifty pence.'

'You shouldn't do that,' said John. 'It isn't right to make money out of someone's funeral.'

'Why not?' said Jim. 'Undertaker's do, and after all, I am family.'

'You still shouldn't do it. Granddad was allergic to cats. Besides, someone's sure to notice if there's a dead animal lying in there with him.'

'They won't see it,' said Jim forcefully, 'I'm going to push it to the bottom between the lining and the wood.'

That evening, Dave's cat was lying beneath the silk lining under Mr Woodward's legs.

'Do you know of anyone else who's got a dead pet that needs a funeral?' Jim asked Dave, as he saw him to the door. 'If you do there's room for several more in the coffin.'

'Why don't you advertise on the newsagent's notice board?' said John sarcastically.

Jim shook his head dismissively. 'I can't do that, Gran might see it; she's always scanning those adverts looking for cleaning jobs.'

Dave put the word around that there was coffin space available for dead pets.

Luckily, Jim's Gran wasn't in when he answered the door to several small children, each carrying a dead pet. Four of the luckless animals seemed to have died from natural causes, two looked as if they had met their deaths in accidents, and one mangy looking cat in an advanced state of decomposition, had obviously been lying around for several weeks.

'Why didn't you bury it when it died?' asked Jim, as the boy handed him fifty pence and the dead cat.

The boy wiped his hands on his jumper. 'How could I? He's been missing for weeks. I only found his body yesterday morning.'

'Can I come to the funeral?' asked a small girl tearfully, as she watched Jim wrap her hamster in cling film.

'Of course you can,' he said good-heartedly, 'but it's going to cost you another fifty pence, and you will have to make your own way there.'

Tears appeared in Gran's eyes, when she looked down at Granddad on the day of the funeral. 'You always were an awkward man,' she sobbed. 'But why did you have to go and die under your own coffin?' Then, a frown appeared on her brow. 'There's something wrong,' she said turning to look at Jim.

Jim's heart missed a beat. Blimey, he thought, she's noticed the bumps in the coffin lining.

'It's his cheeks, they're too hollow. Your Grandfather never had sunken cheeks.'

John, who had been thinking the same as Jim, breathed a sigh of relief. 'I know why he looks like that,' he said trying to sound casual. 'He hasn't got his false teeth in.'

'You're right,' said Gran. Then, she looked at Jim again. 'Will you run upstairs and get them. You'll find them in a glass on the table beside the bed.'

The room was in darkness, except for a thin beam of light that had found its way in through a gap in the curtains. Like a miniature searchlight, it lit the table beside the bed. Water spilled on the floor, when Jim, with a look of disgust on his face, fished out the dentures with two fingers. Clasping them firmly in his hand, he made his way back down the stairs.

'There you are Gran,' handing her the teeth, he wiped his wet hand down the leg of his trousers.

'Thank you Jim,' she said, then, parting granddads lips, she slipped the teeth into his mouth. 'He looks more like your Granddad now.'

Mrs Kreamer could see that her husband was in a flaming mood. 'What's up love?' she asked. 'Did you get out of the wrong side of the bed this morning?'

'I wish I hadn't got out at all,' he grunted angrily. 'Thanks to blooming Damien and the Guy he made last bonfire night, I've got to go down to the charity shop to see if I can buy a new black suit.'

'What do you want a black suit for?'

'I'll need one won't I, if I'm going to follow at Mr Woodward's funeral?'

'You hardly knew the man, so why do you want to go to his funeral?'

'It's a matter of respect, besides, there's sure to be plenty of food and drink after and I won't get invited unless I follow.'

'What are you going to follow in? We don't have a car and if you use the new burger and ice cream van, it's going to look *disrespectful.* And knowing how you're always looking for the opportunity to pick up a few quid, you'll probably want to sell burgers at the cemetery.'

Mr Kreamer grinned. 'A white van following a hearse and a line of black cars will be a bit of a novelty, but it shouldn't matter if there is a burger and ice cream van at the end of the line. After all, it's the thought that counts.'

'Are you going on your own, or do you want me to come?'

Kreamer looked at his wife and shook his head. 'Percy Grant wants to come with me; he's never been to a funeral before.'

'Has he got a black suit?' enquired Mrs Kreamer doubtfully. 'Or is he thinking of going in a pair of black boxers?'

'I doubt if he has got a suit,' Kreamer replied. 'I've never seen him wearing one; I've never seen him wearing black boxers either.'

Mrs Kreamer picked up a pair of Priscilla's wet knickers and threw them in the tumble dryer. 'Neither have I,' she said. 'Thank goodness.'

'Are they burying Mr Woodward today?' Fifteen whispered to Sixteen.

'Of course they are,' Sixteen replied. 'That's why there's a hearse parked outside, and there's no need to whisper, after all they can't hear us.'

'Has Mr Kreamer and Percy Grant been invited?'

'I hope not. What made you ask?'

'They've been tying black ribbons on the new van.'

'You're kidding,' said Sixteen.

'No she's not,' said Fourteen. 'I've been watching them do it, and what's more, they are both wearing black suits.'

'Did they look like they were under the influence of cannabis?' asked Sixteen nervously.

'They didn't look any different than usual; they always seem to be walking on air to me. But I think the ice cream man was taking it seriously; I didn't hear him swear once during the hour it took for them to decorate the van, and he seemed to be in a melancholy mood.'

'History is going to be made here today,' shouted Dunroaming. 'This will be the first time that a white burger and ice cream van decorated with black ribbons has followed a funeral.'

'Can you hear me Ten?' Sixteen shouted loudly and disrespectfully considering there was a hearse parked outside his front door. 'Has the noisy lorry that has just pulled up outside you got anything to do with the funeral?'

'Of course it hasn't.' Ten shouted back. 'Lorries don't follow funerals. It's delivering the crucial part of the inventors environmentally friendly machine that he hopes will earn him a fortune by converting rubbish into a gas that will be used to fuel cars.'

'White ice cream and burger vans don't usually follow funerals either,' said Dunroaming. 'But today is going to be an exception to the rule.'

'Is that the part that's on the lorry?' asked One softly. 'If it is then it looks like the tumble dryer that I've got in my kitchen, the one which Mrs Kreamer uses to dry Priscilla's wet knickers, but the one on the lorry is a whole lot bigger.'

'You're right,' said Ten. 'It is a tumble dryer; the inventor said he bought it from a launderette that closed down last October. He believes it was a bargain; it only cost two hundred pounds. To buy it new would have been more like a thousand.'

Sixteen sounded concerned. 'I hope he has the decency to wait until the coffin has been put in the hearse before he starts building his confounded machine.'

'I doubt if it will ever get built,' Nine said cheerfully. 'Mr Ledger my tenant, told his wife last night that the health inspector will be round this afternoon to check on the inventor. If he finds that Ten is in a filthy, dangerous, condition, which it is, he has the authority to order the inventor to clean up the house or face eviction.'

'The health inspector is definitely going to find me in a filthy, dangerous, condition,' said Ten. 'I'm ashamed to admit it, but I smell vile, and I'm overloaded with all sorts of scummy, grubby, grimy, mucky rubbish, in fact I can't wait for the health inspector to arrive.'

'I wonder how many skips it will take to clear you?' said Nine.

'I feel like cheering,' said Ten. 'And if there wasn't a hearse standing outside Sixteen, then I would.'

'You can cheer if you want,' said Sixteen graciously. 'Mr Woodward isn't in the hearse yet and even if he was, he wouldn't hear you.'

There was a strange look in the undertaker's eyes as he fastened the lid. Had he noticed that granddad had moved an inch or two higher up the coffin since he had laid him out, or was it because he wasn't too happy at the thought of burying someone in a coffin made from bits and pieces of salvaged wood.

'I wonder what he would have said, if he had seen the menagerie of dead animals lying under the wedding dress lining.' whispered Fifteen.

Someone pressing their thumb on the front door bell broke the silence in the room.

'Be a good boy John and go and see who it is,' said Gran, 'I expect it will be the florist with more flowers.'

She couldn't have been more wrong. The boys standing on the doorstep didn't have any flowers, the one with his thumb still on the bell push had a dead pigeon in his hand, and the other was holding a dead rat.

'You're too late to use Granddad's coffin,' whispered John. 'They will be carrying him out any minute now. So it looks like you will have to find someone else who is having a funeral, or you could bury them in your own back gardens.'

The one with the rat gave a disappointed sigh. 'He's beginning to pong a bit,' he said. 'Will you ask Jim if he knows of anyone with a relative who's going to be buried in the next couple of days? And if he does will he give us their address?'

With the front room looking like a tent at the Chelsea Flower Show, the coffin standing on two trestles in the middle looked strangely out of place. Tears welled in Gran's eyes as she walked to the sideboard and pulled out a bottle of champagne. 'We were saving this to drink on our Golden Wedding day,' she said, holding it up for all to see. 'It won't be happening now, so I'll take it with me, and share it with him at the grave.'

'Get that coffin into the hearse as quick as you can.' Mr Wakeman whispered to the pallbearers. 'And cover it with flowers. Our reputation will be up the spout if people along the route see the coffin and think it's one of ours. Trade has been bad enough lately, without that.'

Jim tapped his lips with a finger. 'You've forgotten something Gran,' he whispered. 'You haven't got your teeth in.'

'I would forget my head if it wasn't screwed on,' she said with a sheepish grin, then, she started to make her way up the stairs. 'I know where they are, they're in a glass on my side of the bed.'

A couple of minutes later Gran came down shaking her head. Holding out a set of dentures for Jim to see, she said. 'Do you know what's happened? When you went upstairs for your Grandfather's teeth, you picked the wrong glass. Now, he's going to be buried wearing mine.' Then, with a shrug of her shoulders, she slipped her dead husbands teeth into her mouth.

Jim looked horrified. 'You're not going to Granddad's funeral wearing his teeth are you?' he gasped.

'I haven't got much choice, have I,' she replied. 'He's wearing mine, and I can't go to his funeral looking gummy.'

'You'll be uncomfortable wearing Granddad's teeth.'

'I'll be embarrassed as well, if they fall out when I'm talking.'

Jim searched in his pocket. Handing her a stick of chewing gum, he said. 'Chew on this for a couple of minutes Gran, and when its soft, put Granddads teeth in, it will help to make them stick.'

Gran looked at John as she climbed into the funeral car. 'Why are they here?' she asked, pointing at the children gathered around the hearse.

'I think they've come to pay their last respects,' he lied, throwing a dagger like look at Jim. 'Granddad was a very popular man.'

The funeral procession moved slowly down the close, once around the corner it gathered speed. Some of the children following their pets in the hearse broke into a run, but they had to give up the chase. Their legs were no match for the speeding hearse, funeral car, and the white burger and ice cream van tastily decorated with black ribbons.

Four who had made their way to the church earlier, were waiting at the cemetery gates. Silently they followed the cortège along the drive.

'What are those children doing here?' asked Gran.

Jim shrugged his shoulders and gave John a sly wink. 'It's like John said, Granddad was a popular man.'

After the graveside service, Gran opened the bottle of champagne and poured some of the liquid on granddads coffin. 'Goodbye love,' she said raising the bottle to her lips. Before she had time to feel any of the bubbles going up her nose, the earth suddenly gave way beneath her feet. Screaming as she fell, she landed on top of the coffin with a loud groan and an almighty thud. Then Granddad's teeth flew out of her mouth and landed on the coffin lid.

'I don't think Granddad likes Gran's teeth very much,' Jim whispered to John. 'It looks like he's trying to claim his own set back.'

Jim wasn't the sort of boy who would let the grass grow under his feet. While he was looking around the cemetery on his way out, he got his next moneymaking idea.

'I've just thought of another way we can make a load of money,' he whispered to John.

'It didn't take long for you to come up with another crazy scheme, did it? I hope you are not thinking of asking me to help you. If you are, then, you can forget it.'

Jim looked at him and grinned. 'How do you know it's a crazy scheme? You haven't heard it yet.'

'John stuck his hands over his ears and pressed them tight to his head. 'Don't tell me what it is,' he pleaded. 'I don't want to hear. All of your moneymaking schemes so far have been barmy. So why should this one be any different?'

'Are you sure you don't want to hear what it is?' Jim whispered.

'Of course I'm sure,' John said firmly. 'If I wanted to hear what it is, I wouldn't be holding my hands over my ears.'

'Okay, if you don't want to come in on it with me, then, I'm going to ask Damien Kreamer. When I tell him all about it, I'm sure he'll jump at the chance to make a load of easy money.'

'You can ask him if you like,' said John, 'I don't care. But with him helping you, it's sure to end in disaster.'

'This is probably the best day of my life,' shouted Ten, as the public health inspectors van drove out of the close. 'The inventor has been given a week to clean me up. If he hasn't complied by then he will face eviction.'

'It's a shame in a way,' said Dunroaming. 'We will never know if the inventor really was what he claimed to be, and the world will never benefit from his environmentally friendly rubbish into gas machine.'

'How long has Mrs Woodward's grandson Jim been friendly with Damien?' Dunroaming shouted across the close to Sixteen.

'I don't think they are friends.' Sixteen shouted back. 'What makes you say that they are?'

'They're standing outside One with their heads close together whispering, and as far as Damien's concerned that can only mean one thing, he's up to no good. You can bet your foundations he's going to lead that nice boy Jim into trouble.'

Dunroaming couldn't have been more wrong. It was Jim who was doing the leading this time.

'I wouldn't take any notice of Dunroaming if I was you Sixteen,' said One. 'We all know that she's got a nasty suspicious mind.'

'They're planning something,' Dunroaming said haughtily. 'And whatever it is, it's sure to be bad. That Damien is the kind of a boy who gets his kicks going around puncturing bouncy-castles.'

'Don't you ever give anyone the benefit of the doubt?' asked One. 'Maybe Jim's telling Damien about his Grandfathers funeral.'

'If they are talking about the funeral, then surely they would look a bit more serious than they do, Damien is grinning like a demented Cheshire cat.'

'You know what's wrong with you Dunroaming?' shouted Sixteen. 'You've never forgiven Damien for the time he stuck those two bananas up the exhaust of your owner's car.'

'You lot can't hear what Damien and Jim are saying because

you're all slightly deaf and they're talking in whispers, which is suspicious in itself. However, I'm the youngest house in the close and I still have exceptionally good hearing. In fact it is so good, I've just heard Damien say to Jim, that he would meet him outside his house at midnight.'

'We all know that you're the youngest house in the close,' snapped Sixteen angrily. 'We also know, that you shout the loudest.'

Damien closed his front door softly behind him and tiptoed round to the back of the house.

As the local church clock started to strike midnight, he reappeared again pushing Priscilla's old pushchair. With the wheels squeaking every time they turned, he steered it to Number 16.

Jim stepped out from the shadows making Damien jump. 'Doesn't that thing make a lot of noise?' he said.

'It doesn't make half as much as I would have, if I had screamed.' Damien snarled angrily. 'What did you have to frighten me for?'

Jim grinned in the darkness. 'I was just testing you,' he said. 'You won't be much use to me if you're easily scared.'

'Where are we going?' asked Damien. 'And why did I have to bring Priscilla's old pushchair?'

'I'll tell you later,' Jim whispered mysteriously. 'If I tell you now, you might not want to come.'

'I told you they were planning something,' said Dunroaming, as the two youngsters and the noisy pushchair turned the corner. 'I wonder where they're going.'

'Wherever it is, they shouldn't be going there,' said One. 'Not at this time of the night.'

'I can't see how we're going to make loads of money pushing a squeaky wheeled pushchair along the roads at midnight.' Damien was beginning to sound like he wanted to go home. 'How far have we got to go?'

'As far as the cemetery,' said Jim.

When Damien stopped walking the wheelchair stopped squeaking. 'I'm not going to the cemetery,' he said. 'Cemeteries are creepy places, especially after dark.'

Jim sat down in the pushchair. 'I said you wouldn't want to come if you knew where we were going.'

'I'm not going to the cemetery,' Damien said again.

Jim looked up at Damien, 'My idea could make us both millionaires before we're thirty. So if you want to be a millionaire, then, start pushing towards the cemetery.'

With Jim sitting in the pushchair and Damien steering, they continued on their way towards the cemetery. This time, the squeaking had stopped.

'This old thing only squeaked because it was empty,' said Jim, pleased that he had conquered the noise.

Damien stared down at the back of Jim's head. 'Will your idea really make us millionaires before we're thirty? If it does, that will really be something. My dad isn't a millionaire yet and he's nearly forty two.'

Taking turns to sit in the pram, the two would be millionaires pushed the almost silent vehicle towards the cemetery.

Jim pressed his head against the cemetery railings and stared in. 'Look at all those lovely flowers,' he said to Damien.

Damien got out of the pushchair. 'You didn't bring me here to look at flowers, did you?'

'Of course I didn't. We came here to pick them.'

'They've already been picked. Most of them are standing in vases on graves.'

Jim opened the gate and pushed the squeaking pushchair into the cemetery. 'They won't be for much longer.'

The cemetery was dark and full of frightening shadows, the sound of gravel crunching beneath their feet and the squeak, squeak, squeak, of the prams wheels, gave Damien a reason to doubt the wisdom of his partnership with Jim. 'Why are we really in here?' he whispered.

Jim sighed and pushed the pram into the shadow of small tree. 'I suppose it's time I told you my money making idea. Look around and tell me what you see.'

Damien peered into the darkness and shivered. 'Graves and gravestones,' he said. 'All I can see are lots and lots of graves and gravestones.'

'And flowers,' said Jim. 'Don't forget the flowers, there are hundreds of them, and they're standing around in vases waiting for us to load them into the pram.'

The darkness shrouded Damien's puzzled look. 'What are we going to do with them, when we get them in the pram?'

'We'll take them home to the shed at the bottom of my Gran's garden.'

Damien looked even more puzzled. 'What will we do with them, when we get them in the shed?'

'We're going to make them into bouquets and take them to the hospital tomorrow morning, and then we're going to sell them to the hospital visitors when they go in to visit their sick relatives and friends.'

Damien could already see a flaw in Jim's plan. 'Hang on a minute,' he said. 'We will need white paper to wrap them if we are going to make bouquets and we haven't got any, unless you're thinking of using toilet paper. We've got rolls and rolls of that at home.'

'I know that we will need white paper,' said Jim irritably. 'But that's not a problem. Do you know where your dad keeps the keys to his van?'

The puzzled look returned to Damien's face. 'Of course I do, he hangs them on a hook behind the front door.'

'There are sheets and sheets of white paper in your dad's van; he uses them to wrap the burgers when he sells them. All you've got to do when we get home is lift the keys off the hook open the van and borrow thirty of forty sheets.'

Damien looked nervously over his shoulder. 'Alright,' he agreed, 'I'll get the paper. 'Now let's go and get the flowers, I don't want to hang around in this place for longer than I have to.'

Sticking a hand in his trousers pocket Jim pulled out a fistful of elastic bands and handed them to Damien. 'I'm the one who's going to do the picking, you can do the packing,' he said bossily. 'I looked around the cemetery this afternoon when we were burying granddad so I know where the fresh flowers are. Your job will be to put an elastic band around each bunch when I bring them to you, then, stand them in the pram. Let me know when we've got about thirty bunches, then, we'll go home.'

'I don't think much of your fantastic money making idea,' said Damien despondently. 'You said we will both be millionaires before we're thirty.'

'And so we will,' Jim said softy, as he moved stealthily from grave to grave taking half the flowers from each vase. 'We will do this every weekend, and as long as we only take half of the flowers out of each vase, no will ever know that the flowers we are selling haven't cost us anything.'

'We'll have to start buying the white paper to wrap them in,' said Damien. 'I don't think my dad will miss the thirty sheets that I'll be borrowing this week, but I won't be able to do it again, he doesn't sell that many burgers you know.'

Jim had started looking towards the future. 'When we leave school, we will have to do it full time if we want to become millionaires. That will mean moving around the country, but we'll have hundreds and hundreds of cemetery's to choose from, so we'll never be short of flowers.'

'We will need a trade name,' said Damien. 'All big businesses have trade names.'

Jim started to giggle. 'You're right,' he said. 'And I've just thought of a great one. Let's call ourselves. (Dead good flowers).'

At 1.15 a.m. on Sunday morning with Damien walking beside him, Jim steered the flower-loaded pushchair into Piddle Close.

'I'll take the flowers round the back to the shed,' whispered Jim, 'while you nip into your house and get the keys to your dad's van. When you've got the paper, bring it to the shed.'

'Couldn't I bring it tomorrow morning?' Damien asked with a yawn. 'I'm really tired.'

Jim shook his head. 'We've got to wrap the flowers tonight,' he said. 'I want to be out of the close and on my way to the hospital by ten o'clock.'

Working silently and in darkness, the two would be entrepreneurs wrapped the flowers and stood them up in the pushchair.

'I'll see you at nine,' said Jim, as he turned the key in the door of the shed. 'And don't be late.'

'Its half past two already,' Damien said with a yawn. 'If I'm going to see you at nine, then I'll have to be up at eight, that means I'm only going to get five and a half hours sleep.'

'I wonder what mischief those boys were up to last night,' said Dunroaming, as bleary-eyed Damien walked out of the house with two slices of bread and jam in his hand.

'He's never been up this early on a Sunday morning before,' One replied. 'So it looks like they are going to finish what they started last night.'

'I would really love to know what they've hidden under that pushchair cover,' said Dunroaming. 'It isn't often you see two boys pushing one, so it must be something important to them.'

'I'm curious as well,' said One. 'They took it with them when they went out last night, and they've got it with them today.'

'I know it isn't Priscilla,' Dunroaming said in alarm. 'I can see her hanging halfway out of her bedroom window waving Damien goodbye.'

Looking like two male Eliza Doolittle's. Jim and Damien stood outside the Hospital gates. 'Lovely fresh cut flowers,' shouted Damien, in what he believed to be a street trader's voice. 'Buy them here from us; we're cheaper than the shop inside.'

Standing alongside the pushchair counting the takings, Jim looked at Damien and smiled. 'We've only got three more bunches to sell,' he said happily. 'Then we can go home.'

Suddenly Damien stopped shouting and pointed towards the Hospital entrance. 'Do you remember the man who bought the last bunch of flowers you sold?'

'Of course I do. He gave me a twenty pence tip.'

'He's hurrying towards us waving the flowers around in the air.'

'He's probably coming back to buy another bunch,' said Jim. 'He said they were good value, and he knows that I only had three bunches left.'

'He's very red in the face, and he doesn't seem to be too happy. In fact I'd say he's hopping mad.'

'Have you come back for another bunch Sir?' asked Jim, as the man grabbed hold of him by the shoulder.

For several seconds the man stood staring at him angrily, then, throwing his flowers at the pushchair, he bellowed. 'You got those rotten flowers from the cemetery didn't you?'

Diving for cover behind the pushchair, Jim said recklessly. 'They aren't rotten mister. We only got them last night.'

'Just look at that!' The red-faced man thrust a black-edged memorial card into Jim's hand. 'When my mother-in-law took the paper off the flowers and read the words REST IN PEACE, she grasped her chest as if she was about to have another heart attack. "You evil Devil," she screamed. "I hate you." Then, she threw the flowers back at me and burst into tears. Before I had a chance to explain a doctor ordered me out of the ward.'

'Would you like your money back?' asked Jim begrudgingly. Then, when he noticed that Damien was showing a clean pair of heels halfway along the road, he turned and ran after him.

If Jim had been brave enough to look back, he would have seen the man pick up Priscilla's pushchair and the three remaining bunches of flowers. 'If I ever see you outside this hospital selling flowers again,' he shouted, as he hurled the pushchair and flowers after the fleeing boys. 'Your mothers and fathers will be bringing you flowers, when they come to visit.'

Glaring angrily at each other, Damien and Jim walked into the close.

'I think they've been arguing,' said Dunroaming.

'That doesn't surprise me one little bit,' One answered in reply. 'Damien likes arguing, he argues with everyone he comes into contact with, and when there isn't anyone around, he argues with his own shadow.'

'I wouldn't be surprised if he's arguing with his dad soon,' said **Dunroaming cheerfully**. 'When they went out this morning they were pushing Priscilla's pushchair, now they've come back empty handed.'

'I suppose they've taken it to one of those Sunday car boot sales and flogged it.'

'They couldn't have done that. Who would be daft enough to pay good money for that rust bucket on wheels?'

'Let's face it,' said **One**. 'We're never going to know what those two were up to last night, nor will we ever know what's happened to the pushchair.'

###CHAPTER THIRTEEN###

December 3rd

Dunroaming had been waiting for almost an hour for Two to show some sign of life. When the curtains moved slightly in the front room window, she shouted across the road. 'I noticed that your tenant went out early this morning, carrying a brightly wrapped parcel. Where on earth would he be going at that time of the day?'

Two looked across at Dunroaming. 'Don't you ever go to sleep? I can't imagine what you would want to stay awake all night for.'

'It's nice and peaceful in the close most nights and it's good to be alone with ones thoughts occasionally. Sometimes I get to see things that the other houses miss. If I had been asleep, I wouldn't have seen your tenant go out at half past six. You must admit it's a bit strange; it isn't something he does very often. In fact I can't remember him ever going out that early before.'

'Would you believe me if I told you he went to catch a bus to go to work?'

'You're trying to pull my leg, aren't you? Your tenant doesn't go to work. He's retired.'

'Even if I wanted to pull your leg I couldn't, you're a house, and houses haven't got legs.'

'I know that don't I? It was just a figure of speech.' Dunfoaming didn't say any more after that. She had always found it hard holding a conversation with Two.

Leather upon stone, and laboured breathing, were the only sounds disturbing the silence as the portly old man hurried along the road. The knuckles of his left hand stood out white against the grey of his overcoat as he clasped the collar tight against his throat to keep out the early morning chill.

Misty breath clouded his watery eyes and a deep sigh of relief escaped from his lips when he came to a halt outside the brightly lit entrance of a large department store.

His red-cheeked face suddenly broke into a smile when he glanced down at the large brightly wrapped parcel gently swinging back and forth on a string wrapped around the fingers of his right hand. Slowly, he lowered the parcel to the ground, and then cupping his hands together; he raised them to his mouth and puffed warm air into them. This time his sigh was one of pleasure.

Richard didn't have to start work until ten o'clock but today he had deliberately arrived early, he had many things to do before the toy department manager arrived.

For the next two hours, he made his way around the toy department, picking up tricycles, bicycles, computer games, dolls, Teddy bears and many other toys that took his fancy. At the checkout, he pulled a thick wad of fifty-pound notes from his pocket and passed them to the cashier. 'Would you please see that the toys I have just purchased are put in Santa's Grotto,' he said, as she handed him his receipt.

In the staff changing room, Richard took an old, tatty, Santa suit, and a long, straight, cotton wool beard from his locker. A happy grin broke on his face, as he rolled them into a ball and dropped them into a black plastic bag. With shaking hands, he eagerly ripped the paper from the parcel he had carried into the store.

Seated in front of a mirror, he smiled with satisfaction at the change brought about by the realistic looking white beard, and the brand new

Father Christmas outfit that he'd had tailored to fit his portly figure. After fastening a wide black leather belt, around his roly-poly belly, Richard stood up and nodded approvingly at his reflected image. Today, he was really going to enjoy sitting in Santo's Grotto.

When he had retired three years ago, Richard didn't think he would need to work again, but the lack of money to buy Christmas presents for his five grandchildren had forced him to scan the adverts in the local paper for a temporary job. Strange as it may seem he had been the only would-be-Santa to apply.

Beaming into the mirror Richard pulled the red hat over his curly white wig. 'Now I really look like Father Christmas,' he mumbled, then, picking up a hand-bell he turned and opened the door.

Happy cries of 'Ho! Ho! Ho!' echoed around the toy department as the bell ringing Father Christmas made his way towards the grotto.

Before entering the tinsel covered cave, Father Christmas looked up at the painted sign above the entrance. 'Santa's Grotto,' he read, '£2 per child, £5 with gift.' Richard reached up and pulled the sign down. 'Not today,' he whispered, then, turning the sign over he wrote on the back. SANTA'S GROTTO -------ENTRANCE—AND--TOY'S—FREE.

Soon, a long queue of happy, chattering, children, was snaking its way around the toy department.

'What would you like for Christmas?' Santa asked the wide-eyed little girl standing beside him.

'Please Santa; I would like a doll's pram.'

Red faced with anger, the toy department manager strode into the Grotto holding the altered sign. 'Who gave you permission to let everyone in free of charge?' he snarled, waving the board under Santa's nose. 'You've given away so many expensive toys; every kid in the store is thinking that you really are Father Christmas. What I would like to know is who is going to pay for them?'

Santa gently took hold of the little girls hand and walked with her to the pile of toys standing in the corner. 'You can pick any present you like,' he said. 'And if your mother tells me that you've been a good girl for most of the year, I'll be bringing you a lovely dolls pram when I call at your house on Christmas Eve.' With a broad smile playing on his face and his eyes twinkling with delight he stood at the Grotto entrance waving goodbye to his new friend. When she was out of sight, he turned to the irate manager and said. 'For three years I've been playing Father Christmas to the young children who come into this store. It has been the best seasonal job anyone could wish for, it would have been better however, if I hadn't had to look at the disappointed faces of children leaving the grotto without a present because their parents couldn't afford to pay the extra three pounds.'

The manager looked as if he was about to explode. 'So you decided to let every one in for *nothing* and give them all a *free* toy.'

Richard returned the manager's angry glare with a smile, pointing at a small cash register standing on a table by the door, he said. 'If you would like to check that till you will find that I have paid the two pounds entrance fee for every child who has visited the grotto today.'

The manager gave Richard a puzzled frown. 'What about all those expensive toys you have been giving away? Who's going to pay for them?'

Richard handed him the receipt for the toys. 'As you can see they were all purchased in the toy department, so if your Christmas bonus is linked to the takings, you'll probably find that it's a little higher this year.'

The manager gazed at the receipt with his mouth wide open. How can you afford it,' he gasped. 'You've spent thousands of pounds.'

Richards smile broadened. 'The looks on those children's faces as they walked away with their toys, has made it money well spent.'

'But how can you afford it?' the manager gasped again.

Beneath his false whiskers, Santa's face broke into a smile. 'Five and the bonus,' he said. 'The ticket that I bought for last Saturday's lottery came up with five and the bonus.'

The manager shook his head in disbelief. 'It must have paid out thousands,' he mumbled.

'Hundreds of thousands,' confirmed Richard. 'Which means that I won't need to work anymore. So you will have to find yourself a new Santa.'

'You can't let us down now,' pleaded the manager. 'There are only three more weeks to go before Christmas Eve and where will I find a Father Christmas as good as you?'

Richard called in at the manager's office on the way out. 'This is for you,' he said, handing him a large box.

'Is it our Father Christmas Suit?' the manager asked gloomily.

'It is now,' Richard replied with a smile.

Outside the store, Richard swung the black bag he was carrying over his shoulder. As he walked away, he said to himself. 'I know how embarrassing and uncomfortable it feels having to wear the shoddy red suit and cheap cotton wool beard that the store provides, that's why I'm taking it home with me to throw in my rubbish bin. They say that fair exchange is no robbery, that's why I have left my brand-new de-luxe outfit with the manager. Now, if he ever gets a new Santa, at least he will be dressed in style.'

'I'm sorry that I've been so long writing my story,' said Four. 'I don't have a very good imagination and I don't know any long words, so it's been hard for me to make one up. In the end I decided to write a children's story that would be suitable for eight years olds, which is also the age of all of the houses in our close.'

'Not me,' said Dunroaming. 'I'm younger than the rest of you; I was only built a couple of years ago.'

'You had better not listen to my story then,' Said Four. 'It will probably be a bit too old for you. It's about a circus clown called Hobo. It's titled. The vanishing rabbit.

With a happy smile on his face, Hobo the clown rested his back against the trunk of a tree; with his eyes closed, he sat listening to the sound of his sausages, eggs, and bacon, sizzling in the frying pan.

He had been working hard all morning, helping to erect the Big Top. Now it stood ready, waiting to welcome the audience to the first show.

116

Hungry rumblings had been coming from his tummy, whilst he had been lighting the fire. Now the delightful smell of the food cooking in the pan was making him feel very hungry.

'I say old chap, you may not be aware of it, but you are making it awfully hot for me.'

Hobo looked around in surprise, but he couldn't see anyone. Then, he heard the voice again.

'I hope you won't mind me telling you this, but you have built the fire to cook your dinner over my living room, and it is getting unbearably hot in there. So would you *please* put it out?'

Lowering his eyes to the ground, Hobo saw a large, white rabbit peering at him from the entrance of a burrow.

'Was that you speaking?' He asked, not really expecting an answer.

The rabbit twitched its ears several times, then, it said. 'Of course it was me. Who else could it be, when there are only two of us here?'

Hobo gasped in surprise. 'Rabbit's can't talk, he said. 'Whoever heard of a talking rabbit?'

'Have you ever read the story of Alice in Wonderland?' asked the rabbit.

'Of course I have, Hobo replied. 'I should think everyone has read that book. When I was at school, it used to be my favourite.'

'If you have read Alice in Wonderland, then you must know that rabbits can talk.'

'But the white rabbit in Alice wasn't real; he was only a character in the book.'

'You can believe that if you want to,' the rabbit said irritably. 'But, I happen to know that he was real, as a matter of fact he was an ancestor of mine.'

Hobo thought the time had come to change the subject. 'I am very sorry if my fire has caused you discomfort,' he said. 'I didn't realize that anyone lived down there. If I had known, I would have built it somewhere else.'

'And where would you expect me to live, if not down there?' asked the rabbit. 'Up a tree like a bird or a squirrel?' Then, the rabbit pointed at some houses standing at the edge of a field. 'I suppose you live in one of those posh places over there,' he said enviously.

'No I don't,' Hobo replied, pointing in the opposite direction towards the circus. 'My home is that blue caravan, with the words (**Hobo the Clown**) painted on the side.'

'Are you a clown?' shouted the rabbit gleefully. Hopping from his burrow, he stood in front of Hobo on his hind legs. 'Are you a real live clown? Honestly, are you really a circus clown?'

'I am,' Hobo, answered with a smile.

'Great! Wonderful! Marvellous!' said the rabbit. 'I have always wanted to meet someone who works in a circus.'

'Why did you want to meet someone who works in a circus?' asked Hobo, with a frown.

'To ask how I can get a job,' the rabbit said excitedly.

'Do you really want to work in a circus?' laughed Hobo. 'What kind of work would you be able to do? Can you sing and dance as well as talk?'

'Of course I can, in fact I'm quite a good singer, but unfortunately my dancing isn't very good.' He patted himself on the chest. 'But I don't want to be a singing, dancing rabbit. I want to be a magician.'

'*You* want to be a magician? Now you're talking daft, rabbits can't be magicians.'

'Why can't they? Rabbits work for magicians, don't they? Magicians sometimes pull them out of hats. So why can't a rabbit be a magician?'

'Do you know any tricks? If you want to be a magician, you've got to be able to do magic tricks.'

'I can show you one right now if you like.'

'Right,' said Hobo. 'What kind of a trick are you going to do?'

'I'm going to make myself disappear. All I need to do is say the magic words, *down, up, gone.*' Bending at the waist the rabbit repeated the words. As he straightened his back, his feet legs and body disappeared. Hobo stared in amazement. '**Goodbye,**' said the rabbit, then, his head disappeared as well.

'Well! Well! Well!' said Hobo talking to himself. 'That was a brilliant trick; I wonder where he has gone?'

'I haven't gone anywhere, I am right here in front of you.' Slowly the rabbit's head reappeared.

'That was very clever,' said Hobo. 'But you will need more than one trick to amuse an audience.'

The rabbit's hind legs, body, and finally the front paws reappeared. 'I can do more than one trick,' he said, boastfully. 'Just watch this.' Waving his front paws over the suitcase standing at Hobo's feet, he whispered. 'Go.'

To Hobo's surprise his suitcase vanished from sight. 'Oh, dear,' he said. 'I do hope you will be able to make it return. All of my circus clothes were in that case.'

'Don't worry, I will soon bring it back,' said the rabbit, his voice full of confidence. Waving his front feet over the spot where the suitcase had disappeared, he said. '**Suitcase return,**' and the suitcase reappeared at Hobo's feet.

Hobo sighed with relief, at the return of his property.

'Would you like me to make your dinner disappear as well?' The rabbit asked pointing at Hobo's dinner of sausages, eggs and bacon cooking on the fire.

'No thank you,' said Hobo with a laugh. 'It will disappear fast enough when I eat it.'

'Is there anything else you would like to see vanish?' asked the rabbit.

'Your vanishing tricks are really excellent, but can you conjure things out of thin air like a real magician?'

'Buck the Magical Rabbit, can do anything a magician can do,' the rabbit boasted.

'Is Buck your real name?' asked Hobo.

'No.' said the rabbit. 'My real name is Robby. Buck the Magical Rabbit is going to be my stage name when I work in a circus. Now, Mr Hobo, I want you to keep your eyes fixed on my left hand and watch closely. If my last trick amazed you, then, this one will make your eyes pop out.'

'Rabbit's haven't got hands,' said Hobo. 'They have paws.'

Buck the Magical Rabbit waved his two front feet mockingly at Hobo. 'What are these then, if they are not hands?'

'I have already told you,' said Hobo. 'They are paws.'

'Are we going to stand around talking about hands and paws all day?' said Buck rudely. 'Or would you like see my trick?'

Before Hobo had a chance to reply, Buck, laid a paw flat on the ground. When he lifted it again, he was holding a shiny, black, top hat. 'What do you think of that?' he said, placing it on his head.

'Odzookins!' Gasped Hobo in amazement. 'That is the best trick I have ever seen. I can't see any reason why you shouldn't get a job in the circus as a magician with talent like that. If you would like to come with me, I will introduce you to the owner of the circus. You will have to show him a few of your tricks, but once he has seen what you can do, I'm sure he will employ you as one of his main attractions.'

'Do you really think so?' said Buck excitedly, as he backed into the burrow. 'I am going to get my things; you won't go away will you? I will only be a minute.'

Hobo sat at the entrance to the burrow, chewing on a sausage waiting for Buck the Magical Rabbit to return.

'Okay! I am all packed and ready to go,' the rabbit said with a smile, as he dragged a suitcase from the burrow. 'But I mustn't forget this.' Reaching down he plucked at the grass. Suddenly the smile disappeared from his face. With a worried look, he started patting the ground around him, then, his paws moved faster, as if he was searching for something. 'Where is it?' he shouted angrily at Hobo, his paws running over the ground to his left and right. 'What have you done with it?'

'Done with what?' asked Hobo.

'My cloak, my lovely invisible cloak, the one that I use for my tricks. I left it here on the ground.'

'I don't know what you are talking about,' said Hobo. 'I haven't seen any cloak.'

'Of course you haven't seen it,' screamed the rabbit. 'How can you see it, if it's invisible? What I want to know is what have you done with it?'

Hobo started to laugh. 'Is this some kind of a riddle? First, you say that I can't see it, then, you ask what I have done with it. How can I possibly do anything to something that I cannot see?'

'You're a thief, that's what you are,' the rabbit screamed hysterically. 'You want my lovely cloak for yourself. Give it back to me.'

'Let us be sensible about this,' said Hobo patiently. 'You say that the cloak is invisible and now you cannot find it. Would you please tell me, what is an invisible cloak?'

'Well,' said the rabbit trying to regain control of his temper. 'I have, or maybe I should say, I had a cloak that was invisible and when I covered anything with it, the thing that was covered became invisible and appeared to disappear.'

'Appeared to disappear?' Hobo repeated the rabbits words with a frown.

'Don't pretend to be confused,' the rabbit shouted, 'You know perfectly well what I mean.'

'So that's how you did it? That's how you managed to make yourself disappear? All you had to do was lift the cloak up from the ground. That's why your feet vanished first?'

Buck the magic rabbit raised his head and looked down his nose. 'You're wasting your talents being a clown,' he said sarcastically. 'You should to be a detective.'

'I suppose you had already hidden the top hat beneath the cloak, before you made it appear,' said Hobo.

'That's right, and now I've lost it!'

'Have you lost the top hat as well as the cloak?'

'No you fool, I haven't lost the top hat can't you see that it's still on my head? It's the cloak that I've lost.'

Hobo raised a hand and placed it on the rabbit's shoulder. 'Now, now,' he said, trying to calm him down. 'There's no need to lose your temper as well as your cloak.'

His words of wisdom put the rabbit in a terrible rage. Pulling the top hat from his head, he threw it to the ground and jumped up and down on it until it was flat.

'My oh my,' said the clown. 'You are a stupid fellow. Not only have you lost your cloak and temper, you have also ruined a perfectly good hat. I was willing to introduce you to the owner of the circus, but I don't think I will bother now. To be honest, I don't think you would be suitable for circus work; you haven't got the right temperament.'

After putting out the fire, Hobo picked up his frying pan and suitcase. 'Goodbye Mr Rabbit,' he said cheerfully, as he walked away. 'I hope you manage to lose your bad temper and find your cloak.'

When Hobo looked back, the rabbit was running around in circles, searching for something that he couldn't see.'

'I thought you didn't know any long words,' said Dunroaming.

'I don't.'

'Yes you do. Temperament sounds like a long word to me.'

###CHAPTER FOURTEEN###

December 10th

The boarded up ground floor windows at Number 11, gave the house a cold uncared for look, and after almost a year of illegal occupancy by three drunken squatters, the interior smelt like a council tip.

'My owners are going to have an old fashioned Christmas this year,' Dunroaming said pompously. 'They've invited all of their family and friends to dinner, and in the evening they are going to have a party. Have you any idea what your squatters will be doing Eleven?'

'The same as they usually do I suppose,' Eleven replied. 'During the day, they will eat drink and sleep, and in the evening, they will probably gatecrash a party. I wouldn't be surprised if they let your owners have the pleasure of their company this year.'

In the front room at Number 11, Bob sat on his haunches in front of the remains of a fire with his backside almost touching the glowing embers.

Smithy brushed the dust from a plastic Christmas tree. 'I'm glad I saved these from that skip in town,' he said, 'I knew they would come in handy one day. Christmas just isn't Christmas with out a few decorations and a tree.'

Eric pulled a Santa Claus hat out of a black plastic bag. Grinning at

123

Smithy, he stuck it on his head. 'If we had some artificial mistletoe we could hang it in the middle of the room and take turns kissing each other.'

Smithy snatched the bag from Eric. 'Leave this alone,' he snarled threateningly. 'I've only just pulled it out of Number Two's dustbin. I haven't had the chance to get a proper look inside the bag yet, but it's my property now, and everything inside it belongs to me.'

Eric shrugged his shoulders. 'You can have it for all I care; it's only a pile of old junk.'

A happy smile appeared on Smithy's face when he opened the bag and pulled out a tatty torn Santa suit, a curly white wig, and a long straight cotton wool beard. 'This isn't junk,' he said, fitting the wig on his head. 'Father Christmas suits never date. I can't understand why they threw it away, there's still a lot of life left in it.'

Bob stood up and gave them both a withering look. 'Will you two stop bickering,' he snarled. 'There's no coal or wood to go on the fire, Christmas is only a few days away and all we've got towards it so far is a useless tree, a stupid red suit, and a cupboard that's as bare as a nudists backside. That rubbish isn't any good to us, what we need desperately is something to burn and lots of Christmas booze.'

Smithy tied a topless one-legged fairy with broken wings to the top of the plastic tree and stepped back to admire the result. 'We'll have to go out and do some Christmas shopping then, won't we?'

'We can't do that,' said Eric.'

'Why can't we?' asked Smithy.

'We haven't got any cash.'

Bob grinned across at Smithy. 'What Eric should have said is, we haven't got any cash at the moment, but we will have some soon.'

Smithy fidgeted nervously on his feet. 'The last time you grinned at me like that, I ended up in trouble.'

Bob slipped an arm around his friend's shoulders and gave him a friendly hug. 'Take my word for it there won't be any trouble this time.'

'That's what you said the last time, but I still got arrested.'

Bob hugged Smithy again. 'I'd ask Eric to do it, but he hasn't got the build to do it properly.'

'Okay,' grunted Smithy. 'What crazy scheme have you got buzzing around in your head this time?'

'You've got a Santa suit, and the belly to make a super Father Christmas, all we've got to do now is go to the charity shop in town and pick up a few free toys.'

Eric shook his head. 'You haven't told us what your idea is yet, but I can see a flaw in it already. You don't get free toys at charity shops. You can buy used ones cheap, but they don't give them away.'

'The trouble with you is, you always think negative. They might not give them away, but broken ones, and those that they can't sell, they leave outside the shop in black plastic bags for the bin men to cart away. So if we can get to the shop tomorrow morning before they arrive to collect the rubbish, we'll pick up a couple of bin bags apiece, there should be enough toys in six bags to make quite a few Christmas parcels.'

Eric gave him a puzzled look. 'Why do you want to make Christmas parcels? How's that's going to make money for us to buy booze.'

Bob tapped his brow with a forefinger. 'That's the clever part of my scheme. Once we've made some nice attractive parcels, we'll get Smithy to put on his Father Christmas suit, and then he can stand in the doorway of the Red Lion and sell them to people as they come out for fifty pence apiece.'

Smithy didn't look too pleased. 'Why do I always get the dirty work? I don't want to stand outside a pub selling Christmas parcels. No one will want to buy them anyway.'

Bob looked at Smithy and sighed. 'Sometimes I despair for you two. First, it was Eric, and now you're the one who's thinking negative. Most of the time when customers leave the pub they are too far gone to know what time of the day it is, so if they see a Father Christmas selling presents for charity, there's every chance they that they might cough up an odd 50 pence.'

Smithy was beginning to warm to the idea. 'If we put all of the packages in a black plastic bag, we could call it a lucky dip.'

Bob patted Smithy on the back. 'A lucky dip's a good idea.'

'It won't be very lucky for the people daft enough to buy them,' grunted Eric.

Bob threw him a look at sharp as a dagger. 'People don't mind being conned, if it's for a good cause.'

Smithy seemed to be thinking. 'What charity shall we say it's for? It would have to be a believable one.'

'If you're going to wear that filthy crumpled Father Christmas suit when your selling the lucky dips, then, you could say that you're collecting money for Santa's who have fallen on hard times,' said Eric, with a grin.

Bob rubbed his hands together like a miser who had just found a five pence coin. 'Right, that's the problem of getting the presents solved, now all we've got to do is get down to the charity shop early tomorrow morning and pick up the toys that they've thrown away.'

Smithy walked to the back door.

'Where are you going?' asked Bob.

'To water and feed my reindeer,' he replied sarcastically.

'Just look at them,' Eleven said to Twelve, as the trio of squatters moved the boards on the window to one side. 'The casual way they climb out and walk down the path; anyone would think they actually own me.'

Although it was only a mile into town, Smithy, Eric, and Bob, took turns trying to thumb a lift as they walked. When they were about a hundred metres from the charity shop, they gave up the idea. 'Maybe we'll be more successful on the way back,' Smithy said, optimistically.

Bob grunted. 'If we can't get a lift when we are empty handed,' he said. 'We won't stand a snowball in hell's chance of getting one when we are carrying several black sacks.'

Smithy pointed at the bags stacked on top of each other outside the charity shop. 'It looks like it's our lucky day; there must be at least fifteen bags in that pile.'

'We can't take them all,' moaned Eric. 'That would mean carrying five sacks apiece.'

'We'll have to take them,' said Bob, 'unless you fancy standing here on the pavement sorting through them for the broken toys.'

Smithy scratched his backside and shook his head. 'Aren't you taking things for granted? Maybe they haven't thrown any broken toys away.'

Bob stood with his chin resting in his hand looking at the pile of black bags. 'Right,' he said, having made an important decision. 'We won't take them all. We'll pick up three bags each and be on our way.'

'This is like having our own lucky dip,' said Smithy, as he craftily picked up three of the lightest bags and started walking.

'It sounds like your squatters are coming back.' Twelve whispered to Eleven.

'I was hoping they would forget where they lived, but it doesn't sound like they have.'

'I wish they would forget where they live as well,' Twelve replied with a sigh. 'They're noisy, they smell, and they're always throwing their rubbish into my back garden.'

'I don't want to add salt to your wounds,' said Eleven. 'But I don't like what I'm seeing. From the amount of black sacks they're carrying on their backs, it looks like there will soon be more rubbish flying over the fence into your garden.'

Back in the house, Smithy, Eric, and Bob, eagerly ripped all of the black bags open and tipped the contents on the floor.

Bob sniffed disapprovingly as he stared down at the mountain of junk. 'I can see why they threw this lot away,' he said, picking up a small three-legged wooden horse. 'I feel really sorry for the poor kid who's going to buy this.'

Five hours later, thirty newspaper wrapped parcels of various sizes lay on the floor. Eric picked up one of the largest and gave it a shake. 'You wrapped this one didn't you?' he said looking at Bob. 'It sounds really interesting; can you remember what it is?'

'It's a two thousand piece jigsaw puzzle, and it's going to drive the person who buys it crazy.'

'Why's that?' asked Smithy, as he climbed into his Santa Claus trousers and pulled on his Wellingtons.

'It's absolutely impossible to complete.'

'You can't say that,' said Eric, 'just because you couldn't do it. After all, you're not exactly (The Brain of Britain) maybe there's someone out there who can.'

'I said it's impossible and it is. Even that genius inventor who lives at Number 10 wouldn't be able to put it together. There are three different jigsaws; two with five hundred pieces and one with a thousand, all three puzzles have got bits missing. To make it even harder, I've put the three puzzles in a two thousand piece jigsaw box that was empty when we found it.'

'I remember that box,' said Smithy. 'It had a picture of the leaning tower of Pizza.'

Bob grinned at the others sadistically. 'I hope whoever buys it doesn't try to follow the picture, if they do it will drive them absolutely bonkers, the three puzzles in that box, are a field of bright red poppies, two tigers fighting, and three kids on a beach building sandcastles.'

Smithy picked up one of the presents he had packed. 'The kiddy that gets this won't be too happy either. It's on old artist paint box with brushes without bristles, and tubes of paint that have been squeezed dry and, there's also a yo-yo without a string.'

'You'll be wasting your time trying to sell them,' said Eric. 'No ones going to buy a lucky dip wrapped in newspaper.'

'You're right,' said Bob. 'They don't look very Christmassy.'

Smithy picked up a roll of flowery wallpaper and threw across the room to Eric. 'Wrap them in this,' he said. 'It will brighten them up a bit.'

The Father Christmas standing outside The Red Lion sneezed and wiped his nose on the sleeve of his red jacket.

'How's it going?' asked Bob.

'Blooming awful, I'm freezing cold, I've got the shakes, my nose keeps running, and pigeons keep crapping on me.'

'Bob wasn't enquiring about your health,' said Eric. 'He wants to know how many lucky dips you've sold.'

'Eight. But seven of my customers demanded their money back as soon as they took the wrapping off, then, they threatened to beat me up when I said that I couldn't return their money because the parcels had been opened.'

'They didn't actually hit you did they?'

Father Christmas shook his head and sighed. 'I'm sure they would have, if their mother's hadn't stopped them, but I had to return their money.'

Eric brushed some pigeon droppings from Santa's shoulder. 'If pigeons are doing this to you, then it must be a lucky spot.'

'It hasn't been very lucky so far,' Smithy moaned miserably. 'But I'm doing my best. I nearly sold another one just before you turned up, but when the little girl pulled it out of the bag her mother snatched the 50p coin back out of my hand and threw the present on the floor without even trying to open it.'

'Why did she do that?' asked Bob.

'She said it didn't look like it was worth the money because of the Christmas wrapping.'

'What was she talking about? It was wrapped in wallpaper.'

Smithy tutted and shook his head. 'That's what she meant when she said she didn't like the Christmas wrapping.'

'I'll tell what we'll do,' said Bob benevolently. 'I'll get Eric to go back to the squat and put on that elf costume you nicked from the fancy dress shop last year, then, he can come back and be your little helper.'

'That won't do any good,' groaned Smithy. 'He'll only scare the kids. Can't we all go home?'

Bob shook his head. 'The trouble with you is you give up too easily. The reason why they are all asking for their money back is that you let them to open the lucky dips as soon as they pull them out of the bag. You should tell the little darlings that they mustn't open their presents before Christmas Day. Now, the next time someone comes along with their kid, stick the bag right under their noses and with a hearty Ho, Ho, Ho, wish them a Merry Christmas.'

'I've already tried that, and the stupid child ran away screaming.'

Bob and Eric started to walk away. 'Where are you going,' asked Smithy.'

'Back to the squat,' Bob grunted. 'If we stand around here much longer were going to end up frozen solid.'

Eric grinned at Smithy, then, he lifted a hand to his mouth and went through the mime of having a drink.

Two hours later, Smithy actually managed to sell another lucky dip.

As the boy walked away with his parcel, his mother asked. 'What did you think of Father Christmas?'

'Horrible,' the boy replied. 'He's the worse Santa I've ever seen. One of his Wellingtons was black and the other green, his cotton wool beard kept falling off when he was talking, he had a dewdrop on the end of his nose, he stunk of drink, and from the state of his clothes he must have been sleeping with his reindeer.'

'How did we do?' asked Bob, as Father Christmas climbed through the window into the house.

'We?' said Smithy. 'How can you say we? You were only with me for a couple of minutes.'

Bob took a swig from the bottle of cheap sherry he was holding, then, he handed it to Eric. 'Maybe we weren't standing by your side,' he nodded at the bottle of sherry, 'but we were with you in spirit. So tell me, how much did you make?'

Smithy shuffled in his Wellingtons and opened his hand.

Eric glanced down at two 50 pence coins. '£1 for five hours work, now that's what I call really good money,' he sneered sarcastically.

Smithy tipped the remaining packages out of the bag. 'It was more than five hours work. I was standing outside the Red Lion for six hours. And what about the time it took to carry the bags from the charity shop and sort out the toys, and then we had to wrap them.'

Eric picked up the parcel containing the two thousand-piece jigsaw puzzle. 'I'm going to keep this one,' he said.

Bob looked at him and frowned. 'What do you want that for? If I couldn't do it, then I'm damn sure you won't be able to.'

'I'm going to give it to someone as a Christmas present.'

'Do you really dislike someone that much?'

Eric grinned and nodded at Smithy. 'I'm going to give it to Father Christmas; the poor old chap never gets any presents at this time of the year.'

Smithy pointed down at the clothes and parcels littering the floor of the squat. 'What are we going to do with all this rubbish?'

Bob picked up an evening dress and held it against Eric; with a grimace, he dropped it back on the floor. 'The parcels aren't any use to us, so we'll throw them into next doors back garden. But we'll keep the clothes and sleep on them for a month or two, then, when they're too dirty to use as a bed, we'll take them back to the charity shop.'

###CHAPTER FIFTEEN###

December 18th

'Did you hear that terrible racket in the close last night?' Dunroaming, shouted across to One.

'I certainly did, didn't it go on. What was it?'

'Your Damien and his gang were out carol singing.'

'It sounded more like they were murdering Carol, than carol singing. Did they come to you?'

'They started at me and I wish they hadn't, the glass in my windows has been vibrating all night because of them. After they had sung the first few lines of Silent Night, they knocked on the door, when it wasn't opened immediately they kept knocking until it was.'

'Who answered the door?'

'It was Mr Wyatt Jones, and when he asked them what they wanted. Damien said. 'Are you deaf or something? We're carol singing, and we've been singing our heads off out here for about ten minutes.' Foolishly, Mr Wyatt Jones told them that he hadn't heard them, and if they would like to sing one or two of the carols again, then he would gladly put a few coins in their collection bucket. 'We can't sing one or two again,' said Damien. 'Me, Stuart, John, and Jim, only know one and that's the first few lines of Silent Night. My little sister Priscilla usually finishes it singing solo, because she's the only one who knows how it ends.' Then poor Mr Wyatt Jones had to stand there for what must have seemed like an eternity, whilst four boys shouted Silent night holy night as loud as they could at the top of their voices, then, Priscilla finished the carol in a soft whispery voice. When she had finished, Damien rattled their collection bucket under Mr Wyatt Jones' nose and said. 'There you are Mr, I reckon that must have been worth a couple of quid, don't you?'

Mr Wyatt Jones didn't have any money in his pockets, when he walked back into the house to get some, his wife shouted down from the bathroom. 'Who's making that dreadful noise outside.'

'It's carol singers love.' The poor man shouted up the stairs.

'Don't give them anything,' his wife shouted back. 'That wasn't singing. Mr Tom, the cat across the road is more tuneful, and he isn't half as loud.'

'I shall have to give them a few coins.' Mr Wyatt Jones said in a pleading voice. 'I don't think they will go away until I put something in their collection bucket.'

'All right then, you can please yourself, but if you do give them something, make sure that you take it out of your own money. I don't want you wasting any of my housekeeping on that tuneless apology for singing. And will you please get rid of them as quick as you can, I've only just got out of the shower, and there's been a terrible draught coming up the stairs, since you opened the front door.' '

'Did Mr Wyatt Jones go back to the door and put some money in the bucket?' asked One.

'He didn't have to go back to the door, Damien and the others had followed him in. When he turned round, he found them standing behind him.

'Your wife hasn't got much of an ear for good singing, has she?'

said Damien cheekily. 'Maybe she's got some water in her ears from the shower.'

Even though Mr Wyatt Jones hadn't appreciated the singing, he gave all five of them fifty pence each. Then, he made them promise, that they wouldn't come back again until next year. After he had seen them to the door, Damien said. 'When we come carol singing at your house next year. You will have to pay us a pound each, 'cos we will have improved a bit by then.'

Mrs Wyatt Jones came walking down the stairs in her dressing gown, just as her husband was about to close the door.

'Why don't you go and stand outside your own houses and sing to your parents, I'm sure they would enjoy hearing your voices more than us.' She said un-diplomatically.

As the door closed on them, Damien replied. 'You were in the shower when we were singing, so you couldn't have heard us properly. So we've decided to give you a freebie.' Turning to the others, he said. 'Now all together, as loud as you can, Silent Night.' '

Slowly the five children made their way around the close, murdering Silent Night at every house.

'I think it's about time I called Damien, Stuart, and Priscilla in,' Mrs Kreamer said to her husband. 'They've sang outside every house in the close, and now it looks like they are coming to us.'

'Is John and Jim still with them?' Dennis asked, without looking up from his paper.

'No, they're not as hardy or thick skinned as our kids. They went in doors when Bernie Jenkins at Number 12 threatened to take off his leather belt and hit them with it, if they didn't go away.'

'What did Damien say to that?'

Mrs Kreamer smiled at her husband. 'He didn't say anything, but you would have been really proud of him if you had seen it. He walked Stuart and Priscilla to the other side of Jenkins front gate. *Then, they started singing their own version of Silent Night.* After they had sung it several times, Mrs Jenkins came out and gave them some money.'

Dennis Kreamer laid his newspaper on the coffee table beside his chair. 'That proves that Damien was listening when I told him that persistence always pays.' Then, he walked to the front door, opened it and shouted at the top of his voice. 'If you three think, that you can stand outside intimidating us with that horrible noise, then you can think again. Now, come on in, it's time for bed. You can go out carol singing again tomorrow.'

'Did you hear that?' Mrs Wyatt Jones screamed at her husband. 'Those horrible children are going to be out carol singing again tomorrow.'

'Don't worry,' her husband replied calmly. 'They promised that they wouldn't come back to us until next year, and with a bit of luck we will have moved away by then.'

'May I tell my story now?' Five asked the other houses in the close.

'Couldn't it wait until after Christmas?' asked Dunroaming. 'It's always dull and boring once the festivities are over. If you were to tell us your story then, maybe it would cheer us up.'

'I doubt if it would, it isn't a cheerful story, and if I have to wait that long I will probably forget it.'

Dunroaming sighed. 'The decorations, the tree and the lights, have put me in too good a mood to listen to a story if it isn't a happy one.'

'Hang on a minute,' said Five. 'You're not the only house in this close. You don't have to listen to it, if you don't want to. You could always turn a deaf ear, like you do with other things.'

'He's right Dunroaming,' said Six. 'I want to hear it, and I wouldn't be surprised if the rest of the houses want to as well. So you go ahead Five, and if Dunroaming isn't happy about it, then, that's her bad luck.'

'Are you sure?' Five said timidly. 'I don't want to cause any upsets in the close, especially when it's so near Christmas.'

'You go ahead and tell your story if you must.' **Dunroaming** mumbled nastily. 'Like you've just said, I don't have to listen, if I don't want to.'

'Right,' said Five. 'The title of my story is Null and Void.

The bell signalling the end of the round sounded like music in Ronnie Johnson's ears. On legs of jelly, he stumbled in the direction of his opponent's corner before realizing that his stool was at the opposite side of the ring.

Breathing hard, he sat listening as his trainer prepared him for the next round.

The second round, lasted just five punches, all of which landed on Ronnie's chin. With blood, and a sigh, coming from his mouth, he collapsed to the canvas where he lay motionless, like a discarded rag doll.'

'That wasn't a very long story was it?' **Dunroaming** mumbled softly.

'Give the house a chance, she's only just started,' said **Eight**, who didn't like being the centre of attraction and was dreading the thought of having to tell a story himself. 'It isn't easy you know, in fact I don't know if I will be able to do it when it comes to my turn.'

'Thank you,' said Five. 'You're right It isn't easy, especially when there's a house like Dunroaming in the audience.

It was another fight that Ronnie had lost. Of the eight professional fights, he had had so far, his opponents had been victorious six times, whereas he had only won twice.

As he walked across the car park towards his car, Ronnie tried to push the memory of the disastrous fight from his mind.

'Excuse me, Mr Johnson.' He recognized the man as a spectator he had seen sitting in a ringside seat at all of his fights. 'I have a proposition to put to you which I think you will find hard to refuse, especially if you wish to claim the fame and fortune that awaits you at the pinnacle of your career. Of course, you have absolutely no idea who I am, so therefore may I present you with my card.'

Ronnie looked down at the card. (David Holden, Hypnotelepathic Therapist.) The address printed in the right hand corner was too small for him to read in the lights of the car park.

'I have been following your career since your first professional fight, and I have noticed that although you have the skills and physical attributes to become a world champion, your mind's inability to accept pain prevents you from winning. With the use of hypnosis and telepathy, I can help you to overcome that problem. Should you choose to use my services, I guarantee that you will emerge from all of your future fights undefeated and unmarked. If you want to become the heavyweight champion of the world, may I suggest, that you call in at my office on the day before your next fight, then, I will demonstrate my powers.'

On the day before his next bout, Ronnie called in at Mr Holden's office. 'Good afternoon, Mr Johnson.' The hypno-telepathist waved a hand towards a well-worn armchair. 'Please make yourself comfortable. Your presence here tells me that you are interested in the unique service that I am prepared to offer you. First, I must tell you the terms of the contract, then, if you agree, we will proceed. I require no payment for my service until you have won the heavyweight championship of the world. One week after that achievement, you will present yourself at my office with my fee, which will be one quarter of the purse for that fight. I shall also require one quarter of the purse for every fight thereafter. This I believe to be fair. Naturally, you will be curious to know how I am going to earn the money that you will be giving me. First, I shall hypnotize you. Whilst you are in a hypnotic state, I will form a telepathic bridge to your subconscious mind. Then, I will order your deeper levels of consciousness to relay all pain plus the effects of the punches that you receive during your future fights, to my mind. This will leave you free to concentrate

137

on the fights. If you agree with the terms of the contract I will not require your signature on paper, we will seal the deal with a shake of hands. Before you give me your answer, I want you to know that if you accept the contract, I will look upon it as legal and binding until your last professional fight. In addition, I want you to understand that if you should decide to default on our contract, all of the service that I will be providing will be immediately withdrawn. If you should force me to do this, I must warn you, that the consequences will be extremely severe.'

Ronnie hesitated for a moment, he wasn't sure whether he wanted to accept this strange offer, but he was desperate to succeed in his career. He had always dreamt that one day he would become the Heavyweight Champion of the World. Then, with a quick shrug of his shoulders, he held out his hand.

Mr Holden pointed to a settee. 'Please lie down on that settee and make yourself comfortable.'

Nervously Ronnie lay on the settee.

'Now I want you to lift your eyes and gaze at the ceiling light.'

Ronnie raised his eyes.

'You will now count from one to four.'

Ronnie started to count. One- two- three- four.

'Thank you Mr Johnson, it is done.'

Slowly Ronnie opened his eyes.

'You cannot remember what happened, so therefore you are thinking that no change has taken place. To remove that doubt from your mind, I will demonstrate the result of the session we have just had.' Mr Holden then closed his hand into a fist pulled back his arm and punched Ronnie in the eye.

To Ronnie's surprise, he didn't feel the blow at all, but he watched in amazement as Mr Holden's eye slowly began to swell, then, it turned red and closed.

Unable to feel pain when he fought, it took only 21 fights for Ronnie to become the Heavy Weight Champion of the World. His enthusiasm, strength, and ability to absorb pain had beaten all who stood before him. His share of the purse as contender for the title had been the highest ever.

Mr Holden waited in vain for Ronnie to honour the contract, but when the time came for him to pay the Hypnotelepathic Therapist, the new World Champion didn't want to part with a quarter of his Purse. He told himself that Mr Holden hadn't really earned it. All he had done was hypnotize him once.

The Champion decided to defend his title. Three or four big money fights he thought, and then he would call it a day.

Ronnie Johnson sat in his corner, with a deep frown furrowing his brow. He was worried. When he had looked down, he had seen Mr Holden sitting in a ringside seat staring up at him. At first, Ronnie hadn't recognized the Hypnotelepathic Therapist - his features had changed beyond belief. His face now looked like that of a veteran prizefighter, with all of the marks of the violent trade engraved on his face.

It took just half a round and one special punch, to bring a glazed look to Ronnie's eyes. Slowly he sank to his knees. For several seconds, it looked like he was praying. Then, he fell forward on to his face.

The referee rolled him over onto his back and gazed down in horror. From head to waist his body was black and blue, displaying the effects of all the punches he had received in 21 fights.

As they were lifting the ex-champions body over the ropes, Mr Holden, whose face was now completely unmarked, got up from his seat and hurried forward to help. Lowering his head, he whispered in Ronnie's ear. 'Because you defaulted on our contract Mr Johnson, all of the pain, plus the effects of the punches that I suffered on your behalf, have been returned to you. Our contract is now, null and void.' '

'Now can we all forget about telling stories until after Christmas?' said Dunroaming.

'That's not fair,' Six shouted angrily. 'It was my turn to tell the next story, and I've been working on mine ever since Dunroaming told hers. I've put a lot of work into it, and if I have to wait until after Christmas I will probably forget the plot.'

'I reckon you've lost it already.' Dunroaming murmured nastily.

'You can be as bitchy as you like, it doesn't bother me. I'm going to tell my story and I'm going to tell it now. Even if none of you wants to listen, I am still going to tell it. It is titled. No Refuge.

You are alone in the room staring up at the ceiling listening. Desperately you want to lift your head to see if he is still around, but you can't. No matter how hard you try to blink your eyes your gaze stays fixed on the light above. You have already tried to lift your arms and legs but your muscles didn't respond to the commands you gave them. Try harder you can do it, I was in a similar situation as you once, I didn't believe I could do it until I tried. It isn't fear that holds you paralyzed to the bed, the only reason you no longer have any control over your physical structure is, you are dead. That brute of a man you married two years ago always threatened that one day he would kill you, and now he has.'

'Hang on a minute,' said Eight in a puzzled voice. 'If the woman on the bed is alone in the room, and she's dead. Then why is someone talking to her?'

Six sighed at the interruption. 'I don't know, I suppose it's a spirit voice.'

'You must know who it is, after all it is your story.'

'Alright!' said Six snappily. 'The voice isn't meant to be a character. It's a ghostly whisper, which only the person on the bed can hear. If you want me to clarify it even more, it's her spirit guide. Now that I've made that clear, can I get on with the story?'

'I was only trying to help,' said Eight apologetically. 'You want your story to sound believable don't you?'

'Give yourself some time to get used to the fact that you no longer exist as a mortal being,' the voice said. 'Then try sitting up. That's right; just ease yourself out of your upper body. It's going to be a traumatic experience, but you can do it. He's gone downstairs so he won't know what you are doing, but even if he were still in the room, he wouldn't be able to see you leaving your corpse.

Now stand up. It feels like your floating doesn't it. That's because you are. Look down at your feet they are several centimetres above floor. Now turn around and look down at your vacated body. Bend over and take a closer look. You're not breathing are you? That should confirm that you are dead. Yes, he really has ended your life. This isn't one of those out-of-the-body-experiences that some people go through at the point of death. This is the real thing.

You have stepped back in surprise at the amount of bruises on your face and neck. It's all coming back to you now, as you spiritually relive the pain you suffered when he grasped hold of your throat with one hand and squeezed whilst repeatedly punching you with the other.

141

Now try walking. Move over to your dressing table and look into the mirror. It's amazing isn't it, walking didn't take any effort, and doesn't it feel wonderful not having to drag an aching body around?

You're surprised to see your reflection in the mirror. You always thought that ghosts were transparent, but you look exactly the same as you did when you were alive.

Now move your eyes from the mirror and look around the room; it's empty, except for you and your corpse, which he has left lying on the bed like a discarded rag doll. The pink candlewick dressing gown, the last present he bought you has fallen open, revealing more bruises on your legs and feet.

If you're feeling distressed at the way your glazed eyes stare vacantly up at the ceiling, close them. Just bend down and touch the lids with the tips of your fingers. You can do it; after all, you didn't believe that you could leave your body until you tried.

Death doesn't seem to have affected your hearing; you've just heard noises coming from downstairs.

You want to go down to see what's going on, but you're worried about opening the door the creaking hinges sound like screeching rats. In the past, they always warned him when you were leaving the room. Don't be afraid, in your particular state of being you don't need to open and close doors, disembodied spirits are able to pass through them.

It is pitch dark on the landing, but downstairs a shaft of light is escaping through a gap in the kitchen door.

There is no need to tread cautiously as you descend, the wooden treads won't groan when you place your feet upon them. Even if you were to jump up and down, they wouldn't make any sound, you're a spirit now and spirits haven't any weight. Not that it would matter if they were to creak a little, he wouldn't be able to hear above the noise he is making pulling up the floorboards in the kitchen. That's where he intends to hide your body, until he can find a permanent place to bury you, somewhere miles away from here.

The light from the kitchen is still playing on the hallway floor and wall even though you are now standing in its path peering into the room.

Stripped to the waist, red faced and sweating profusely, the brute who was once your husband is kneeling on one knee gazing into the hole he has just created.

It doesn't seem possible that this creature is the same man you married two long years ago. When you first met, love was blind; it never allowed you to see him for the beast that he really was. Foolishly, you ignored the signs of a drinking problem. The first time you saw him really drunk was on your wedding night that was when he revealed the person he had been hiding from you.

You should have fled from the house the next morning and sought refuge in a home for battered wives, but you didn't dare, you were too frightened of the consequences if he should catch you. After that, it was too late. At first, his beatings were followed by tearful remorse, but he would be hitting the bottle again before the tears had time to dry on his face. Almost every night you ended up cowering in a corner with your hands covering your face as he used his knuckles and anything else that came to hand to plant new bruises on top of the old. Drink was no longer the excuse for attacking you. Now, he found pleasure in your pain.

He will get away with killing you, unless you do something about it. No one in the village is going to miss you. Why should they? They

don't even know that you exist. Your husband never told any of the locals that he was married; they believe him to be a single man living alone
at the farm. Now the question is. What can you do about it?

Walk into the room, don't worry he won't see you you're a ghost.
Did you notice that the moment you stepped into the kitchen he
looked nervously over his shoulder and frowned. Is he aware that your
disembodied spirit has entered the room?

The claw hammer he was using to pull up the floorboards is lying
beside him; see if you can pick it up.

You doubt if you will be able to, after all, if you can walk through
closed doors then surely your fingers will pass through the wooden
handle.

Maybe they will, but you won't know the answer until you try.

See! You are able to pick it up, and strangely, you can feel your
fingers gripping it in the palm of your hand.

How is it possible? It takes physical force to lift a hammer.

Spirits use telekinesis; you are able move objects by the power of
thought.

Now, you are wondering, if I can feel the handle of the hammer in
my hand, would I feel pain if I were to hit myself with it.

The only way you will find the answer to what you are thinking, is
to do it.

It hurt didn't it. Even though the head of the hammer passed
through your arm, it hurt. This poses another question. If you are dead,
then how are you able to feel pain?

The answer is simple. Pain is a mental impression, a sensation of
acute physical hurt, in life you experienced it many times, in death you
remember how it felt.

Touch your face with the back of your hands notice how cold they are. If you were to place them on his bare back, would he feel your icy touch?

He shivered, so he must have felt them, and then, he quickly turned his head and looked over his shoulder again. Was he expecting to see someone standing behind him? How would he have reacted if he had been able to see you staring hatefully into his eyes?

He's climbing out of the hole.

Now he's going upstairs to collect your body.

Do you intend to follow him, or are you going to wait until he comes down again?

You've decided to follow him up the stairs.

Your murderer is only two steps in front of you unaware that you are behind him with a hammer in your hand. There is no reason why he should suspect that you are there, your feet don't make any noise on the treads, and he knows that you are upstairs lying dead on the bed.

Isn't it a great feeling having him at your mercy? It would be so easy to swing the hammer and smash it into the back of his head. However, you don't intend to do that, the first blow would probably kill him and if it did he wouldn't suffer, and what you want most of all is to return some of the pain he gave to you.

The screeching rat hinges greeted him like an old friend when he opened the bedroom door.

His hand was shaking when he picked up the bottle of whisky that he had been drinking just before he killed you, and he looked nervously around the room before he unscrewed the stopper and lifted the bottle to his lips. Can it be that he senses your presence in the room? How would he react, if he were to turn around and see his hammer floating at waist height above the floor?

This time, he won't put the bottle down on the bedside table until it is empty, then, he is going pull your body off the bed and drag it down the stairs.

He's swaying drunkenly back and forth staring down at your lifeless body, without any sign of remorse.

Drop the hammer. He's bound to turn around when he hears it hit the floor.

The sight of the hammer lying on the floor seems to have sobered him; he is wondering how it got up here when he left it downstairs.

Now, walk over to the bedside table and knock the whisky bottle over.

There's a puzzled nervous look on his face. First, the hammer that he had left downstairs appeared mysteriously on the bedroom floor. Now, the bottle that he had just put on the bedside table has fallen over of its own accord.

Shrugging his nervousness to one-side, he drags your body off the bed by the feet. The puzzled look becomes a twisted smile, when your head hits the floor.

Now, he's pulling you towards the door.

On the landing he stares back into the room, he's still wondering how the hammer came to be in the room when he left it in the kitchen.

You're watching him descend the stairs dragging your body behind him. You wince as if in pain each time the back of your head hits a tread with a sickening thud.

You were about to follow him down the stairs but you have changed your mind; you will join him down in the kitchen later, after you have picked up the hammer.

Contemptuously he rolls your corpse into the hole under the floorboards, then, he looks up in time to see the flying hammer come crashing down on the top of his head.

You hear yourself scream every time that you hit him, but he cannot feel the pain anymore. He's dead.

It was a mistake to kill him. You could have haunted and hurt him for the rest of his natural life.

For almost ten minutes, you've been staring down at his corpse thinking, wondering if this is the first time; a ghost has actually committed murder?

Now you are looking at him in alarm. You were about to turn and walk away when you noticed a slight movement in the upper half of his body. It happened to you, so you know what to expect. He is about to vacate his mortal remains.

Alarm turns to fear, when his disembodied spirit sits up. Fear becomes panic, when he turns his head looks up and gives you a smile that is similar to the one he had on his face just before he ended your life. This time, like the last, it's a warning of what is to come.

Why did you stop to pull back the bolts? In your panic to get out of the house and away from him, did you forget that you are able to walk through closed doors?

Now that you are on the outside, where do you intend to go? If you are able to leave the building, then, so can he, and that vicious smile told you that he will be seeking revenge. Now that you both exist in the spirit world he has the whole of eternity to find you, and out here in limbo, there is nowhere to hide, nor are there any homes for battered wives. '

'I thought your story was very good,' said Two condescendingly.

'It was better than very good,' Six snapped, in reply. 'You might all think that I am patting myself on the back, but my story was brilliant.'

'Self praise is no recommendation,' Five mumbled to herself softly. She was convinced that her story about the boxer was easily the best so far.

'I'm beginning to wish that I hadn't suggested that we all make up a story and tell it,' said Two. 'There won't be any ordinary conversation around here until every house has told their stories, and we're not even half way yet.'

'You'll be getting ordinary conversation from me,' said Eighteen. 'I'm not even going to try to make up a story. And I'll bet there are other houses in the close who don't want to make up one either.'

'Well I don't for one,' said Eight. 'What about you Nine, do you want to tell a story?'

'I'd sooner have a hole in my roof,' she grunted in reply.

Then, Ten said, that he thought the idea had been stupid in the first place, and Eleven, Thirteen, Fourteen, Fifteen and Sixteen agreed. Seventeen didn't say anything; a loud snore from her chimney told the other houses that she was fast asleep.

'I Want to tell one,' said Seven. 'I've been working on it ever since Dunroaming told the first one and what good for her is good for me.'

'And I'm going to tell a story too,' Twelve said dramatically.

'Alright! Alright!' Shouted Dunroaming. 'We can't stop the houses that want to tell stories from telling them, but how about waiting until after Christmas.'

###CHAPTER SIXTEEN###

Christmas Day

'Cor,' gasped Ten. 'Isn't it pretty? I've never seen so much snow in my life before, it must have been falling all night.'

'It isn't pretty,' said **Fourteen** gloomily. 'It's blooming dangerous. It must be at least twenty centimetres deep on our roofs and the weight of all that snow will be testing the strength of our roof joists, and if Twelve really is infested with woodworm his roof could cave in at any moment.'

'I thought it would be repaired by now,' said **Twelve** gloomily. 'When the house doctor inspected it in October, he said he would be back in a day or two to fix it.'

'That was eight weeks ago,' said **Dunroaming.** 'Why haven't they operated on you? Woodworm eat really fast you know and they are always hungry. Your rafters must be running alive with the greedy little larvae by now. I'm sure that if I had anything as dangerous as woodworm, my owners would have had it fixed immediately.'

'My tenants aren't rolling in money like yours,' **Twelve** snapped angrily. 'If it had happened in April or May I'm sure they would have had it done by now, but October is too near Christmas and Christmas is always an expensive time, so they've had to cancel it until around Easter next year.'

Dunroaming tutted loudly. 'They're taking an awful chance ignoring it like that, those woodworm have probably been working up in your loft for a couple of years already.'

'If they've been up there for that long and the roof is still intact, then, I doubt if a few more months will make much difference.'

'A Merry Christmas to all of the houses in the close,' said Three. Then, bringing the subject back to snow, she said. 'I wonder why I haven't got any snow on my roof.'

'It's all those electric light bulbs burning day and night in your loft,' said fourteen enviously. 'They've made your tiles too hot for the snow to settle.'

One had been silently admiring the beautiful white carpet outside her front door. 'Doesn't virgin snow look lovely,' she said. 'No one has yet disturbed it with their feet.'

'Enjoy its beauty while you can.' Dunroaming said nastily. 'It isn't going to last much longer, any second now and chaos will be breaking out in the close.'

'What makes you say that?' asked Two curiously.

'As soon as that menace Damien wakes up and sees snow, he's sure to come rushing out, and then he'll start throwing snowballs. And knowing him, he will probably make them by packing snow around a rather large stone.'

One responded quickly. 'You've developed a fixation about that boy haven't you? As far as you're concerned, he can't do anything right. Why don't you give him the benefit of the doubt occasionally, maybe where snow is concerned he will play with it like any other normal child?'

'I suppose he would if he was normal, but he isn't, is he? He's a monster.'

One glared angrily across the close. 'One of these days, you and I will be having a humdinger of a row. I don't like Damien much either, but it's unfair to pick on him for nothing.'

'It might be for nothing at the moment, but let's see if you're singing the same tune, when Damien sees the snow.'

'He's already seen it; he was looking out of the window at five o'clock. But I doubt if he'll be out this morning, he's too busy tearing the wrapping off his Christmas presents to bother about a bit of snow.'

'O.K,' said Dunroaming. 'Just give him hour or two to break the presents he's been given, and then he'll be out.'

As it happened, it was ten o'clock in the morning and there were snow-men standing in most of the front gardens, before Damien poked his head outside the door.

'What did you get for Christmas?' asked Jim, as he scooped up two handfuls of snow pressed them into a snowball and threw it at Mr Tom, who had foolishly stepped outside for a quick pee up the front door.

'Not much,' said Damien ungratefully. 'My brother and sister got more than me. I suppose that's because I'm the oldest, and what I did get didn't last five minutes. The blooming things must have been made in China.'

Mr Tom eyed Jim suspiciously, as he made another snowball. 'Are you coming out for a snowball fight?' he asked. Then, he turned and threw the icy missile at the cat. Hissing loudly, Mr Tom turned in mid-wee bashed the cat flap with its head and dashed back inside the house.

'I'll be out in a minute,' Damien replied. 'First I'm going pop out to the back garden, to pick up my dad's spade.'

Waving a spade in the air, Damien walked round the close examining all of the snowmen. 'I'm going to have more fun with this than any of the rotten presents I got for Christmas.' He said to Jim, who was walking beside him with an armful of snowballs. 'While my dad's in the kitchen helping mum stuff the turkey, I'm going to build a snowman that's bigger and better than any in the close, and I'm going to build it where everyone can see it.'

'That's great!' said Jim encouragingly. 'If you're going to build it where everyone can see it, then, you'll have to build it on the roof of your house?'

Damien started shovelling snow into a pile. 'I did think about building it on the roof,' he said. 'But there isn't enough snow up there, so I'm going to throw as much as I can up onto the roof of my dad's van, and then I'm going to build my snowman up there. You can help me if you like.'

Dunroaming looked pointedly across the close at One. 'See!' she said, 'Normal children are quite happy to build snowmen in their gardens and throw snowballs at each other, but not Damien, he wants to build a giant one on the top of his father's van. Like I said, he's a monster.'

###CHAPTER SEVENTEEN###

31st December

'D o you know what today is?' asked Fifteen miserably.

'Nope,' Sixteen replied listlessly. 'And I don't really care. Every day is pretty much the same as any other, to me.'

'Fridays aren't the same as every other day,' said Three gleefully. 'They're different. I really look forward to Fridays, especially Friday nights when they come home from the pub drunk. The close really comes to life then.'

'You're going to be in your element tonight then,' Fifteen replied gloomily. 'It's New Years Eve, so there's sure to be lots of drunken parties in the close.'

'Its going to be another long night without any sleep then.' said Sixteen with a yawn. 'They ought to ban New Year; it comes too soon after Christmas.'

'I rather like it.' Seventeen's letterbox usually rattled when she spoke, but today it didn't.

Sixteen stifled another yawn. 'There's something different about you Seventeen, but I can't quite think what it is.'

'It's my letter box,' said **Seventeen proudly**. 'It doesn't rattle any-more. Mr Pringle my tenant got a set of power tools for Christmas so he fixed it. In fact he's been wandering around the house ever since Boxing Day tightening everything that he found loose, now his wife's complaining that she can't lower the toilet seat.'

'I was talking about the New Year,' said **Fifteen cantankerously**. 'Now for some reason the subjects gone back to Christmas.'

'Personally I want to forget all about Christmas,' said **Seven** miserably. 'And as for the New Year celebrations tonight, I'll be glad when they are over.'

'You surprise me,' said **Eight**, who still blamed Seven for the night when her tenant Mr Peacock threw half a brick at his wife and it went through the front room window. Five months later, small shards of glass were still puncturing peoples backsides when they sat on the seat in the window. 'I thought you liked parties, and Mr Peacock is sure to throw a good one to celebrate the arrival of the New Year.'

Nine giggled loud enough for most of the houses in the close to hear. 'And if Mr Peacock runs true to form, it won't only be a party that he ends up throwing. So let's hope that your tenants have the sense to board up their new window.'

'Mr Peacock's a lovely man,' said **Seven protectively**. 'When he's sober, you couldn't wish for a better tenant.'

'Maybe he is a good tenant when he's sober, but he hardly ever is.' said **Nine**. 'You told me only the other day that he hides a bottle of whisky inside his artificial leg so that he can have a drink close to him if he should wake up during the night.'

'Maybe one of his New Year resolutions will be to give up drink-ing,' said **Eight**.

'What are New Year resolutions?' asked **Seven** in a puzzled voice.

'They're a kind of promise that people make on New Years Eve as the clock strikes twelve. They promise that they will give up smoking or drinking, and some even go as far as to say that they will give up sex. But most of their promises especially the sexual ones are broken before the next day.'

'Why do they make them, if they don't keep them?'

Before Eight had a chance to reply, he heard Dunroaming scream at the top of her voice. 'Bring that back here immediately.'

'Bring what back?' asked Three. 'And who are you yelling at anyway?'

'I wasn't shouting at any of you.' Dunroaming sounded almost apologetic. 'I was trying to get Damien Kreamer's attention.'

'It's a bit pointless shouting at the boy isn't it? Every house knows that humans can't hear us talk, and if they can't hear us talk, then it stands to reason that they won't be able to hear us when we shout.'

Dunroaming felt a bit foolish. 'In my anger, I forgot that the little menace wouldn't be able to hear me.'

'What were you shouting at him for?' asked One. 'He must have done something really bad to make you blow your top like that.'

'The little brat's just stolen my name plate.'

One stared at the house opposite. 'It certainly isn't on the wall where it used to be, so it looks like someone has taken it. But, how do you know it was Damien?'

'I saw him unscrewing it just a minute or two ago, surely you saw him do it as well, after all, you are standing dead opposite.'

'You must have a very high opinion of yourself, if you think I spend all of my time looking across at you,' One replied scornfully.

'You're trying to cover up for him, aren't you?' Dunroaming, shouted. 'You must know that he's got it. After he unscrewed it he hid it under his coat and walked across the road, then, he opened your front door and took it inside.'

'You're right,' said One. 'He has just come in, but I didn't see your name plaque hidden under his coat.'

'Of course you didn't see it,' snarled Dunroaming. 'You wouldn't be able to see it if it was hidden.' The house paused for breath. 'I know what you're doing; Damien is your tenant's son so you are deliberately being obstructive.'

Two, coughed politely before entering the conversation. 'You had better watch what you're saying Dunroaming, if you carry on the way you are going, you will end up accusing One of being Damien's accomplice.'

'That Damien's a menace,' Dunroaming snarled again. 'One, ought to be ashamed to have him living under her roof.'

'What can I do about it?' One replied softly. 'I've been saying for months that the Kreamer's are the worse thing that has ever happened to me. If it was Damien who took your name plaque, then, it's up to your owners to sort it out.'

'They won't know who took it will they, if they didn't actually see him unscrew it from the wall? And if they didn't see him take it, then, how will they know that he's the culprit?'

'They could report it to the police and get them to take finger prints,' said Two sarcastically.

'Don't be stupid. How can they take fingerprints off the name plaque, if it isn't there?'

'Hey, Dunroaming,' said Four. 'Do you remember last September when we voted to drop the Number bit in front of our names? You told us that you hadn't voted because you weren't a Number any longer since your owners had given you a name. Well, now that your name plaque has been stolen and you're no longer a Number, what shall we call you?'

'Let's call her Nameless,' said One.

'Your Damien's going to get into trouble now.' Nameless, shouted across the close.'

'He isn't my Damien.' One shouted back. 'And what has he done this time?'

'While my owners were out, he took the fire extinguisher out of his fathers van, then, he pushed the nozzle through my letter box and turned it on. Now my hall is filled with foam.'

One didn't answer straight away, then, with a giggle she said. 'If Damien did that, then, it must have been crazy foam.'

'Trust you to be flippant about it.'

'I can't help it; the Kreamer's have been living in me for so long, I've developed their quirky sense of humour.'

'That isn't the end of it,' said Nameless. 'After he had filled my hall with foam, he screwed my nameplate back on the wall were it used to be.'

'I knew that Damien wouldn't keep your name plaque, he isn't a thief.'

'Did you say he isn't a thief? He's more than just a thief; he's a grave robber and a vandal. Have you forgotten, just before Christmas he and Jim stole all those flowers from the cemetery? And, do you know what he's done to my name plaque?'

'I haven't any idea,' said One. 'But something tells me, that you're going to tell me even if I don't want to know.'

'He's altered the r to an f and changed Dunroaming to Dunfoaming.'

'That's just youthful high spirits,' said One. 'It's probably Damien's way of seeing out the old year.'

'I am disappointed that you have your nameplate back Dunfoaming,' said Four. 'I thought Nameless suited you better.'

'I'm not looking forward to the prospect of standing in the same place for all my life with nothing to do but talk to the houses in the close,' said Sixteen gloomily. 'I'd like to be able to do something a bit more adventurous. I wish I were one of those mobile homes we were talking about a couple of months ago. At least they get to go places.'

'Standing around is what houses do,' said Fourteen gruffly, *he had developed a bit of a cold, and it hurt when he spoke.* 'Don't go envying mobile homes, most of them would change places with you if they had the chance. It can't be much fun standing in a draughty field for most of your life with different families abusing you week after week. And in the winter you're left all alone for months on end without any heating to keep you warm.'

'Hark who's talking,' said Sixteen. 'You've got your central heating on, but you've still caught a cold. Anyway, I thought mobile homes travelled to different countries and all that.'

'Some of the lucky one's do, but most of them end up in places called Holiday Parks. I don't think you would like them very much they're horrible places with lots of children running around all day screaming their heads off, and you don't like kids very much, do you? In the evenings, most of the adults go out to a place called the clubhouse where they drink and dance for hours on end. Take my word for it; you wouldn't want to be put in a Holiday Park?'

'Perhaps you're right.' Sixteen's gloom seemed to have lifted a bit. 'Maybe it's the thought of another year starting tomorrow, that's getting me down.'

'People are weird creatures aren't they,' said Two philosophically. 'From the fuss they make every New Years Eve, you would think it's the start of a new life, not just another Year.'

Mrs Kreamer intended to see the New Year in alone with her husband. With that in mind, she had made sure that her three children were in bed by nine o'clock.

Damien however had other ideas, ten minutes later; he sneaked out of his room dressed as a baby complete with bottle and dummy. Tiptoeing down the stairs whilst his parents sat in the lounge watching the television, he opened the front door and stepped outside. Closing the door quietly behind him he waited on the doorstep until the road was clear of people. Then, to complete the image of a newborn baby he stuck half of a football that he had turned inside out to give his head a bald look and tied the two strings that he had attached to it under his chin. Holding up the napkin that he had made out of one of his mother's bath towels, he ran practically naked out of the close. He was halfway to the Red Lion before he realized how cold it was. 'I should have worn my coat,' he mumbled.

Every New Years Eve the Red Lion held a free to enter fancy dress competition, with prizes for those who came first, second, and third, the first being a bottle of Champagne, the second a bottle of brandy, the third two bottles of wine. This year Damien intended to enter, he was certain his costume would win one of the prizes, which he intended to sell to his dad.

In the bar at the Red Lion, customers were standing waiting to be served. One of them standing with an empty glass in his hand looking like a thirsty camel, pointed at Mr Bones standing at the end of the bar. 'If I've got to wait until I'm in his condition before I get served, then, I might as well go to the Owl and Duck.'

'You can go there if you like,' Malcolm replied offhandedly. 'But you will find that their beer is four pence a pint dearer than ours.'

Damien managed to sneak into the Red Lion toilets without being seen. Taking up temporary residence in an empty cubicle, he locked the door and sat on the seat shivering with cold until he heard Malcolm shouting for the fancy dress competitors to line up in front of the judges. Several people standing by the toilet doors laughed aloud, when a baby holding up his napkin walked out and joined the end of the line. The infectious laughter drew the judge's attention to the New Year Baby standing with a dummy in its mouth.

'I like the baby,' said Mrs Braithwaite one of the judges, who was sure she had seen him somewhere before. 'He is so cute. I'm going to vote that he is one of the winners.'

'Cute or not. We can't give him a prize,' said Malcolm. 'Anyone can see he's only a child, and we are not allowed to sell or give alcoholic drinks to people under the age of eighteen.'

When Damien heard what Malcolm was saying he started to cry. Past experiences had taught him the value of tears and having listened to Priscilla crying whenever she wet her knickers, which was quite often, his efforts sounded like the real thing. With Damien's imitation of a distressed baby growing louder and louder, Malcolm looked at the other judges in desperation. 'We will have to give him a prize of some sort,' he said, his eyes coming to rest on a Black Forest Gateau standing on the buffet table. 'I think that's the only way we are going to get him to shut up.'

When Malcolm presented him with the large gateau, Damien stopped crying. Taking the dummy out of his mouth, he said politely. 'Thank you Mister, but I would sooner have the bottle of Brandy.'

'You will have what you are given or nothing at all, you little brat.' Malcolm whispered under his breath. 'By rights you shouldn't be in my pub.'

Unfortunately, for Damien, when he let go of his nappy and lifted his hands to accept the prize, the heavy white bath towel slipped to his feet. With both hands occupied holding the gateau, all he could do was step out of the fallen garment and head for the door. Luckily, some kind person pulled the door open to allow the naked teenager to make a quick getaway.

Damien was halfway home and three quarters of the way through the black forest gateau, when the church clock announced the arrival of the New Year.

'Hey One,' Eighteen shouted as loud as he could to be heard above the sounds of music and laughter coming from some of the other houses in the close. 'Damien is walking towards you with his mouth covered in chocolate or something, and he's stark naked.'

'He wasn't naked when he went out.' One replied casually. 'I wonder why he took his napkin off.'

'I doubt if we will ever know, the same as I doubt if his parents will ever know that he's been out.'

Damien undid the strings holding the half of a football on his head. Now completely naked except for his trainers, he placed the half-ball on the empty forest gateau dish, and then he threw it like a Frisbee towards Dunfoaming.

'My owners aren't going to like finding his rubbish,' Dunfoaming said miserably, as the gateau plate and half of a football landed on the front doorstep.

On the other side of the road, naked Damien cautiously opened his own front door and stepped inside.

One gave a sigh of rueful hopelessness. 'There's only one thing left to say,' she said. 'And that's to wish every house in the close, A Happy New Year.'

'Am I included in that?' Dunfoaming asked hopefully.

One didn't bother to reply.

###CHAPTER EIGHTEEN###

1st January

'Good morning One,' said Dunfoaming.

'It was until you spoke,' One replied nastily.

'Damien isn't around creating havoc in the close. Is he ill, or have his parents seen sense at last and locked him permanently in his room.'

'They wouldn't dare do that to him, they'd be afraid of the consequences. If you must know he has a bit of a cold, and he has been sick several times, which is quite understandable considering he ate a whole Black Forest Gateau last night on his way back from the Red Lion. However you were right about him being locked in his room, but it's a case of self- imprisonment.'

'What on earth was Damien doing at the Red Lion last night? Asked Six. 'Don't tell me he was drinking.'

'Believe it or not, he was taking part in a fancy dress competition.'

'How do you know that?'

'I heard him telling his brother this morning.'

'Did he win?'

'Of course he did.' One said proudly. 'Damien always wins.'

162

'If he's locked himself in his room, then he's up to no good,' **Dunfoaming said miserably.** 'Did someone buy him a bomb making kit for Christmas?'

'If someone has, I hope he throws one of the bombs through your front window,' **One mumbled under her breath. Then, loud enough for the other houses to hear, she said.** 'If you must know, he's sitting in his room writing.'

'Is he really writing?' **asked Three excitedly.** 'I wish I could write. If I could, I would write a story about this close.'

'People will be writing about this close one day.' **Dunfoaming said nastily.** 'There's no doubt about that. It's only a matter of time. When you get raided by the police, and the press find out that they've arrested Percy Grant and his parents for farming cannabis in your loft, the papers will be full of stories about you and this close for days if not weeks.'

'You can be certain of one thing,' **said One.** 'Damien isn't writing a story. He doesn't have the talent. The only one with any creative ability living in me is Vincent the artist and that's debatable when you look at some of the pictures he's painted on my walls. '

'Maybe he's writing to celebrities asking for their autographs.' **Suggested Three.**

'Damien collecting autographs.' **Dunfoaming snorted derisively.** 'Don't make me laugh, that's absolutely absurd. The only thing that boy is ever likely to collect is trouble.'

'What are autographs?' **asked One naively.**

'You don't know much do you,' **Dunfoaming said cockily.** 'Autographs are signatures, or to put it in a way that you will understand, they are names. Lots of people collect them. Sometimes if the person is really famous, or if they were famous when they died, they can be worth quite a lot of money.'

'There isn't much point in writing to a person asking for their autograph if they are dead, is there?' said **Three seriously.**

'That's the crazy sort of thing that Damien would do. And personally, I wouldn't be at all surprised if he got one or two replies.'

'If he's writing to celebrities, I wonder how he managed to get their addresses?' said **Four.** 'Surely they wouldn't have been daft enough to have given them to him voluntarily.'

'If they did, then it will serve them right if he vandalizes their house plaques.' **Dunfoaming hissed viciously.**

'He isn't writing for autographs. He wouldn't waste his time doing something like that. He's writing begging letters. And before you ask me who he's sending them to, they are going to the Queen, the Prime Minister, the Leader of the Opposition, and other rich people.'

'He doesn't expect to get replies from them does he?' said **Three.**

'Of course he does. He wouldn't be wasting his time writing them if he didn't. His New Year resolution was to make a lot of money. He's even going to the expense of putting self-addressed envelopes in every letter.'

'You're joking,' said **Dunfoaming.** 'If he's putting self-addressed envelopes in the begging letters he's sending, then he must be an optimist as well as a vandal. Inserting return envelopes doesn't necessarily mean that he will get any replies, and if he is lucky enough to get one or two, he definitely won't be getting any money from the Queen. It seems that everyone except Damien knows that the Queen never handles bank notes or coins of the realm. It's also a known fact that the Prime Minister and the Leader of the Opposition are so tight, they never

ever open their wallets.'

'Hey Dunfoaming!' said Seven 'It's funny that you should say that the Prime Minister and the Leader of the Opposition are so tight they never open their wallets, because my story is about a wallet.'

'Hang on a minute,' said Dunfoaming. 'I thought we weren't going to tell any more stories until after Christmas.'

'Well? It is after Christmas. It's the New Year, and for those of you who want to listen. My story is titled. The Devil's wallet.' After a suitable pause, Seven said.

'Kevin Cassidy's friends had always called him Lucky, now it seemed that his luck had deserted him. Within the space of seven months, he had lost his wife, his house, and his job. Optimistically Kevin believed that things would get better. Circumstances were soon to prove otherwise. With shoulders hunched in despair, his fumbling fingers searched his trouser pockets as he made his way along the road towards his squat. Slowly he dragged his thumbnail along the edge of a solitary coin trying to ascertain its value. The smoothness told him that it was only a two pence piece. 'What good is two pence?' he mumbled, as he forced the coin through a small hole at the bottom of his pocket. The clink of metal on stone signalled the coins arrival on the pavement. Lowering his eyes, he followed the rolling coin's path towards the gutter. His vacant expression became a look of surprise, when the two-pence came to rest alongside a black leather wallet. The wallet hadn't been there a minute or two ago, when he had been earnestly searching the ground hoping to find something of value, he was certain of that. A quick glance around, told him that he was alone in the street. With a gasp of excitement and a shaking hand, he stooped to pick up the wallet. As soon as his fingers closed on the leather, he snatched them away.

It had been hot. Hot enough to burn.

Quickly covering his find with his foot, he raised his tingling fingers to his mouth and soothed them with the tip of his tongue.

Lowering his hand again, he cautiously touched the wallet with the back of his fingers and found that it had cooled.

A mask of disappointment grew on his face, when a thorough search of the leather compartments revealed that his find didn't contain any money, only an address book, and a folded piece of paper.

Kevin flicked through the first few scorched pages of the address book, had he thought to continue turning the pages until he got to the C's, he would have found his own name printed there, with a date written in red alongside.

With a look of disappointment, he returned the book to the wallet and unfolded the piece of paper. Released from the folds, a cheque fluttered to the ground.

Kevin's mouth dropped open in surprise when he picked it up. Pay Kevin Cassidy one thousand pounds, it said.

Seconds later he was cursing his luck, the cheque was unsigned. Mystified he returned his attention to the piece of paper, and found it blank.

He was about to screw it into a ball, when faint writing began to appear. A puzzled frown greeted the arrival of each word. The completed message read. The enclosed cheque will be signed, when the wallet is delivered to the above address.

Although the district was unfamiliar territory, strangely, as if someone was mentally guiding him, Kevin walked straight to the address given on the paper.

Silhouetted against the night sky like a building in a horror film, the large, dark, house, stood at the end of a long gravelled drive. With feelings of apprehension growing stronger with each step, Kevin forced himself to walk towards the house. With every crunching footstep, a voice seemed to be shouting. "Turn back; turn back, before it's too late." Once he stopped and nearly turned around, but the thought of the promised reward that awaited him overcame his concern.

With the cold night air cutting through his clothes, Kevin shivered uncontrollably as he climbed the wide stone steps to the door.

Doubtfully, he lifted the gargoyle headed knocker. For several minutes, he stood with the grotesque head in his hand trying to make up his mind. Then, with a wry grin, he let it fall. Patiently he stood waiting for the door to open. With his patience at an end, he raised the heavy knocker again and slammed it down.

As the door slowly opened, the sound of its creaking hinges made Kevin's flesh creep.

'Good Evening Sir.' The tall thin sallow faced man's clothes told Kevin that he was a butler. His deep-set eyes studied Kevin's face for several seconds, and then they moved down to the wallet in his hand.

'I, I found this lying on the pavement,' Kevin stammered. 'I think someone must have been trying to burn it, because when I picked it up it was hot. When I opened it, I found this note and cheque.'

The butler looked at the piece of paper in Kevin's outstretched hand. 'You wish to claim the reward?' The words slipped from his tongue like the hiss of a snake. As if by magic, a silver salver appeared in his hand. 'If you would please place the wallet and cheque on the tray, I shall return them to the Master.' Before closing the door, he gave Kevin a lopsided grin. 'I shall return in a few minutes with the cheque signed.'

The promised few minutes passed slowly and coldly. They had grown into thirty before the door opened again.

The sound of Kevin's chattering teeth, brought a brief reappearance of the butler's lopsided grin. 'The Master is grateful for the return of his address book,' he said, thrusting the silver salver towards Kevin. 'It is one of his most treasured possessions. As you can see he has signed the cheque, if you wish to pick it up it is yours. However, before you decide to take it, I have been told to offer you a choice of any of the three rewards lying on the tray. As you already know, the cheque is for one thousand pounds. However should you choose the scratchcard that is lying next to the cheque, you will be the winner of ten thousand pounds.'

Then the butler picked up a brown envelope opened it and pulled out a wad of fifty-pound notes. Waving them in front of Kevin's eyes, he said. 'Or you can have two thousand pounds in cash.'

Kevin looked at the money, cheque, and scratchcard. He had no doubt in his mind which to take, after all the cheque was only for one thousand pounds, and past experiences had taught him that the chances of ever winning on a scratchcard were practically nil. Greedily, he said. 'I will take the cash.'

'You were foolish,' the butler said, as Kevin pocketed the money. 'You should have chosen this.' Rubbing the scratchcard with his thumbnail, he showed the card to Kevin. 'As you can see,' the lopsided smile returned to his face. 'As promised, it is worth ten thousand pounds.'

The look of disbelief on Kevin's face became one of surprise, when, after the butler had returned the scratchcard to the tray it burst into flames. Then, along with the cheque, it disappeared in a small cloud of smoke.

When Kevin tried to open a bank account with the cash, the bank manager summoned the police.

'They're not forgeries,' Kevin cried. 'They can't be. All of the numbers are different; at least they were when I checked them.'

'How naive do you think I am?' The Detective Sergeant asked with a grin, as he snapped a pair of handcuffs on Kevin's wrists. 'You must think that I've just flown out of a cuckoo's nest, if you expect me to believe that someone gave you two thousand pounds just for returning an address book.'

As they led Kevin away, he looked down at the envelope in the detective's hand containing the forged fifty-pound notes. 'I wish that blasted envelope would suddenly burst into flames and disappear in a cloud of smoke like the cheque and the scratchcard,' he mumbled softly.'

###CHAPTER NINETEEN###

January 24th

'Hey Eleven,' said Twelve excitedly. 'Have you seen the notice board that's just been erected in your front garden?'

'Of course I have.' **Eleven replied.** 'But I can't read what it says.'

'That's a surprise; I've always thought that you could read.'

'I can probably read better than you, but I can't read what the board in front of me says because I'm looking at the back of it and the words are facing the other way.'

'It say's that you're up for sale by public auction,' **said Dunfoam-ing.** 'It seems that now your owners have finally got rid of the squatters, they also want to get rid of you.'

'Have they actually managed to evict those three?' **Four sounded surprised.** 'I thought it would never happen, and when it did I missed it. Did they go quietly?'

'They got them out on January the fourth. I can't understand how you missed it. They created such a commotion a crowd actually gathered to watch.' **Twelve paused for breath.** 'When the bailiffs first drove into the close I didn't pay much attention. The fun really started when they started hammering on Eleven's front door.'

'I think I know what happened better than you,' snapped Eleven. 'After all they were living within my walls. So maybe it will be better if I tell the story, then, it will be told without exaggeration.'

'Have it your way,' said Twelve, resentfully. 'But it won't sound very exciting without a bit of embellishment.'

Eleven's front door rattled as she cleared her throat. "It's the bailiffs,' Smithy shouted, as two huge men jumped out of the car ran up the path and banged loudly on my door. 'They've come to throw us out.'

'They've got to get in before they can do that,' said Bob, as he picked up the television Smithie had stolen from Four and stood against the door with it in his arms.

'Who is it, and what do you want?' Eric shouted through the letterbox.

'We are bailiffs,' they both shouted back. 'We will give you five minutes to collect your possessions and come out voluntarily, if you fail to do so, we have the power to arrest and hand you over to the police.'

'You can't hand us over to the police,' sneered Eric. 'There aren't any coppers in sight, besides; you've got to arrest us before you can do that.'

'I knew this one wouldn't be easy,' said the bailiff holding the writ in his hand. 'I've had dealings with this trio before. It looks like we'll have to earn our money the hard way.' '

Eleven's front door rattled as she cleared her throat again. 'For five minutes the bailiffs stood looking at the door expectantly. 'They're not coming out Dave,' said the one with the writ. 'So you'd better put your shoulder to the door.'

Dave rubbed his shoulder and sighed. 'Could you do it for me George, my shoulder is still aching from the last job?'

'Sorry mate, but I can't do that. It's your job to break in, and it's my job to serve the writs. Why don't you try using your other shoulder?'

Dave took several paces back and glared at the door. 'That's still aching from the job we did a couple of weeks ago.'

'You should try and get your hands on one of those battering rams the boys in the drug squad use, it would certainly make your job a whole lot easier, and it would save you from suffering so much pain. As for this door, it doesn't look all that strong; you could try kicking your way in.'

'I'm not even going to think about doing that,' Dave replied. 'Some of these doors are tougher than they look. I tried it once and ended up rupturing myself.'

George shrugged his shoulders unsympathetically and pointed at the door. 'Go to it then,' he said callously. 'And try not to scream when the pain kicks in, it might upset the neighbours.'

'Maybe we should try going round the back first?' said Dave. 'You never know there might be an easier way in there.'

George shook his head firmly and turned to look at the gathering crowd. 'That's out of the question,' he said. 'If we go round the back and there's an easy way in, our audience are going to miss the show, and we wouldn't want to disappoint them would we, after all they are going to be our witnesses if this gets a little bit nasty and those three inside accuse us of being rough handed.'

Dave bravely lowered his shoulder and hurled himself forward; as his shoulder thudded against the door, he gave a loud groan. For several seconds he stood flexing his arm, and opening and closing his hand to relieve the pain. 'After I've finished trying to barge this door open,' he stepped back to tackle the door again. 'I doubt I'll be able to lift my hands high enough to rough handle anyone even if I wanted to.'

The fifth time he threw himself at the door it flew open. White faced with pain Dave turned to George. 'Did you hear that crack?' he said. 'I think I've dislocated my shoulder.'

'That's a relief.' George replied calmly. 'When I heard that sickening sound I thought it was broken.' '

'Why didn't you help your squatters out,' said Ten. 'You could have put some pressure against the door to prevent it from opening.'

'Maybe I would have helped to keep the bailiffs out if they had treated me with some respect, but they've abused me since the day they first moved in. There's only so much a house can take you know.'

The sound of loud music coming from one of her bedrooms had made it hard for Thirteen to hear what Eleven was saying. 'What happened after the door gave way?' she asked.

'Bob, the squatter behind the door holding the television dropped it and ran, as George rushed into the house waving the writ. Unfortunately, for George the television landed on his foot.

'You've just assaulted a sheriff's officer.' He screamed. Then, he started hopping around like a grasshopper with only one leg. 'You've done it now, I'm going to phone for police backup.' '

'I've never seen a grasshopper with only one leg.' Thirteen said seriously. 'Come to think of it, I've never seen a grasshopper.'

'When I first saw the three police cars come into the close,' said Twelve. 'I thought that they had come to arrest the drug baron.'

'The crowd that had gathered in the close was even larger than the one we had on bonfire night when Thirteen went up in flames,' said Eleven dramatically.

'That was the worst night of my life,' said Thirteen. 'I thought I was a goner. And the pity of it was I was too distressed to appreciate the crowd.'

'There was a fairly large crowd in the close on the night Mr Pettigrew went up onto my roof to rescue that cat,' Eighteen said boastfully. 'And the fire brigade was called out because he couldn't get down. Did you know that was the first time the fire brigade had ever come into the close?'

'Did the squatters leave of their own accord? After the police cars arrived,' asked Four.

'Of course they didn't,' Eleven said proudly. 'They said they were happy here and they didn't want to leave, in the end the police had to arrest them.'

'Did they go quietly then?'

'My squatter's weren't the type of people to go anywhere quietly, I thought you knew that. It took six police officers to carry the little fat one out, and as they were carrying him down the path he was kicking and punching every one in sight, and he wriggled and twisted his body like an eel until they dropped him. Then, he got up and knocked two of their hats off. Then, he jumped on them and ran back inside me.'

'He didn't really jump on two police officers did he? If he did, then, that's a serious offence.'

'He didn't jump on the police officers stupid, he jumped on their hats. The next time it only took four of them to carry him outside, and he wasn't struggling, in fact he went with them as quiet as a lamb.'

'Something must have happened to calm him down,' said Four. 'Did they beat him up?'

'No, it wasn't anything like that,' Eleven replied. 'They promised that if he behaved and went with them quietly, they would give him a bottle of whisky.'

'What about the other two, did they go quietly as well?'

'They didn't want to, but after the fat one had accepted the bribe, they had to take one as well. So in the end my owners got rid of them cheaply. All it cost them was three bottles of whisky'

'Where did they go when they left you?'

'How would I know? I never leave this spot and I haven't got a crystal ball, but I suppose they went back to the police station.'

'I didn't mean the police officers,' said four with a sigh. 'I was talking about your ex-squatters.'

'I should think they stayed in the cells for the night, I suppose the police kicked them out in the morning. No doubt, they'll come back here in a day or two as they've done in the past, only this time they won't be able to get back in. My owners have learnt their lesson. Sometime today they will be putting metal shuddering on my windows and doors, and then I'll be left looking like Fort Knox until someone buys me at the auction.'

'What's an auction?' asked Seventeen naively.

'You're really ignorant aren't you?' said Eighteen spitefully. 'Don't you really know what an auction is?'

'I wouldn't ask if I did, would?'

'You've been standing in our company for eight years; surely you must have heard us talking about auctions before. An auction means going under the hammer.'

'I bet that hurts,' said Ten.

'I know all about going under the hammer,' said Dunfoaming. 'I saw a programme about it on the television the other day. It means that people go to a hall to bid for houses and when the auctioneer gets the highest offer he hits the table with a hammer.'

'People do really weird things don't they,' said Four. 'Why does the auctioneer have to hit a table?'

'It's to seal the deal,' Dunfoaming said knowingly. 'And in Eleven's case, I should think she will be brought by a property developer for practically nothing.'

'It doesn't seem fair, does it?' said Eleven. 'If houses are treated with respect they can live for two or three hundred years, but the way my squatters have treated me I'll be lucky if I haven't fallen apart in a year or two.'

'What about me?' **Thirteen liked talking about the fire that had gutted one of her bedrooms.** 'If that fire had been allowed to spread to more than one bedroom I'd be a pile of rubble now.'

'In a way your fire was a blessing.' **Dunfoaming said enviously.** 'Now that you've had a complete makeover you're not bad looking, but if the fire had really taken a hold and destroyed you completely, you would have made a really ugly ruin.'

'Cheer up Eleven,' **said Twelve sympathetically.** 'When you come up at the auction, you might be bought by a property developer, and that could have its good side. You might end up having a complete make over like thirteen.'

'A complete makeover sounds really scary,' **said Three.** 'If I ever come up for auction, I hope that I'm not sold to a developer.'

'You don't need developing,' **said Two, in a sexy voice.** 'You're developed enough; you've got a gorgeous ground floor bay window.'

Dunfoaming hadn't finished with Eleven. 'I'm really worried about you Eleven,' **she lied.** 'If you do happen to fall into the hands of a developer, I should think the first thing he will do is completely gut you.'

'He won't have much to do then,' **said Eleven with a laugh.** 'The squatters have already done that.'

Ten slammed one of his upstairs windows to get Eleven's attention. 'It looks like the New Year is going to be an exciting one for you Eleven.'

'How can you say that it's going to be exciting, I'm going up for auction?'

'You've got to look at it in a positive way. You've got rid of those three ghastly squatters, and you're starting out on a new adventure.'

Eleven had been standing with boarded windows and doors for over two weeks, when a large white van pulled up in front of her. Two men dressed in overalls climbed out walked to the back of the van and opened the doors. 'I reckon we should take the boarding off the front door before we unload the van Jim,' said one to the other. 'I've been hearing a few things about this close and none of them are good. From what I've heard, I don't think it will be a good idea to leave doors open or things lying around unattended, there are a few light fingered layabouts living here.'

Jim closed the van doors and locked them. 'When we looked at this house before it went to auction the state of it told us that squatters had been living here for some time. There were hardly any floorboards and no inner doors, in fact, they had used everything burnable to keep themselves warm, but, in spite of all that, it looked like a good strong house, and it seemed to be standing in a nice close. So please don't tell me, that we've bought another white elephant.'

Martin shrugged his shoulders. 'I hope not,' he said downheartedly. 'After all the mistakes we made last year, we can't afford to make another one. If this property doesn't show a profit, it will mean the end of our careers as developers and we could end up out of work as well.'

'Did you hear that?' Dunfoaming shouted across at Eleven. 'The two men in the white van are your new owners, and they think that they might have made a big mistake buying you. One of them thinks that you could be a white elephant.'

'I heard what they said.' Eleven replied with a groan that seemed to come deep from her foundations. 'They can't be very good developers if they don't know the difference between a white elephant and a house, so it won't be my fault if they can't sell me and make a profit will it?'

'Apart from the floorboards cupboards and doors, what will they have to replace to make you saleable again?'

'Practically everything, I'm in a real sorry state. I've still got a bath but it hasn't got a bottom and there's a hole in the floor where the toilet used to be.'

'Have you got a bathroom sink?' asked **Twelve**.

'Oh yes. I still have one of those. But unfortunately it's lying at the bottom of the garden in two pieces.'

'What about your central heating?'

'The boiler and radiators were sold two weeks after my ex-squatters moved in. The kitchen sink is also at the scrap metal dealers, the squatters dumped it outside his yard after he told them that it was worthless.'

'It sounds like your new owners will have to spend a cart load of money before you'll be saleable again,' **said Dunfoaming cheerfully**. 'Unless they think that you're not worth the outlay, and they sell you on again just as you are.'

'They won't do that will they? Who's going to buy a house that's in my condition?'

'Your new owners were silly enough to buy you at the auction, so if they decide that you're not worth developing and put you up for auction again, I'm sure that the auctioneers will be able to find somebody just as stupid as them.'

'I wouldn't worry about it if I was you,' **said Ten kindly**. 'Whatever happens they will never pull you down, they couldn't do that even if they wanted to because you are joined to Twelve, and even if you weren't, I doubt if they would do anything as drastic as that. Although they were daft to have bought you in the first place, I'm sure that they will have enough sense to know that a piece of land with a house standing on it, is worth more than a plot on it's own.'

'It isn't very nice not knowing what's going to happen to you.' Eleven said miserably.

'Personally I think you're very lucky, most of the houses standing in this close haven't had any attention for years. If your new owners decide to smarten you up and sell you on, then you are going to have a really exciting experience, and although they won't admit it, I can tell you now, the female houses are going to envy you being pampered by two hunky builders.'

It had taken Martin and Bernard three weeks to complete Number 11's transformation. During the course of those weeks, most of the houses in the close had been looking on enviously, as new doors, floorboards, cupboards, a new bathroom suite and kitchen, were carried into the house. At night before the developers went home they carefully replaced the metal grills on the windows and doors.

'I don't think your new bathroom suite is very good quality.' Dunfoaming said maliciously. 'It you ask me it must have been the cheapest they could buy. When I saw them carrying the bath it didn't seem to have much weight to it, and it looked like it was too small to hold much water and, I reckon it's too thin to take the weight of a full-grown man. All you can do is hope that the family who finally buy you, are not on the plump side, 'cos if they are, they won't be able to take too many baths in safety.'

'I doubt if they will want to use the bath.' Eleven replied defensively. 'My developers have sensibly decided to fit a super-de-luxe shower in the bathroom as well.'

###CHAPTER TWENTY###

February

'Good morning Fourteen,' said Eight courteously. 'I thought your tenant Jenny, looked really beautiful when she went out this morning.'

'She's a beautiful girl,' said Fourteen proudly. 'But that nurse's uniform she has to wear when she goes to work doesn't do her justice.'

'She wasn't wearing her uniform this morning.'

'I know that. She's hardly going to wear it on her day off is she?'

'Is she going to meet that Doctor Goodheart?' asked Eight, trying to make his question sound casual. 'Is she having an affair?'

'No, she isn't! Doctor Goodheart is a married man. How did you get the impression that Jenny was seeing him?'

'Most of the houses in the close were talking about it last September when he called and stayed for the day.'

'All that the houses in this close ever do is gossip. They really would have had something to gossip about, if he had stayed for the night.' Fourteen snapped angrily. 'Anyway last September was ages ago.'

'They could have been carrying on since then, it's not unknown these days for single women to sleep with married men, in fact its common practice.'

'Jenny isn't that sort of a girl, she has her standards. If she couldn't get a man of her own, she wouldn't go out of her way to steal someone's husband.'

'I should have thought she would have a steady boyfriend by now. She must be heading towards her thirties.'

'She could have one for all we know, or maybe she hasn't met the right one yet. Then again, maybe she isn't interested in men. Not all women have to have a man you know, some are quiet capable of managing without them.'

Fifteen invited herself into the conversation. 'Mrs Braithwaite who lives in me couldn't live without them; she's man mad she is. As soon as her husband walks out of the door to go to work in the morning, she is on the phone inviting another man over. You wouldn't believe me if I went into all the details, but I've seen and heard things that would make your roof tiles curl.'

'What sort of things are you talking about?' **asked eight naively.**

Fifteen lowered her voice to a whisper. 'What they do to each other, goes way beyond the conventions of normal sexual behaviour.'

'**Eight sounded shocked.** 'Even if you were willing to tell us what they do, I wouldn't want to hear. What goes on in our tenants bedrooms is their business not ours, but it must be really filthy if it goes beyond the conventions of normal sexual behaviour.'

'It's not fair to leave us hanging in the air like that,' **said Dunfoaming.** 'If you're not going to tell us what they get up to, at least you can tell us who she invites over. Is it someone living in the close?'

'Even if I gave you twenty guesses I doubt if you would get it right.'

'If it's someone living in the close, I wouldn't need twenty guesses, there are only nineteen houses.'

'I already know who it is,' **said One.** 'So I don't need any guesses. Percy Grant the drug baron isn't a stranger to her bed; he's been having it away with her on a regular basis since bonfire night.'

'How do you know that?' **Fifteen sounded surprised.**

'I heard him boasting about it to Kreamer a couple of weeks ago.'

'If he told Kreamer that, then he's a liar,' **blurted Dunfoaming.** 'I'm standing dead opposite three, and if Percy Grant had been going up to Fifteen on a regular basis I would have noticed.'

'What you've just said isn't strictly true either,' **said Eighteen.** 'How can you be standing dead opposite Three, if I am?'

Three decided the time has come to end the scandalous conversa-tion. 'The reason you haven't seen Percy strolling up the close to visit his bit on the side is because he doesn't go in the front way, he's too crafty for that. He waits until the coast is clear then he climbs over the small wire fences that separate the gardens out the back.'

Eighteen did a quick bit of mental arithmetic. 'That's eleven fences he would have to climb over before he got to her house, and Percy Grant doesn't seem to be a very athletic man. It's a wonder he has enough strength left to do something that goes beyond the conventions of normal sexual behaviour, after climbing over eleven fences.'

Fourteen had been watching Jenny as she walked down the road. When she turned the corner and walked out of the close, he said. 'I hope she's gone to the library for another book, I've finished the one that she was reading.'

'How can you read a book?' **said Four.** 'You haven't got hands, so how do you turn the pages?'

182

'I don't have to turn any pages. I read over her shoulder.'

'You lucky thing,' said Thirteen enviously. 'I'd love to be able to read a book, but all my tenants ever want to do is watch television.'

'I think you're lucky to be able to watch television,' said Fifteen with a sigh. 'I wish Mrs Braithwaite would turn hers on more often. I'm sick and fed up with having to watch and listen while she and Percy Grant grunt and groan their way through their sessions of abnormal sexual behaviour.'

'You still haven't told me where Jenny's going,' said Eight forcefully.

'I haven't told you because I don't know, and even if I did I wouldn't tell you. Maybe she really is going to the library.'

Jenny's eyes darted from one beautifully painted figure to the next.

'Have you made your mind up?' asked the young man standing beside her at the garden centre. 'Who's it going to be? Are you going to buy, Happy, Bashful, Dopey, Grumpy, Sneezy, Sleepy, or Doc?'

'It will have to be Snow White,' said Jenny. 'If I were to take one of the seven dwarfs, it would break up the gang.'

The man shook his head sadly, then, cupping a hand under Jenny's elbow, he guided her away from the figures. 'If you take Snow White,' he whispered. 'It will break their hearts. She is like a mother to them. And although she doesn't know it, they are all secretly in love with her.'

For several seconds they both stood staring at the tableau deep in thought. Then, a smile suddenly grew on the young man's face. 'If you were to buy the complete set,' he said. 'I would be able to give you an excellent discount, and then everyone will be happy.'

Jenny returned his smile. 'Everyone except my bank manager, my account is already in the red for this month.'

The young man shrugged his shoulders disappointedly. 'If you've made up your mind that you are only going to buy Snow White, then I shall have to turn all of the dwarfs around the other way.'

'Why have you got to do that?' asked Jenny with a puzzled look.

'If their backs are turned, they won't be able to see me carry her away.' As if it had been an afterthought, he added. 'I only hope that she doesn't start screaming for help when I do.'

Jenny shook her head and laughed. 'You're absolutely crazy, fancy treating garden ornaments as if they are human.'

A serious look replaced the man's smile. 'Don't let them hear you say that,' he whispered. 'They don't know that they are made of concrete, they think that they are the same as us.'

Jenny pointed at the free delivery within ten-mile notice. 'Does that still stand, if I only buy Snow White?'

'Even if you only buy the witches poisoned apple, I will still deliver it free of charge, as long as you live within a ten mile radius.' The young man replied as he took Jenny's money and rang it up on the till.

'My name's John,' he said, as he ran a finger down his delivery book and wrote Jenny's name and address at the bottom. 'Will it be all right, if I drop Snow White off tonight at seven?'

True to his word, John's van arrived at Jenny's front door dead on the stroke of seven.

'Hey Fourteen. A white van has just pulled up outside your front gate. Is Jenny having something delivered?' asked Thirteen nosily.

'It isn't any of your business really is it? However, you are going to see what it is when the driver carries it into the house, so I might as well tell you. Jenny has bought a beautiful ornament for my patio out the back. That's where she was going when she went out this morning, when Eight narrow-mindedly thought she was going meet Doctor Good-heart on an illicit date.'

After John had carried Snow White through the house, he stood her on the patio and kissed her gently on the cheek. Trying hard not to smile, he said. 'That was a goodbye kiss from all of the seven dwarfs.'

John and Jenny stood talking and laughing on the doorstep for almost an hour. When he finally drove off in his van, he had discovered that they both had the same crazy outlook on life. He also knew that she was single, had no steady boyfriend, and he wanted to see her again.

When Jenny answered the ringing doorbell at seven o'clock on Tuesday evening, she was surprised to find John standing on the doorstep with Happy cradled in his arms.

'There must be some mistake,' she said. 'I didn't buy any of the dwarfs.'

John looked down at the figure in his arms. 'I'm not delivering,' he said apologetically. 'I've brought him along to ask if he could see Snow White. He has been so miserable since she left. Just look at his face. I ask you, is anyone going to buy him looking like that? I'm sure he will start smiling again, if he could see her for just a few minutes.'

On Wednesday, it was Bashful's turn to visit. 'He's so shy, I doubt if he will even say hello,' said John, as he stood him in front of Snow White.

John was right, Bashful didn't speak, but his painted cheeks seemed to take on a deeper blush.'

It came as no surprise to Jenny, when John turned up on Thursday evening with Grumpy. 'The poor little fellow is more cantankerous than ever, now that Snow White isn't around,' he said.

Jenny was about to leave the house for her usual Friday night out with friends, when John turned up with Dopey.

'I was just on my way out,' she said, standing back to allow him to carry the concrete figure into the garden.

'I shouldn't have sold Snow White without the seven dwarfs,' he said, as he stood Dopey in front of Snow White. 'With all of this carrying them back and forth so that they can see her,' John nodded down at Dopey. 'You must think that I'm as daft as him.'

On Saturday evening, when John arrived with Sneezy, he found Jenny waiting at the door.

'You shouldn't have brought him,' she said, with a look of concern. 'He seems to have such a dreadful cold.'

'I didn't want to, said John. 'But he created such a fuss. He said that he had asked Doc's advice. And Doc had told him that a drop of fresh air and a visit to Snow White would be better than any medicine he could prescribe.'

As John walked down the drive with Sneezy in his arms, Jenny called after him. 'If you are thinking of bringing Sleepy tomorrow, I hope you've figured out a way to keep him awake.'

Jenny stood in her doorway watching John load Doc into the van. 'Thank you for allowing all of the dwarfs to visit Snow White,' he said with a grin. 'Now that they know she is well looked after, I don't think they will be bothering you in the future.' Then, with a quick wave of his hand, he drove off.

Jenny was watching television when the doorbell rang. Let it be John, she thought as she walked to the door. 'I suppose it's your turn to visit Snow White,' she said, before he had time to open his mouth.

John thrust a bunch of roses into her hand. 'That's not why I'm here,' he said. 'Everyone knows that Snow White belongs to the seven dwarfs. The reason I am here, is because I wanted to see you.'

'It must be wonderful to have a real romance and go walking in the moonlight with the one you love,' Eleven said with a sigh, as she watched Jenny and John walking down the street with an arm around each others waist.

'Blow the romance thing,' said Thirteen. 'I wouldn't like any of that slushy stuff. I would just settle for a walk in the moonlight.'

'I wouldn't want any slushy stuff either,' said Fifteen. 'Watching Mrs Braithwaite and Percy Grant has put me off of slushy for life.'

'Just to be able to walk would be enough for me,' Dunfoaming mumbled to herself. 'But I suppose running would be better. If I was able to do that, then, I would be out of this close and be away from you shabby lot for ever.'

Sixteen rattled one of his open windows angrily. 'Just listen to yourselves. Eleven wants to have a romance and go walking in the moonlight. Thirteen would be happy just to go for a walk. Fifteen has had her fill of slushiness, and goodness knows what Dunfoaming wants, because she didn't say it loud enough for any of us to hear. I don't know what's come over all of you lately your beginning to sound just like your tenants; none of them seem to be happy with what they've got either.'

'I wouldn't say that exactly,' **said Fourteen.** 'Since my tenant Jenny met John, she's more than happy; in fact she's walking on cloud nine. I wouldn't be at all surprised if there's a wedding in the close in the near future.'

Eleven sighed again. 'I'm quite happy. I just thought it would be nice to have a romance and go for a walk in the moonlight, but I wouldn't mind walking on cloud nine instead. Cloud nine, sounds like it's soft and comfortable.'

'If it's a romance you want,' **said Two in his sexiest voice.** 'Then, I'm the one for you. Unfortunately, a walk in the moonlight is out of the question, but if you are partial to a love song or two, if you will pardon the pun, I'm sure that my beautiful singing voice will sweep you off your feet. Apart from that I'm also the handsomest house in the close.'

'You don't half like blowing your own trumpet, don't you,' **said Dunfoaming, acidly.**

Two's sexy voice became a sneer. 'I would be doing myself an injustice if I didn't. But don't you worry Miss Dunfoaming, no matter what the circumstances; I will never blow my trumpet in your direction.'

###CHAPTER TWENTY-ONE###

'Have you any idea where Mr Kreamer and Percy have gone?' **One asked Three.** 'They've never taken the burger van out at one o'clock in the morning before.'

'It's no good asking me what they are up to,' **Three answered irritably, annoyed that she had been aroused from her sleep.** 'All I know is that Kreamer told Percy that he had some work to do tonight. He said because it was a two-man job he would need an assistant. He also told him that if he didn't want to be in on it it didn't matter, as he knew somebody who would jump at the chance to earn some real money.'

'Percy must have said that he would do it, because they've gone out together.'

'Did he ask Kreamer what the job was?'

'If he did, I didn't hear him, but you can bet your life it's something dodgy. I can't imagine where they could possibly sell ice creams and burgers at this hour of the morning.'

'It will be even later when they get there. It's one o'clock already, and they've only just started out.'

Three yawned sleepily. 'No doubt we'll find out where they've been when they return. Until then, I have only two words to say. Goodnight One.'

'You haven't told me what this job is yet.' said Percy as he climbed into the seat beside Kreamer. 'Nor have you told me how much I will be earning.'

Kreamer turned his head and gave Percy a lopsided grin. 'If it all goes well, you will be two grand the richer by midday tomorrow. I'll tell you all about it as we go along.'

'Well?' said Percy, after they had been travelling for about ten minutes. 'Where are we going, and what have I got to do to earn this two thousand quid? Whatever it is, I've got a funny feeling that it won't be legal.'

Dennis shrugged his shoulders. 'Legal is boring, and it doesn't pay very well. All we've got to do is pick up a package and drop it off at an address in London before eight in the morning.'

'What sort of a package is it?' asked Percy suspiciously.

'It's going to be a wet one.' Dennis replied with a grin. 'We've got to fish it out of the sea.'

Alarm bells had started ringing in Percy's head. 'If we're going to fish it out of the sea, then, it definitely isn't legal. It had better not be Heroin, or Cocaine, if it is then, you can count me out. I don't want anything to do with mainline stuff, that's too heavy for me. I'm too young to spend nine or ten years of my life locked in a room that isn't much bigger than a toilet.'

'I thought you knew me better than that.' Dennis sounded hurt. 'I wouldn't have anything to do with class A drugs either. I've got three kids to support. If you must know. It's a couple of hundred kilos of cannabis.'

'Two hundred kilos of cannabis in a package floating in the sea, how the hell do you expect us to lift in into the boat? I doubt if an Olympic weight lifting champion would be able to lift that much.'

'You won't have to lift it into the boat,' said Dennis. 'You'll be doing the rowing. I didn't think of asking before we set out, but you can row can't you?'

'I haven't done any recently, but I used to pull a boat over the water quite often when I was younger.'

'That's all right then, you concentrate on the rowing, and I'll worry about the package and how we're going to get it ashore. However, if it will set your mind at rest we won't be lifting it into the boat. I'm going to release it from the buoy that it will be anchored to, and then I'll tie it to the back of the boat and we will tow it to the shore.'

'I can't help but notice that you keep saying we, but it isn't going to be we is it? It's going to be me. I'm the one who will be doing the rowing, and dragging two hundred kilos of cannabis through the water isn't going to be easy, in fact, it's going to be bleeding hard.'

'But it will be worth it. Two thousand pounds is a nice chunk of cash.'

'How far have we got to go to pick up this package?'

Either Dennis didn't hear, or he pretended not to.

'I don't know if you've realized it or not, but a white burger van like this stands out like a pregnant woman in a crowd of skeleton's at this time of the morning, and you've had your jingle playing ever since we started out.'

Kreamer gave Percy a sheepish grin. 'I've got so used to hearing them; I sometimes forget to switch them off.'

'How far do we have to go to pick up this package?' Percy asked again.

Dennis switched off his chimes and turned the radio on. 'It's only six miles to the Wayling Bay, maybe a nice bit of music will help you to relax.'

'We're not going to Wayling Bay to pick up the package are we? The sea around that part of the coast can be very rough at this time of the year.'

'The weather forecast said the sea will be calm. It nearly always is, when there's a full moon.'

'Whose bright idea was it to pick up the stuff tonight? Didn't they know that there would be a full moon?'

'The boys we are working for are professionals; they run on a tight schedule. They don't give a damn if there's a full moon or not. If they say that they want the package fished from the sea tonight, then tonight it's got to be.'

Dennis and Percy sat silently listening to the music, until they reached the roundabout that separated Melderton from Wayling Bay.

'I hope you've realized that we will need a boat, before we can row out to sea and pick up that package. Please don't tell me that we've got to steal one from the harbour.'

Dennis tutted loudly. 'I've just told you, the people we are working for are professionals. It's all been arranged, there will be a boat waiting for us on the beach.'

'Have you any idea what sort of boat it will be?'

Dennis turned his head looked at Percy and grinned. 'It won't be The Queen Mary, or anything like that, but they guaranteed that it would suitable for the job. Before we started out, they told me on my mobile that they've hidden it between two rocks on the beach at the bottom of the cliffs, and when we've brought the cannabis ashore, I've got to sink it.'

Dennis parked the van in a deserted car park near the beach. Slipping his arm around Percy's shoulder, he whispered in his ear. 'I can't see anyone around, can you?'

Percy shook his head. 'There won't be any coppers hanging around at this time of the morning. As for the locals most of them are Londoner's living in holiday homes, and if I know Londoner's, they will all be tucked up in bed fast asleep by now.'

Dennis nodded in agreement. 'This is what we will do. As soon as we've brought the package ashore, I will leave you on the beach to guard it while I come back here and pick up the van. Then we will sink the boat, lift the cannabis into the van and be on our way. It's as easy as that.' *Dennis didn't know it at the time, but as easy as that, wasn't going to be all that easy.*

Percy stepped back in surprise, when they found the boat. 'You were right when you said it won't be the Queen Mary,' he gasped. 'But at least they could have left a decent boat. You can buy these things in any seaside shop for about twenty quid; it isn't much more than a boat-shaped Lilo. I wouldn't even trust it to take my weight in a swimming pool, but your friends expect the two of us to take it to sea and pick up a package weighing about two hundred kilos.'

'It won't be weighing *about* two hundred kilos.' Dennis said gravely. 'It will weigh *exactly* two hundred kilo's. I told you that the people we are working for are professionals.' He looked at his watch. 'When the package is put into the sea in about ten minute's time, it will weigh two hundred kilo's, and when we deliver it they will expect it to be the same weight. If it isn't, they will say that it's been tampered with, and then they will take it out of our hides.'

'So, I won't be able to open it up and take a bit out for myself?'

'You could, if you wanted to.' Dennis said seriously. 'But to do that, you would have to be tired of life.'

'I was only joking. I wouldn't tamper with it even if I could; I've got plenty of my own growing up in the loft.'

Together they picked up the red rubber boat. 'I hate shingle beaches,' Dennis whispered, as they carried it down to the sea. 'They make too much noise.' Then, he looked at Percy. 'Where are the oars?'

'Don't ask me? How would I know? You're the one in charge.'

'You'd better go back and see if you can find them,' said Dennis. 'We won't get very far without them; perhaps they fell out of the boat when we were carrying it here.'

Moaning to himself about the size of the boat, Percy made his way back to the rocks. 'If the oars are the ones that were made to fit the boat, then I doubt if they will be much bigger than the spades kiddies use to make sandcastles on the beach,' he mumbled. After searching for a several minutes, he found the oars lying with two lifejackets behind a   large rock. 'I was right about the oars, 'he said in disgust. 'My mum's got wooden spoons in her kitchen that are bigger than these.'

Percy stood looking up at the moon. 'It's almost as bright as day. I wish it was darker.'

'Don't worry about it being light, no one's going to be looking out to sea at this time in the morning, and even if someone is, I doubt if they would be able to see us.'

'Don't talk stupid,' Percy snapped angrily. 'Of course they'll be able to see us. If we're bobbing about on the waves in a red rubber boat in full moonlight, they won't be able to miss us. In fact, we're going to stick out like an inflamed boil on a nudists bum.'

Dennis slipped his life jacket on and tied the strings. 'Alright then,' he said. 'Let's be off.'

'Give me a chance to put my life jacket on,' said Percy.

'You don't need a life jacket. You won't be moving about in the boat like me. You'll be doing the rowing, and a bulky jacket will slow your arm movements down.'

'Percy held out his hands. 'Look at these,' he said. 'They're shaking like a couple of jellies on a plate, and I'm not even sitting in the boat yet. When I am, I will probably be shaking from head to toe. There will be plenty of arm movement then, even if I am wearing a jacket. And I hope you're not thinking of moving about in the boat, 'cos if you are, you'll be taking it to sea on your own.'

'What are you afraid of? You can swim can't you?'

Percy pointed at the huge incoming waves. 'It's these breakers that I'm afraid of, haven't you noticed the size of them? I'm terrified that one of them might wash me overboard.'

Dennis looked at the waves breaking on the beach. 'Those aren't real waves,' he said calmly. Then, he pointed out to sea. 'That's where you're going to find the real waves.'

Reluctantly Percy climbed into the boat and sat down. 'You'll have to push the boat out until you're up to your waist, then, you can jump in.' he shouted.

'There's no need to shout,' Dennis whispered. 'I'm standing right behind you. Voices can carry a long way on a quiet night.'

Dennis pushed the boat off the beach and climbed aboard, but before Percy could get to work with the oars, a wave carried them back to the shore.

Five attempts later, Dennis panted. 'It's no good. I'm never going to launch this blasted thing with you onboard, you'll have to climb out and give me a hand.'

'I can't do that. I have to be ready to start rowing. Maybe you'll be more successful if you walk further into the sea before you climb in.' Percy suggested helpfully. 'If you keep pushing until you're up to your chin we will be in much deeper water.'

'I'll give it a try, but if that doesn't work, then you'll have to get out and help. We can't afford to spend the rest of the night trying to get out to sea; we've got to deliver the package before eight in the morning.'

Percy looked down at the head that seemed to be floating on top of the water. 'We should be deep enough now, so climb in and I'll start rowing.'

With Dennis, hanging half in and half out, Percy pulled expertly on the oars. 'It's tougher going than I thought it would be, and the sea's getting really rough. I thought you said the forecast was for calm water.'

Dennis looked up at the sky. 'It looks like you are going to get your wish,' he said gloomily. 'It will be really dark in a moment or two; the moon is just about to disappear behind those stormy looking clouds.' As the words were leaving his mouth, the storm broke.

With the red rubber boat bobbing up and down like a demented duck on a water spout at a fairground shooting range, Percy managed to be sick three times during his first five minutes of rowing.

Baling like mad with the wind in his face at the blunt end, Dennis unfortunately copped the lot. 'If you have to be sick again,' he snarled angrily. 'Will you try and do it over the side.' Then, he poured the contents of the baling pot into his lap to wash away Percy's supper.

'I can't help it,' moaned pale-faced Percy miserably. 'I used to get terribly seasick when I went rowing as a boy and I was only on a pond in the park.'

Half an hour later, having lost the battle to keep his breakfast, lunch, and supper inside him, Percy shipped the oars. Looking down sorrowfully at the blisters on his hands, he tucked them under his armpits in a vain attempt to relieve the pain.

Dennis glared at him contemptuously. 'Don't sit there with your hands stuck under your arms like you're imitating a chicken. The marker buoy must be out here somewhere, look around and see if you can spot a small flashing light.'

Percy rubbed his stomach and groaned. 'I daren't move my head, if I do I'll be looking at the waves and then I'll be throwing up again. I've been sick so many times it's left me feeling weak and exhausted, at the moment I don't think I've got enough strength to row back to the beach. However, I might be all right if I can sit here for a few minutes and have a short rest.'

'You can rest for as long as you like after we've found the package and we're on our way to London.' Dennis turned his head and pointed at a wave heading towards them. 'And I don't think you will have to row the boat back to the beach either, the speed those waves are moving towards the shore, they will carry us back, all you will need to do is steer.'

Percy breathed a sigh of relief. Steering is a lot easier than rowing he thought. Then, the boat tipped dangerously when Dennis leaned to his left to pull out the mobile that had started ringing in his pocket.

Grasping the sides of the boat in panic, Percy shouted. 'What are you doing? Let the bleeding phone ring, it's probably some drunken git wanting to order a burger and chips and asking if you can deliver.'

'Dennis's face grew red with rage. 'You should have rang me earlier!' he shouted into the phone. 'If I had known that the package hadn't been left for us to pick up, I wouldn't be sitting in a small rubber boat in the middle of a boiling sea with a rower who keeps being sick all over me looking for a buoy that doesn't exist. What do you want us to do now?'

'Look at the size of that wave coming towards us, it's as big as a house.' Percy shouted hysterically. 'It's going to capsize us.'

Dennis dropped his mobile and stared at the wave in disbelief. 'If it does,' he bellowed back. 'Hang on to the boat for dear life, and kick hard with your legs for the shore, and let's hope that the tide will take us in.'

Percy gave him a terrified look. 'What if the boat gets washed away?'

'Then, we will have to swim back to the shore, won't we? I hope that you're a strong swimmer.'

'I can swim better than I row.'

'You can hardly swim at all then.' Dennis sneered sarcastically, as the wave reached them.

For several seconds the boat floated on top of the wave. Then, it turned over throwing it's passengers into the sea. When they surfaced, the boat was several metres away.

'How are you feeling?' asked Dennis through chattering teeth.

'How do you think I'm feeling? I've been sea sick since we started out, now I feel as weak as a kitten, the water's bleeding freezing, the boat that we should be sitting in looks like it's a mile away, and from what I gathered from your phone call, the job has been called off.'

Dennis swam until he was alongside Percy. 'Are you always like this when you go out on a job? You haven't stopped moaning since I picked you up.'

'I think I've got a right to moan. It's the middle of the night and I'm fighting for my life swimming in a rough sea about a mile from land. My hands are red raw from rowing a boat that wasn't sea worthy, and the package we were supposed to pick up wasn't even put into the sea. And I expect that when I finally get to the shore, that's if I *ever* get there, you're going to tell me we won't be getting paid because we didn't pick up the package.'

Dennis spat out a mouthful of salt water. 'We can't expect to get paid for a job that we didn't finish.'

Percy stopped swimming and started treading water. 'It wasn't our fault, we couldn't do the pick up was it?'

Dennis floated past Percy on the crest of a wave. 'Instead of moaning about not getting paid, we should count ourselves lucky.'

Percy started swimming again in an attempt to catch up with Dennis. 'I can't understand your thinking,' he shouted. 'How can you say we were lucky?'

'The boat that was supposed to drop the package off, was picked up by the coastguard just after it started out. If it had been a few hours later, they would have been picking us up instead.'

To add insult to injury, the storm clouds drifted away and the sea became calm, just minutes after angry waves carried Dennis and Percy onto the beach and dumped them there.

Half an hour later, Percy rolled over on his back. Opening his eyes and looked up at the cloudless sky. Then, he turned his head and saw Dennis kneeling beside him. 'Thank God you're alright.' Dennis sounded relieved.

Percy sat up. 'It's nice to know you care.'

'Who said I cared? I was worried in case I had to give you mouth to mouth resuscitation.'

Percy screwed his eyes into a squint and looked along the beach. 'I was hoping we had seen the last of that thing,' he grunted, pointing at the red rubber boat floating lazily on the water several metres away.

Dennis got to his feet walked to the boat and pulled it ashore.

'Are you going to sink it?' asked Percy hopefully.

Dennis gave the boat a quick once over. 'There's nothing wrong with it, so I think I'll take it home with me.'

'Take it home with you? What are you going to do with it

when you get it there?'

'I'm going to give it to the kids. Then, at least the night won't have been completely wasted.'

'What use will it be to them? You never take them to the beach and there aren't any rivers near by.'

'I wasn't reckoning on them using it as a boat. I'm going to put it in the back garden. It will make a nice trampoline.'

'What about me,' said Percy. 'What am I going to get for all my work?'

'You won't be getting any money, that's for sure. But you've already got something that money can't buy.'

Percy's brow creased in a puzzled frown. 'I'd like to know what it is.'

'You've got memories of an experience that you're never going to forget,' Dennis replied casually.

'I see the Burger van has returned,' said Dunfoaming, as two very wet men climbed out of the front and slammed the doors irritability behind them. Water oozed out of their shoes and wet footprints followed them as they made their way to their front gates.

'Percy sloshed his way up the path to his front door, and then he glared across at Dennis. 'I hope you never ask me to go out on a job with you again, 'cos if you do, I can tell you now, the answer's going to be no.'

Dennis shrugged his shoulders dismissively. 'You wouldn't have said that, if you had the two thousand pounds that I said you would earn in your pocket.' Then, he turned the key in the lock and walked indoors.

###CHAPTER TWENTY-TWO###

'Buenos días,' said Dunfoaming.

Two gave her a puzzled look. 'Buenos, what?'

'Dias,' repeated Dunfoaming. 'I said Buenos dais. It's Spanish for good morning. I'm trying to learn the language.'

'What on earth are you trying to learn Spanish for?' asked Three. 'I doubt if any Spanish houses will ever be moving into our close.'

'I'm not exactly learning it properly; I'm just picking up a few words here and there. It doesn't hurt to extend ones vocabulary, does it? But my owners are taking it seriously, they've got phrasebooks and records, and a Spanish lady is going to come here once a week to teach them.'

'Are they thinking of selling up and moving to Spain?' asked One hopefully.

'They're not going to move there permanently, they're going to buy a holiday villa in Benidorm. That's why they're learning to speak Spanish. They want to be able to mix and converse with the locals in their own language.'

'It will be quite an achievement if they ever learn to speak Spanish good enough for the people in Benidorm to understand them,' grunted Three. 'From what I've heard the locals around here can't understand them when they speak English.'

'That's because they talk all hoity-toity like they have plums in their mouths,' said Two. 'No doubt they are understood in the posher part of the town.'

'Is there a posher part of town?' said Six. 'Well that does surprise me, I've been around here all of my life and I didn't know that.'

'If your owners are really going to buy a villa in Spain.' said One. 'I wish you could bog off with them as well.'

'Is bogoff a Spanish word?' asked Dunfoaming naively.'

'You tell me,' One grunted in reply. 'You're the one who's learning Spanish.'

Dunfoaming stood silent for some seconds, then, she said. 'Yes, it is a Spanish word. I've just worked it out. It means the toilet is out of order.'

'No it doesn't,' said Eight. 'It isn't a real word, it's a made up one. I doubt if you would be able to find it in any dictionary. My tenant's wife works in a supermarket, and I heard her telling her husband that bogof means, buy one get one free. Supermarkets seem to be doing it a lot these days; it's just a crafty way to get their customers to buy more than they really need.'

'My owners are flying to Spain next week on a viewing trip,' Dunfoaming said loud enough for all of the houses in the close to hear. 'If they purchase a property they will probably live here in the summer, and winter abroad.'

'With the world in the state it's in, it isn't a good time to buy property abroad,' said Eighteen mournfully. 'The bottom has fallen out of the market. In fact, it isn't sensible to buy property anywhere just now. Your owners could lose thousands of pounds.'

'It's not as bad as all that is it?' gasped Eleven. 'If it is, I can't see myself ever being sold.'

'I can't see you ever being sold either,' **Dunfoaming said with a sneer.** 'Even though they've tarted you up a bit, you're still the dowdiest looking house in the close.'

'You know what it will mean if your owners are daft enough to buy a villa in Benidorm don't you?' **said One.** 'Every winter from now on, you are going to be alone and empty. That means long cold days and nights with no central heating. You'll be absolutely freezing.'

'I wouldn't take any notice of One if I was you,' **said Eleven.** 'You won't be alone and empty for very long, nor will you be freezing. When my ex-squatters hear that your owners have bought a place in Spain and they are going away for the winter, the three of them will be moving in before your owner's plane has left the runway. Then, you will find out just what it was like, when they were living in me. I can tell you one thing for sure; you won't be so fanciful after they've been maltreating you for a month or two.'

'You must think that my owners are crazy, they wouldn't leave me alone and unattended in this close for more than a day. If they do buy a place in Benidorm, they are going to contract a twenty four hour a day security firm called "Home Guard" to protect me from Damien and people like your squatters.'

'My ex-squatters,' **Eleven corrected.** 'They're my not living in me anymore.

'They might be able to protect you from Eleven's ex-squatters,' **said One in a serious voice.** 'But it will take more than a security firm to stop Damien getting inside you once he knows that your owners have gone and left you unoccupied.'

###CHAPTER TWENTY-THREE###

Saint Valentine's Day

'You'll never guess what my tenant has bought,' Twelve said to Thirteen.

'I don't have to guess, I've already seen it in your back garden. What on earth did he have to buy one of those things for?'

'I think it's a Saint Valentine's gift for his wife.'

'I thought Saint Valentine's gifts were supposed to be romantic.'

'They are.'

'You'd have to have a fantastic imagination, to find anything romantic in a gift like that!'

Young Bob Jenkins knew that his Dad was pleased with himself, when came into the kitchen after finishing work grinning like a quarter of a watermelon. When he had left in the morning, he had been moaning about having to go to work on Friday the Thirteenth when all sorts of unfortunate accidents would probably happen.

Taking hold of his wife's hand, he said. 'I want you to come into the back garden with me, Florrie. Friday the thirteenth has turned out to be a lucky one after all. I've managed to buy you a Valentine present with a difference and it was a bargain. I'm sure you're going to love it.'

Florrie sounded surprised. 'It isn't Saint Valentine's Day until tomorrow, and it's the first time you've ever bought me a Valentine present,' she said. 'In fact it's the first time you've every bought me a present of any sort, what have I done to deserve it?'

Bob knew there was going to be trouble ahead, when he heard his mum scream. 'I hate it; I really hate it, what made you think I would like a skinny thing like that? I've always known you were a bit soft in the head, but soft or not and I don't care if it is a present for me, you're not going to bring that mangy mutt into the house.'

Bob walked into the garden. 'Mum' he said. 'If you have always known that Dad was a bit soft in the head, then, why did you marry him?'

'God knows,' she replied glaring at his dad.'

'He's not a mangy mutt,' Bernie mumbled in defence of the dog. 'He's a thoroughbred racing greyhound.'

For the next ten minutes, Bob stood listening in admiration as his dad practiced the art of gentle persuasion.

'Just imagine,' he said, 'parading him around the track before the start of a race and then cheering him on to win. Then after we have had a glass or two of champagne, we will go and collect the price money. Sometimes it can run into hundreds of pounds, and when he starts winning the really big races it could be thousands.'

'This poor creature won't be winning any races big or small,' Florrie replied with a sad sigh. 'Just look at him, the poor things so thin you can see his ribs. If I were to keep him, I would have to take him out for a walk sometimes, and the neighbours will be sure to see, and when they do they will think that we've been starving him then, they would report us to the RSPCA.'

'Greyhounds are meant to be thin,' said Bernie. 'Even when they are at the peak of fitness, they look half-starved.'

Bob heard the sound of defeat in his mum's voice, when she said. 'If I let you keep him he will have to live out here in the garden, so it looks like you will have to build him a kennel.

Bob thought that his dad was pushing his luck, when he said. 'You won't be letting *me* keep him love you'll be letting *yourself* keep him, he's your dog. I bought him for you as a Valentine present.

When Bob's mum agreed that, they would keep the dog. Bob realized that his Dad wasn't the only one in the family who was a bit soft in the head.

'I think it's only fair to warn you,' Twelve said loud enough for his immediate neighbours to hear. 'You'll probably be hearing a lot of sawing and banging tomorrow and it will probably last for most of the day. My tenant has persuaded his wife to keep the greyhound on the condition that he builds him a kennel.'

'If my tenant hadn't died under that wardrobe, he would have been able to build him a kennel in a couple of hours,' said Sixteen with a touch of pride in his voice. 'He was a skilled joiner and a master craftsman. He made his own coffin out of bits and pieces of scrap wood.'

'It's a pity he's dead isn't it?' Thirteen said coldly. 'We could have put up with him sawing and banging for a couple of hours that would hardly have bothered us at all. But if your tenant is going to be bashing away with a hammer for a whole day, we're going to suffer aches in our roofs and attics.'

As Bob's soft-in-the-head parents sat at the table planning the greyhound's racing future, Bob stood at the kitchen window admiring his dad's latest acquisition.

'One of the first things we will have to do, is find out if he jumps over hurdles or runs on the flat.' said dad. 'Then we can start racing him on one of those unlicensed tracks.

Bob tried not to smile when he said. 'I know the answer to that question Dad. He's a hurdler.'

His father gave him a puzzled look. 'How do you know that?' he said.

'By the way he's just jumped over the garden fence.'

Both parents rushed outside, in time to see the greyhound disappearing over Number 7's fence.'

Either Bob's mum couldn't, or she didn't want to hide the sound of relief in her voice, when she said. 'Oh well, that's that problem solved. With a bit of luck, we're never going to set eyes on that walking bag of bones again.'

'How can you say that,' said Bernie sadly. 'He was the only present I ever bought you.'

Unfortunately, luck wasn't on Florrie's side. Half an hour later the fence jumping greyhound returned, proudly carrying a dead white rabbit between its teeth.

'Where did you get this?' asked Bernie, pulling the rabbit from its mouth.

'I know where he got it,' said Bob. 'It's Samantha Pettigrew's pet. She lives at Number 4.'

Florrie glared at Bernie. 'It's your dog,' she shouted. 'You'll have to go and tell Mr Pettigrew that it's killed his daughter's pet.'

'It isn't my dog, it's yours.'

'It's yours now. I've just given your present back. And I want you to promise that you'll never buy me a present again.'

'You won't be able to tell him about the rabbit until Sunday night,' said Bob. 'They've put their cat Mr Tom into a cattery for the weekend and gone to visit friends in Cornwall. When they get back and find the rabbit dead, Samantha is going to be terribly upset. Especially when she finds out it how it died; she thought a lot of that rabbit, she's had it since it was a few weeks old.'

'Bernie had laid the dead rabbit on the kitchen table. With his ear resting against its body he seemed to be listening for a beating heart or some small sign of life.'

'Why don't you try giving it mouth to mouth resuscitation?' said Florrie coldly.

'I would if I thought it would do any good,' he said, 'but it would only be a waste of breath.' Pulling several small pieces of grass from the rabbit's mouth, he casually dropped them on the kitchen floor. 'I'm afraid this poor old bunny won't be eating any more grass, it's definitely dead.'

With a distasteful look, Florrie picked up remains of the rabbit's last meal and dropped them in the treadle bin. 'You had better put that rabbit somewhere safe until you can return it to the Pettigrew's when they get back tomorrow. From the look on that greyhounds face, I would say that the only reason he brought it back here was so that you could skin it for him to eat.'

'It's going to be an exciting day tomorrow, when my tenants get back from Cornwall.' Fours voice sounded a bit higher than usual. 'There's going to be hell to pay, when Mr Jenkins brings back Samantha's dead pet rabbit and tells them that it was killed by his greyhound.'

'Mr Jenkins is a gravedigger isn't he?' said Five.

'That's right,' Twelve answered proudly. 'He's one of the best in the country. In fact he was the one who dug Mr Woodward's grave.'

'So why doesn't he just bury the rabbit somewhere and say nothing about it being killed by his dog? Surely that would be the easiest and most sensible thing to do.'

'You're right of course.' Twelve agreed. 'But how often do humans do easy sensible things?'

'I saw the greyhound jumping over the fences with it in its mouth,' said Six. 'And when it landed in our garden, it didn't half frighten Mr Speedwell's pigeons.'

'I shouldn't think there were any pigeons in your garden for it to frighten,' Three said bitchily. 'They seem to spend all of their time roosting on my roof.'

'I've told you why they do it,' said Four. 'It's because your roof is the warmest around these parts, and if there's one thing that they really like, it's to feel warmth beneath their feet.'

'Dad!' said Bob. 'I've just had a great idea. If you take the dead rabbit around all the local pet shops tomorrow, I'm sure you will be able to find one that's identical in colour and size. And then tomorrow night, after the neighbours have gone to bed, you can climb over their fences to Samantha's garden, then, you'll be able to put the new rabbit in the dead one's hutch.'

Bob's dad was so pleased with the idea; for one dreadful moment, Bob thought he was going to kiss him.

'Did you hear that dog barking last night Fourteen?' asked Thirteen.'

'I certainly did, I thought it was never going to stop.'

'It was worse for me,' said Twelve gloomily. 'The creature was sleeping in my kitchen.'

'Sleeping? I wish it had been sleeping. If it had been sleeping, I wouldn't have this terrible pain in the roof.'

At eight o'clock, with the dead rabbit lying in a plastic bag, Bernie Jenkins left the house to begin his search for the live rabbit that would replace the dead one. It was five o'clock in the afternoon before he returned with a rabbit that could have been the dead rabbit's twin. The pet shop owner had kindly offered to take the dead one off his hands and bury it in his back garden, which was now a pet's cemetery.

Bernie glared down at the dog. 'It's taken me all day and cost me £25 to find a replacement rabbit for the one that you killed,' he snarled. 'And, I had to pay the greedy pet shop owner £10, to have the dead one buried.'

'Never mind darling,' Florrie said sarcastically. 'You'll get all of your money back again, when *your* greyhound wins his first race.'

On Sunday morning at two o'clock when Bernie believed that, all of his neighbours would be fast asleep. Looking like a nervous would be burglar; he climbed carefully over his neighbours' fences carrying the live white rabbit in a cardboard box.

Standing with the dog in the kitchen doorway watching, Bob suddenly realized that his mother had been right – his Dad really was soft in the head.

'Hey Ten,' Eleven whispered softly. 'I think a burglar has just climbed over my fence into your garden. What are you going to do about it?'

'There's isn't much that I can do, is there? There isn't much point in shouting that there's a burglar in the garden, if only houses can hear me. But if he tries to break in, I suppose I could make my windows and doors creak really loud and hope that it alerts my sleeping tenants.'

'You've got a crazy inventor living in you; surely he doesn't need you to alert him to a break in. He must have invented and installed something that would wake him if someone tried to force an entry.'

'You would think that just looking at all of the junk lying in your back garden, would to be enough to tell any would-be burglar that he would be wasting his time,' laughed Eleven.

'He wouldn't be wasting his time if he was a scrap dealer,' sniggered Nine.

'A break in isn't something to laugh at,' said Seven. 'I'd be really nervous if it was happening to me.'

'There isn't anything to worry about,' said Twelve. 'That man climbing our fences isn't a burglar. It's only my stupid tenant making his way to Four's back garden with the white rabbit that he's going to use as a replacement for the one that his dog killed.'

A few days later, when Bernie called in at the Red Lion for a quick drink, he noticed Mr Pettigrew standing at the bar staring thoughtfully into a pint of beer.

Bernie gave him a friendly pat on the back. 'Cheer up Kieth,' he said. 'You look like you've got all the worries of the world on your shoulders.'

Kieth lifted his eyes and gave him a weary smile. 'Something's puzzling me, and no matter how hard I try I just can't figure it out.'

Thinking that he might be on to a free pint, Bernie said craftily. 'You know what they say, (two heads are better than one, and a problem shared is a problem halved.) If you care to tell me what's worrying you, maybe I will be able to help.'

Mr Pettigrew shrugged his shoulders hopelessly. 'Last Friday I took the family away to Cornwall for a long weekend. Before leaving, I went into the back garden to check that my daughter Samantha had left enough food and water for her pet rabbit. Sadly, I found the poor thing dead in its hutch. I couldn't just leave it lying there, so I quickly dug a hole at the bottom of the garden and buried it. I didn't want to spoil Samantha's weekend so I decided that I wouldn't tell her about the rabbit until we returned from Cornwall.' He lifted his glass to his lips, when he returned it to the top of the bar, it was half-empty. 'Now, I know that you're not going to believe this, but it's true. When we returned home on Sunday evening the rabbit was back in its hutch alive and kicking.'

Bernie gave him a doubtful smile. 'You're kidding.' He said. 'Dead rabbits can't come back to life.'

Kieth shrugged his shoulders again. 'Maybe they can, and maybe they can't,' he said with a frown. 'But, that's not what's bothering me. What I would like to know, is how did it managed to get back inside its hutch and lock itself in.'

###CHAPTER TWENTY-FOUR###

March 1st

'I haven't been able to see too well lately,' **Dunfoaming mumbled**. 'I think it's about time my windows were cleaned.'

'I know how important it is for you to see everything that is going on in the close,' **said One**. 'Having dirty windows can be very frustrating. I had my ground floor windows cleaned two days ago. Mrs Kreamer paid Damien two pounds to do them, but she wasted her money. I could see quiet well before he started, but now everything's a blur. Luckily, for me she wouldn't let him do the upstairs she was frightened that he might fall. So I can still see what's going on in the close.'

'When you pay peanuts, you only get monkeys.' **Dunfoaming replied** venomously. 'It's a pity that she didn't let him do the upstairs as well, then, you would be in the same condition as me. But at least when mine are cleaned, they'll be done by an expert.'

'I wish my windows had been cleaned by a monkey,' **said One with** a sigh. 'A monkey would have done a better job.'

'Damien came knocking on my front door yesterday, with a bucket of water in one hand and a sponge in the other,' **said Two**.

'You must admit the boys a trier,' One replied, with a touch of admiration in her voice. 'Did he want to clean your windows?'

'I haven't a clue. My tenant has had dealings with the little devil before, so he pretended that he wasn't in.'

'I say, One,' Eleven said in an excited voice. 'If you can't see out of your downstairs front windows then you couldn't have seen the people who came to view me yesterday.'

Before one had a chance to answer, Dunfoaming said. 'I did, I saw them. Their faces were alive with expectation when they got out of the car and stood looking at you. Then they went in. Half an hour later, when they came out again, they didn't seem to be at all impressed. I suppose they didn't like the bathroom.'

'That just goes to prove that most of your talking comes out of your waste pipe. It was the bathroom that they liked most all. The kids really loved the super-de-luxe shower; in fact, they liked it so much they wanted to try it there and then. At first, the woman had her doubts about the bath; she thought it seemed a bit on the small side.'

'What I did I say when I saw them carrying the bath through your front door?' Said Dunfoaming. 'I told you then that it seemed to be a bit on the small side, and I reckoned it was too thin to take the weight of a full grown man.'

Eleven decided to ignore Dunfoaming. 'When the lady got into the bath to try it out she said there was only enough room for one, so her husband wouldn't be able to take a bath with her in the future. But it didn't matter that much, she said. As there was more than enough room under the shower for two.'

'Oh dear.' Dunfoaming groaned. 'Don't say that we are going to have another family from Hell living in the close.'

'Actually,' said Eleven, imitating Dunfoaming's posh voice. 'They will probably bring a bit of class to this close. The adults are profession actors.'

Twelve seemed to be impressed. 'Are they really? Are they famous? Do they get asked for autographs and that sort of thing?'

'I thought I recognized the ladies face,' said Ten. 'I'm sure I've seen her on the television. I think she was in that house programme once or twice, but I can't remember what it's called.'

Twelve could hardly contain his excitement. 'I think I know the one that you mean, it's my favourite. Is it called Coronation Street?'

'Coronation Street isn't about houses,' Dunfoaming said authoritatively, 'it's a soap. The programme that you are probably thinking about is called Homes under the Hammer. Isn't that right Eleven?'

'It's no good asking me,' Eleven replied. 'As you all know, my ex-squatters stole a television once, but I've never actually seen one when it's been working.'

'You're in for a treat then,' said Ten. 'If the people who have been viewing you turn out to be your new owner's, and if they really are professional television actors, then they are sure to have a television. After all they will want to see themselves working, won't they? But be careful, television is very addictive. At first, it's a novelty and you want to keep watching it all of the time. But after a while when you realize that most of the programmes aren't really all that good, it's too late, because you are already hooked. Believe you me; I'm the one who knows. It's got to the stage where I even enjoy watching the adverts.'

A furniture van followed by a car drove into the close and stopped outside Number 11.

'Hey Dunfoaming!' shouted Eleven. 'It seems like you got it wrong as usual. My poor quality bathroom suite didn't put the actress or her family off. If it's them who are moving in, then they must have gone ahead and bought me.'

Dunfoaming stared across at One. 'That's good, Eleven,' she said begrudgingly. 'And if, they really are professional actors, and not ice cream and hamburger sellers. Then, perhaps we will be getting a better class of person living here, after all, but I think they must be (as mad as March hares) to move into this close.'

'They are actors,' Eleven said excitedly after the furniture van had been unloaded and driven away.

'How did you manage to find out so quickly?' asked Ten.

'Molly their daughter, was unpacking one of the boxes when she found a photograph album. She sat looking through it for a few minutes. Then, with a frown, she pulled a photograph from the album, and passed it up to her mother. 'This is a picture of you, isn't it mummy?' She said. 'Why are you dressed as Cinderella?'

As Sylvia, her mother, gazed down at the photo, her eyes took on the faraway look of someone remembering the past.

'That photo was taken just after I met your father,' she said, 'during my first starring role in pantomime.'

Sitting down beside her daughter, Sylvia fitted the picture back in the album. 'It was my first big audition and I was feeling really nervous as I went through my routine. After I had finished I hurried off the stage almost on the verge of tears.'

'Why was that mummy?' asked Molly.

'I was disappointed with my performance. Inwardly I knew that I could have done better, I felt that I had let myself down. I had been hoping that the audition would have opened the door to a part in a professional production.

"If I were the director of the pantomime you would certainly be included in the cast. In my opinion you've definitely been the best so far." The young man, who had spoken those words of comfort, was leaning nonchalantly against a piece of scenery waiting to go on stage. In the brief second that our eyes met, I knew that I had fallen in love. In the dressing room, I quickly changed from my leotard into street clothes. I was anxious to get back into the wings as quickly as I could. I wanted to watch the man who had stolen my heart do his audition. I positioned myself in front the piece of scenery he had been leaning against, and as he walked towards me at the end of his audition, I winked at him and said. If I were the director, you would certainly be included in the cast, in my opinion you have definitely been the best so far.

As he returned my wink, he whispered. "You're only saying that because it's true, and if you're still here after I have changed, I'm going to be brave enough to ask if you would like you to come with me to the pub opposite the theatre for a drink."

Half an hour later we were sitting facing each other in the bar toasting our success. As we were leaving the theatre, the director had called us back, to offer us parts in the pantomime.

It was like a dream come true. I just couldn't believe it; he had given me the part of Cinderella.

Early next morning Edward and I met outside the stage door, after wishing each other the best of luck, we strolled hand in hand into the theatre.

For the next six weeks, we worked hard preparing for the show. During that time, we became inseparable.

We performed the full dress rehearsal in front of a specially invited audience of local schoolchildren. It was a night to remember. The beautiful scenery, the wonderful costumes and glittering coach, helped to bring the story of Cinderella to life. The children's laughter and applause during the show, told the cast that the pantomime was going to be a huge success. Having Edward around lifted my performance; his presence gave me the self-confidence that I had been lacking before.

Although it was only a small provincial theatre, the pantomime was a success beyond our wildest dreams. Although we had been playing to full houses at every performance, it came as a surprise when we were asked to extend the run.'

Sylvia reached down and stroked her daughter's golden hair. With a sad sigh, she said. 'All good things come to an end. On the day of the last show, smiles were absent from the faces of most of the cast until we walked on stage.

Two months had past since the first dress rehearsal and because it was so romantic, the memories of what happened on that last night will remain crystal clear in my mind forever. At the end of the show, the audience gave us a standing ovation. Before the curtain came down for the last time, each member of the cast walked forward to take his or her final bows. Suddenly Edward took me by the hand and led me to the footlights. Then, in front of everyone in the theatre, he dropped to one knee and proposed. At first the audience and cast were shocked into silence, you could have heard a pin drop.' '

'It's like that around here sometimes.' Dunfoaming interrupted rudely. 'When all of the kids are at school, this close is so quiet you would be able to hear a pin drop, but when they get home and start playing out in the evening. It's so blooming noisy, I doubt if you would be able to hear a bomb drop.'

'I knew you wouldn't be able to keep quiet for very long.' Said Eleven. 'Now I've forgotten where I was up to.'

'Edward had just dropped to one knee and proposed,' said Twelve excitedly. 'What happened next?'

'According to Sylvia, everyone in the theatre started laughing.

'What part was Daddy playing in the pantomime?' asked Molly. 'Was he Prince Charming?'

Sylvia smiled at her daughter. 'No darling,' she replied. 'A lady always plays the Prince in pantomime that's the tradition, but your father will always be Prince charming to me.'

Molly looked puzzled. 'Why did everyone laugh, when he proposed?'

'The reason they laughed was because it looked so funny. When your father dropped down on one knee and asked me to marry him, he was dressed as one of the ugly sisters.' '

'Neither of my new owners have been on television,' Eleven sounded disappointed when she talked to Ten, the next day.

'I knew it,' said Dunfoaming. 'If they were famous television actors, they wouldn't have bought a house in this close. They would have bought a really expensive one, in a decent respectable neighbourhood.'

'If they aren't television actors,' said Ten. 'Then what do they do for a living?'

'They're actors, like I said, but they're not television actors, they might be one day, but neither of my new owners have appeared on television yet. Silvia works for a repertory company who owns a small theatre a few miles from here. Edward is more of a comedian than an actor. He works mainly in clubs and pubs. On Friday night, he will be appearing at the Social Club in town. And on Saturday and Sunday he will be performing at the Ruby Club, and the Woodman Public house at Melderton-On-Sea.'

'And what will he be doing for the rest of the week?' asked Dunfoaming.

'How do I know?' said Eleven. 'They only moved in yesterday, but I don't suppose he has to work more than three evenings a week to earn a good living, comedians are quite well paid you know.'

###CHAPTER TWENTY-FIVE###

March 12ᵗʰ

'Hey Dunfoaming.' One shouted across the close. 'I heard a lot of swearing coming from you this morning, were your owners having a bit of a tiff?'

'I don't want this to become general knowledge,' Dunfoaming whispered. 'It was more than a bit of a tiff. When Mrs Wyatt Jones got her hands around her husband's throat, I thought it was going to end in murder.'

'We haven't had a murder in the close yet.' One whispered back. 'At least we haven't had one that we know of, if we were to have one, it would make this close really famous.'

Dunfoaming sounded shocked. 'I wouldn't want one to happen inside me. Murders are really ghastly.'

'Why did she try to kill him?' asked eighteen who had been straining to hear what was going on. 'He must have done something really bad, if she wanted to kill him. They've been together for all of their married lives haven't they.'

'Of course they have silly. If they hadn't they wouldn't be together now would they.'

'They could have broken up and got back together again, lots of couples do that. I've heard that some people get married five or six times.'

'That wouldn't be to each other though would it? Surely, after a marriage has failed more than once. They would have learnt their lesson.'

'I've heard that some film stars get married several times to different people, it's like a kind of hobby with them.'

'That's all right I suppose if they can afford it, marriage is very expensive you know.'

'Mr and Mrs Wyatt Jones' wedding cost them thousands of pounds.' **Dunfoaming said snobbishly**. 'On the day, she wore a dress that cost two thousand and the reception cost a fortune as well.'

'Surely the brides father picked up the tab for the reception, didn't he?' **said Seventeen**. 'That's what they usually do.'

'Mrs Wyatt Jones hasn't got a father, he ran away just after she was born.'

'He probably didn't want to pay out for a costly reception when she grew up and got married.' **said Eighteen**.

'Then there was the honeymoon,' **said Dunfoaming**. 'That cost Mr Wyatt Jones a couple of thousand pounds. They went on a Caribbean cruise you know.'

'Some people are really lucky aren't they?' **said Sixteen** enviously. 'Mrs Wyatt Jones went on a Caribbean cruise, for her honeymoon. But poor Mrs Woodward, who is living in me, had to spend most of her married life with her husband's coffin in her wardrobe.'

'For all you know she could have gone on a Caribbean cruise for her honeymoon as well,' **said Fifteen**. 'You weren't even built when she got married so you wouldn't know.'

'That's where you are wrong, 'cos I do know where she went on her honeymoon. On the day Mr Woodward was buried I heard her telling young John and Jim that the day she will always remember was her honeymoon when they both went up the Thames on a boat.'

'That's a kind of a cruise, isn't it?' said Seventeen sympathetically. 'But I bet it didn't cost anything like two thousand pounds.'

'We're getting away from the subject a bit here,' said One. 'I wanted to know why I heard a lot of swearing coming from Dunfoaming last night.'

All of Dunfoaming's windows rattled when she gave a loud sigh. 'They aren't getting on very well at the moment; it doesn't take much to start a row. With the economic climate the way that it is at the moment, Mr Wyatt Jones is frightened that he might lose his job, and his wife is worried that she might be getting to old to have a baby.'

'She isn't pregnant is she?' said One.

'I don't think so, but she could be, because she did tell Mr Wyatt Jones that she has been feeling broody lately.'

'That doesn't mean she's pregnant,' said Two. 'Although she could be, because chickens get broody when they want to sit on and hatch eggs.'

Dunfoaming's windows rattled again. 'I don't think she wants to sit on eggs, but I reckon she would love to be able to sit on Damien's head.'

'Why would she want to do that?' asked One in surprise.

'He's been at it again hasn't he? This time he has sneaked into my back garden and stolen two pairs of Mrs Wyatt Jones' knickers. What with her being broody, and the knickers going missing, that's what started the row this morning.'

'When did it happen?' asked Two.

'They went missing sometime during the night. They were hanging on the line at eleven o'clock because I noticed that they were blowing in the wind. Mrs Wyatt Jones realized they were gone when she went out early this morning to bring them in.'

'It sounds like we've got a bare-arsed robber living in our close,' shouted Four humorously.

'Whoever it was isn't bare-arsed any longer,' Three said in reply. 'Now they've got two pairs of knickers to wear.'

'It isn't a laughing matter,' Dunfoaming shouted across at Four, then, she turned her attention to One. 'You always seem to be nosing across the street at me One, so tell me, did you happen to see your Damien sneak into my back garden during the night and steal the knickers from my clothesline?'

'How many more times have I got to tell you, he isn't my Damien, and why would he want to steal knickers off your line?'

'That boy would do anything to cause trouble, and if he didn't take them then somebody did.'

'I can't see why anyone should want to steal Mrs Wyatt Jones' knickers,' said Eighteen. 'I've seen them flapping around on the line often enough and I can honestly say that they have never struck as something that would be worth stealing.'

'The knickers that were stolen last night were special.'

'What do you mean special?' said Seventeen. 'Knickers are knickers, what on earth can be special about them?'

'There's something special about Priscilla's knickers, said One. 'And that's the smell, especially when her mum puts them in the tumble dryer after she's wet them.'

'They were silk, designer knickers that Mr Wyatt Jones bought for her when they were on their second honeymoon last year in France.' said Dunfoaming. 'And they were really expensive they cost £60 a pair.'

'It seems like Mr and Mrs Wyatt Jones have been learning Spanish for nothing, doesn't it,' said One.

Dunfoaming sounded puzzled, when she said. 'I don't get your point. What has learning Spanish got to do with silk designer knickers?'

'If they are not getting on very well, then they won't be buying a holiday home in Benidorm.'

Mr Hugh Wyatt Jones always called in at the Red Lion for a drink on his way home from work. He liked to sit in the inglenook with the regulars chatting about the events of the day. Laying his drink on the table, he spat at one of the logs blazing in the fire. Silently he sat watching the bubbling spittle until it disappeared, then, he turned to John Duckman. 'That Damien has been up to his tricks again, this time he's stolen some of my wife's underwear from our clothes line.'

'Maybe it wasn't Damien,' Duckman replied. 'It could have been those gypsies camped on the sports field that did the stealing. They wouldn't think twice about nicking your false teeth if you opened your mouth in front of them.'

'Those people camped on the sports field aren't gypsies,' said Maggie, one of the inglenook's regulars. 'They are travellers. Gypsies are a different kind of people.'

Hugh spat at the log again. 'Gypsies or travellers, they would have a job stealing false teeth from me. I haven't got any.'

'Yes you have,' said Maggie. 'You've got that gold one in the front.'

Duckman frowned at Hugh's gold capping. 'I wouldn't let them see that if I was you, they are so light-fingered they would have that nugget out of your mouth and you wouldn't even know that it had gone.'

Hugh touched the gold tooth self-consciously with his tongue. 'If it was those gypsies who stole my wife's fancies, then a couple of their women are probably strutting around the sports field today, wearing expensive silk knickers.'

Maggie looked doubtfully at Hugh. 'You're kidding us. Your wife hasn't got any expensive silk knickers.'

'Not now she hasn't, but she did have last night. I bought them for her last year when we were on our second honeymoon in Paris, and they were very expensive. They cost £60 a pair.'

'Dave Rawle another Inglenook regular turned his head and winked at Duckman. Then loud enough for everyone in the inglenook to hear, he said. 'I knew you had a good imagination when you told me that your wife is the best looking woman in Dorset, but I hope you don't think that anyone in this room is going to believe that you actually paid out £120 to buy her two pairs of fancy drawers.'

Hugh licked his left index finger and drew it across his throat. 'May I drop dead on this spot if I'm not telling the truth. But I wouldn't have paid out that much if my wife hadn't taken advantage of my poor state of health.'

'You wasn't ill in Paris, was you?' said Maggie. 'Aren't you the one who's always boasting that you've never had a day's illness in your life?'

Hugh looked slightly embarrassed. 'I was out of my head at the time. I had been drinking too much cheap French wine.'

Duckman lifted his glass to his mouth. 'I can understand that,' he mumbled. 'Too much wine does tend to loosen ones purse strings.' His pyramid shaped Adam's apple moved rapidly up and down as he drank. The full glass that he had lifted it to his lips was almost empty when he put it down.

Dave stared at the half inch of liquid lying at the bottom of Duckman's glass. 'How can you say that? You must have had at least six pints since we came in, and I've been sitting here next to you for about five minutes with an empty glass in my hand, it doesn't seem that those six pints have loosened your purse strings.'

Duckman wiped his lips with his thumb. 'Beer affects me in a different way to wine. If I were drinking wine, I would probably have treated every one in the bar by now. Then, he lifted the glass to his lips again and drained it. 'It's about time someone told those people to move on. We haven't been able to have a game of football since they parked their caravans on the sports field.'

'I wouldn't want to be the one who has to tell them to leave,' said Hugh. 'I'm afraid of those gypsies. They have strange powers. God knows what would happen if one of them was to give you the evil eye.'

'Don't talk daft!' Duckman picked up his empty glass and walked to the bar.

Malcolm lifted the sandwich that had begun to curl at the edges from the skeleton's plate and threw it into the black plastic bag that he kept behind the bar. 'You don't really believe in all that nonsense, do you Hugh?'

Hugh joined Duckman at the bar. 'It's not nonsense Malcolm, those people really can dish out curses and foretell the future I can vouch for that, I had a weird experience with a gypsy a few years ago.'

Duckman raised his eyebrows, and grinned at Malcolm. 'Come off it Hugh, you've never had a weird experience in your life.'

'Hugh is right you know,' Maggie interrupted. 'Romanies can foretell the future. A fortune-telling gypsy told me once that a tall, dark, handsome stranger would sweep me off my feet and the next day I met my Jimmy when he knocked me over coming out of a tobacconist.'

'Hang on a minute,' said Duckman. 'Jimmy isn't tall and dark.'

'That's true,' said Maggie. 'He isn't. However, he is handsome, and at the time, he was a stranger and he did sweep me off my feet because I ended up sitting on my backside in the gutter. So her prophesy was ninety per cent right, wasn't it? You can't argue with that now, can you?'

Hugh looked down at his open hand. 'It's amazing how she knew what was going to happen, just by gazing at the lines in the palm of my hand.'

Malcolm laid a fresh cheese and onion sandwich on Mr Bones' plate. 'What on earth did you go to a fortune-teller for? I thought it was only women who believed in that sort of crap.'

Hugh sighed. 'I didn't want the blooming gypsy to tell my fortune. She tricked me into having it done.'

A smile spread slowly across Duckman's face. 'Are you actually admitting that you've been conned by a woman?'

Maggie nudged Mrs Jackson another inglenook regular sitting with her elbow. 'They have all been conned by a woman, at some time or other.' She whispered.

Hugh returned Duckman's smile. 'Buy me a drink and I'll tell you all about it.'

'You must be joking. You've never ever told me anything that's been worth the price of a beer.'

Malcolm pulled up a pint and placed it in front of Hugh. 'Have this on the house,' he said. 'A good story is always worth a pint.'

Hugh took a quick swig of his free beer then wiped his lips with the back of his hand. 'I was walking through the Arndale Centre in Luton.' He looked pointedly at Duckman. 'For the benefit of those who hardly ever set foot outside this town, the Arndale is a large enclosed shopping centre.'

'What were you doing in Luton?' asked Maggie.

Hugh sighed and took another mouthful of beer. 'It hasn't anything to do with the story, but I was visiting my sister.'

Mrs Jackson lifted her seat and plonked it down nearer to the fire. 'I didn't know you had a sister. Is she older than you?'

Hugh sighed again. 'Do you want to hear this story or not?'

'Just ignore them,' said Dave. 'You know what women are like when they get together. Can't you see they're trying to set you alight?'

Duckman pretended to scratch his nose. Under the cover of his cupped hand, he whispered to Malcolm. 'She's going to catch herself alight, if gets any closer to that fire.'

Hugh waited until he had their attention again. 'I was about to walk into Marks and Spencer's, when this gypsy woman came up beside me and waved a small silver clad bunch of heather in front of my eyes. "Lucky white heather," she said. "Buy some lucky white heather Mister; it will change your luck." You're talking a load of rubbish, I said. White heather isn't lucky.'

Leaning forward in her seat to say something, Mrs Jackson acciden-tally tipped her gin and tonic into her lap, before the liquid had a chance to soak into her dress she brushed it back into her glass with the back of her hand. Then, with an embarrassed, brown-toothed smile, she said. 'What did she say, when you told her that?'

'She didn't say anything; she just kept waving the heather in my face. Why should I buy your sorry looking heather? I said. Just because you say, it's lucky. I have a whole bed of it in my back garden, and it's never brought me any luck. The blooming woman however was persistent she wouldn't take no for an answer. "Buy some lucky white heather Mister," she kept saying.'

'My wife's a bit like that,' said Duckman. 'She never takes no for an answer.'

Maggie conjured up a scalding look and threw it at Duckman. 'Trust you to bring sex into the conversation, that's all you men ever think about. Go on,' she said, turning her attention back to Hugh.

'Just to get rid of her, I took a 50 pence piece from pocket and dropped it into her outstretched hand.'

Dave carried his glass across the room, and joined Hugh and Duckman at the bar.

'Do you know what she did then?'

Maggie and the others sitting in the inglenook answered Hugh's question with a shake of their heads.

'The cheeky cow pushed the sprig of heather into my buttonhole. "I'll need another 50 pence Mister," she said. "My lucky white heather costs £1." '

'I've always thought you were a shrewd man,' shouted Maggie. 'You should have offered to keep her supplied with heather from your garden.'

The smell of scorching material followed Mrs Jackson as she planted her feet firmly on the floor and pushed her chair away from the fire. 'Maggie's right you know,' she said. 'You missed a golden opportunity. You could have made enough money to buy your wife another two pairs of expensive silk knickers.'

Hugh's eyes darted across the room and came to rest on Mrs Jackson, then; a sickly smile appeared on his face. 'This happened a few years ago, I hadn't even bought the knickers then.'

Mrs Jackson grinned sheepishly back. Lifting her glass, she said. 'I'm sorry. I get a bit confused at times; put it down to old age.'

Hugh raised his eyes and stared at the ceiling above Mrs Jackson's head. 'More like too many G and T's,' he mumbled, then, he took a couple of quick swigs of his beer. 'Several curious people had gathered around us, and they all seemed to be looking at me. So I felt in my pockets for another 50p. "I can change a £5 note if you like," she said, as if her eyes had already scanned my trouser pockets and found them empty. Like an idiot, I opened my wallet and pulled out a £ 5 note.'

Duckman shook his head in disbelief. 'Surely you don't expect any of us to believe that you actually pulled a £5 note from your wallet?' he said, loud enough for everyone in the bar to hear. 'I've known you all my life and I've never seen you pull a note from your wallet. No, hang on a minute I'm lying. I did see you do it once, but it was only a sick note to give to the teacher at school.'

The sickly smile reappeared on Hugh's face when he stationed his eyes on Duckman. 'As soon as she saw the fiver, she snatched it from my hand and stuffed it in her pocket.'

Malcolm placed a fresh pint in front of the skeleton and poured the old one away, then, with a grin, he said. 'Her hand must have moved like greased lightning if she managed to snatch a fiver from you.'

Deciding to ignore Malcolm's remark, Hugh looked at the empty glass in Malcolm's hand. 'It was a waste of good beer, throwing that one away. Why didn't you offer it to one of us?'

'It was flat. You wouldn't want to drink flat beer would you? Besides, I've just given you a free one.'

Hugh glanced down at the remains of his beer. 'So you did,' he said. 'I'd forgotten that. Now can I finish my story? Before I had a chance to ask for my change, she grabbed hold of my wrist and stared down at my palm. "I see in your hand, that you are going to be lucky today." Lucky, I said. How can you say that? I've already lost £5 50 and the day has only just begun. Then, she pulled my hand closer to her, and said. "Our futures are written in our palms. Yours tells me that you will be buying a scratch card today, and that card is going to make you richer by £200." If you can see me wasting my money on a scratch card, then you can't be very good at telling fortunes, I said. The gypsy grinned and shrugged her shoulders. "You won't be wasting your money. You're going to spend £1 to win £200, and your good luck isn't going to end there. Tomorrow you will double what you won on the card, when you place it on a greyhound called Franklyawinna. Then, you will successfully chase your luck, when you put all of your winnings on dog number four in the fifth race at the same meeting." '

Hugh gave a sad sigh. 'Who knows? Maybe things would have turned out different if she hadn't been holding a baby in the crook of her arm, and if a lump of soggy bread hadn't fallen from the baby's mouth into the palm of my hand. "I wish you hadn't done that," the gypsy said, when I pulled my hand from hers to shake off the soggy mess. "You have just shaken the images of the future from your hand. However, I saw enough to tell me that you will be going to Epsom racetrack. In the last picture, I saw you standing in front of a track-side bookie laying everything you had won on a horse called Talented Pickpocket." Is it going to win? I asked. "I don't know," she replied. "You shook the image from your hand before I could see the result, but I did see you at Epsom, and the first meeting is in two days time. So it looks like you will be there to see the result for yourself." Can I have my change now? I asked hopefully. She gave me a queer sort of look. "What change is that Mister? You only gave me £5 50, and I always charge £4 50, for fortune telling, and £1 for lucky white heather." I didn't want my fortune told, I said. "Of course you did," she replied. "You wouldn't have given me £4 50, for nothing, and before today is over, you are going to realize that it was the best money that you have ever spent." Rather than enter into a slinging match over a few pounds, I decided to mark it down to experience. As I turned to walk away, I'm sure that the baby winked at me, and although it was too young to speak, I swear I heard it whisper. "You're a right sucker, aren't you?" '

Hugh picked up the skeleton's beer with one hand, and the cheese and onion sandwich with the other. Grinning cheekily at Malcolm, he took a large bite out of the sandwich. 'Nice strong onion,' he said. Then, he washed it down with three quick gulps of the beer. 'There you are Malcolm, your little tableau looks more realistic now,' he said, as he laid the remains of the beer and sandwich, in front of Mr Bones.

Duckman looked at the skeleton and shuddered. 'What on earth are you going on about? There's nothing realistic about a skeleton having a beer and a sandwich in a pub. It gives me the creeps. I can't understand why Malcolm leaves it sitting there at the bar. It ought to be buried in a cemetery where it belongs.'

Leaving his empty glass standing in a small puddle on the bar, Hugh walked back to the table and lifted his coat off the back of a chair.

'You're not going home, are you?' asked Dave.

Hugh glanced at his watch. 'I've been here for nearly an hour and a half. If I don't get back soon my wife is going to put me in the doghouse. I told her that I was only going to have a quick one, and then I was going to see if I could find out who stole her fancy knickers.'

Disappointment showed on Dave's face. 'You can't go yet, you haven't told us the end of the story.'

'You might just as well stay and tell us what happened,' said Maggie. 'If you're thinking of walking around the town lifting ladies skirts looking for your wife's fancies, you're going to get yourself into an awful lot of trouble.'

'What do you think I am?' Hugh grunted indignantly. 'I wouldn't go around skirt lifting. I was thinking of making a few discreet enquiries.'

Mrs Jackson wiped her nose with the back of her thumb. 'I'll tell you what I'll do Hugh. If you will stay and finish the story, I'll let you have the knickers that I'm wearing, and if you ask Maggie nicely, maybe she will let you have hers as well.'

Hugh dropped his bottom lip in disgust. 'No thanks. I'd sooner be in the doghouse.' Then, he pointed at Duckman. 'If you can get that tight git to buy me a pint; I'll stay a bit longer and tell you what happened, even if it does mean facing the wrath of my wife.'

Everyone's eyes turned towards Duckman, who was busy studying the ceiling. For almost a minute he resisted their gaze, then, he raised his hands in the air and turned to Malcolm. 'I suppose you had better pull one up for him,' he said, begrudgingly. 'Otherwise those two will end up taking off their drawers and throwing them at me.'

Hugh draped his coat over the back of the chair, and sat down at the table.

'Well?' asked Dave. 'Did you go and buy a scratch card?'

'Of course I did, I had to, didn't I?'

Once again, Duckman glanced up at the ceiling, this time he shook his head in disbelief. 'How could you have been that stupid?' Lowering his eyes, he fixed them on Hugh. 'The gypsy had already taken you for £5 50, so you went and spent another £1 on a scratch card.'

'I only did it to prove to myself that gypsies can't really tell fortunes.'

Duckman paid for the drink carried it over to the table by the fire and laid it down in front of Hugh. 'I'm beginning to see you in a different light,' he said. 'I've always known that you don't like spending your money, but I never thought the day would come when you would deliberately throw it away.'

Hugh lifted a bit of froth with his finger and licked it. 'As I had never purchased a scratch card before, I had no idea what to do until I read the PLAY INSTRUCTIONS. **(Rub off the latex. Find three like amounts to win that amount.)** I scratched the ticket with my thumb nail and studied the symbols.'

'And found that you hadn't won a thing,' interrupted Dave.

'You're wrong,' said Hugh. 'The gypsy had been right. I'd won £200. The next day I went into a betting shop and scanned the list of runners at the various greyhound meetings. I could hardly believe my eyes when I found one running under the name of Franklyawinna. I have to admit, my hands were trembling when I passed my betting slip and £200 across the counter. Luckily I didn't have too long to wait, as the gypsy had said, the dog was running in the first race.'

Mrs Jackson spilled her gin and tonic again, when she leaned towards Hugh. 'Did it win?'

Hugh raised his pint towards Duckman in a gesture of thanks, then, laid it back on the table. 'When the race results were posted on the board, they showed that Franklyawinna had romped home first. 'You will successfully chase your luck, when you put all of your winnings on dog number four in the fifth race at the same meeting.' With the fortune-teller's words ringing in my ears, I wrote out another bet. The counter clerk didn't make any comment when he accepted it, but I knew from the way he raised his eyebrows when he handed me the receipt, that he thought I was on a loser.'

Duckman gave Hugh a knowing grin. 'I bet you ended up wishing you hadn't chased your luck.'

'I left the betting shop after the fifth race, with £1,200 in my pocket, so I had no reason to wish that.'

'You must think we were born yesterday, if you expect us to believe that you once won £1,200 gambling on dogs.' Dave shouted to Hugh.

Mrs Jackson grinned at Dave. 'If anyone's daft enough to believe that he once forked out £120 on two pairs of fancy knickers, then I can't see any reason why they shouldn't believe that he's telling the truth'

Hugh folded his arms and sat back in his chair. 'There's not much point in going on, if you think I'm lying.'

Duckman glared at Mrs Jackson and Dave. 'You've upset him now, say that you believe him, otherwise he won't tell us the end of the story and I will have bought him that drink for nothing.'

Dave returned Duckman's glare with a doubtful smile. 'Of course we believe him, what he's told us so far is so unbelievable it's got to be true.'

Duckman turned to Hugh. 'What about Epsom?' he said. 'Did you go? The gypsy said she saw you standing in front of a track-side bookie putting all of your winnings on a horse called Talented Pickpocket.'

Hugh's face became a picture of abject misery. 'Of course I went; I didn't have any choice, the gypsy had already told me that I would. I arrived at the track in a quandary, I didn't know what to do, the gypsy hadn't been able to see if Talented Pickpocket had been a winner or not.'

'Was there a horse with that name running?' asked Duckman excitedly.

'Of course there was, and I wasn't a bit surprised, everything the fortune-teller had told me, had come true. I was standing near a bookie trying to make up my mind if I should chance all of the £1,200, when a man with his arm in a sling bumped into me. "I'm sorry Sir," he said. Then, he looked down at his arm, groaning painfully, he hurried away.'

'Well?' asked Dave. 'Did you put all of your winnings on the horse?'

'I was going to, but when I reached into my pocket for the money, it wasn't there. The police officer I reported my loss to, shook his head sympathetically. "Apart from the horse running under that name, there are several talented pickpockets working this racecourse today. It seems to me, that you have been taken for a ride by one of them." '

For almost a minute Hugh sat in silence holding his hands in front of the blazing logs staring into the fire. He jerked back into life, when Mrs Jackson leaned over and prodded him in the ribs with a finger. 'What happened then?'

'I didn't have enough money left to place a bet, but I stayed and watched the race, and I certainly wasn't cheering, when Talented Pickpocket romped pass the winning post five lengths in front of the others. Then above the roar of the crowd, I heard the gypsy woman shouting. "Lucky white heather, lucky white heather, buy some lucky white heather and change your luck." '

Hugh's spitting log had almost burnt away. After gazing at the remains thoughtfully for several seconds, he said to Duckman. 'I'll bet you a pint, I could hit it again.'

Duckman looked at Hugh and shook his head. 'Don't you ever learn? I should have thought you'd be off of betting after Epsom.'

Mrs Jackson gave Hugh the evil eye. 'Spitting on fires is a filthy habit. Do you spit on the fire at home?'

'Of course I don't. We've got electric fires in doors, if I was to spit on them, my wife would kill me.'

'You can certainly tell a good story,' said Dickie Dickinson, who had been sitting silently in the inglenook nursing half a pint of best bitter. 'Was it really true?'

'I know that the bit about the expensive silk knickers is,' grunted Duckman. 'He showed me the receipt. And I wouldn't be at all surprised if he's framed it and hung it up in their bedroom, just to remind his wife how generous he is.'

'I've never told anyone about a strange experience I had a few months ago with a true Romany gypsy, and I swore to myself that I never would. However, most of you seem to believe Hugh's story, so maybe you will believe mine as well. And I won't be expecting any of you to buy me a drink, because I always like to buy my own.'

Mrs Jackson looked at the glass in his hand and shrugged her shoulders. 'You've had that same glass in your hand, since you came in an hour and a half ago, so I don't suppose you will even think of buying a drink for any of us, but we won't be offended if you should offer, and I doubt if any of us will refuse.'

Dickie looked at her coldly. 'My Aunt Millie doesn't get many visitors,' he said, 'so whenever I turn up on her doorstep she is always pleased to see me. "Come on in," she says with a smile as wide as a Cheshire cat's, "you must be tired after your long journey." '

'It serves her right if she doesn't get many visitors,' interrupted Mrs Jackson, 'she shouldn't have moved away. When she lived here, she had so many men knocking at her door they must have wore out several knockers.'

Dickie shook his head and glared at Mrs Jackson through half closed eyes. 'As I was saying, she always gives me a big smile and leads me into her front room, then she pats me on the shoulder and whispers the words I dread to hear. "Make yourself comfortable on the settee Richard, while I go and make you a nice hot cup of tea." '

Mrs Jackson nudged Maggie in the ribs with her elbow, and waved to attract Dickie's attention. 'Is your aunt Millie losing her memory a bit with old age?'

Dickie half closed his eyes again and sighed. 'What are you going on about now?'

'You've just said that she calls you Richard, when your name is Dickie.'

'She calls me Richard, because that's my name. It's only you drunken lot in here who call me Dickie.'

Mrs Jackson looked surprised. 'I never knew that. I've always thought that your real name is Dickie.'

In an effort to steer Dickie back to his story, Maggie said. 'Why do you dread hearing Millie say she's going to make you a nice hot cup of tea? Don't you like tea?'

Dickie shuddered. 'Of course I like tea, everyone likes tea, but the stuff my aunt makes tastes really vile, it curdles the stomach. I've no idea what type of tea leaves she uses, but they taste like they've been grown in the Devil's back garden, and blended by a witch.'

'If it tastes as bad as that, then why do you drink it?' asked Duckman.

'I don't have much choice really she brings it into the room and stays with me until I've drained the cup. One time, I asked if she had any biscuits. When she went into the kitchen to get them, I poured what was left in my cup into a pot plant standing beside the settee. A couple of hours later, all of its leaves dropped off.'

Mrs Jackson looked at Dickie and grinned. 'There's an easy way out of your problem. Why don't you tell her, that you prefer coffee?'

Dickie shook his head. 'I can't take a chance like that, what if her coffee turns out to be worst than her tea?'

Duckman stifled a bored yawn. 'What has all this got to do with gypsies?'

'Just give me a minute; I'm getting to that part. Whenever I visit my aunt, I always go to the market that they hold on the green. Like most village markets, it's small but interesting and sometimes you can manage to find a bargain. I had never seen gypsies selling at the market before, so it came as a surprise to see a genuine Romany standing behind a stall selling vacuum flasks. The colours of the flasks were so bright they dazzled my eyes, but apart from the colours, they didn't seem to be any different from flasks that I had seen in shops. The stallholder looked at me and smiled. "Are you looking for a Thermos with a difference?" he asked. "If you are, then you've come to the right place." I can't see anything different about them, I said, they look the same as flasks you can buy in the shops. The old man picked up a red one, and waved a hand over some of the others. "These may look like ordinary flasks, but they're not, they're special. That's why they're priced at £50." '

Everyone around the table had started to show an interest. 'You're having us on,' said Hugh. 'He didn't really expect you to pay £50 for a flask. No one would pay that kind of money for a flask.'

Mrs Jackson looked at Hugh and grinned. 'They would if they were rich and daft like you.'

'I'm not rich,' Hugh grunted, 'and you know it. And why are you calling me daft?'

'Aren't you the one who paid £120 for two pairs of fancy knickers?'

Dickie smiled at the fire, as if he was sharing a joke with the flames. 'Your prices are a bit unreal I said. I can buy a flask that size in any hardware shop for a fiver. The gypsy laid the Thermos back on the stall. "It's not the size that counts," he said. "Even if it was only half the size; it would still be worth its weight in gold." I don't know where you come from, I said. But it can't be from around these parts; otherwise, you would know that if anyone were to pay that kind of money for a vacuum flask, they would have to be off their trolley. The gypsy shrugged his shoulders. "You'll be more than willing to pay £50, when you see what my special flasks can do. Pick up any two flasks you like, then, follow me into my caravan and I'll give you a demonstration of their worth. Once you've seen them work their magic, you'll agree that they're worth every penny that I'm asking." '

'You didn't go into his caravan, did you?' gasped Mrs Jackson. 'Didn't your mother ever tell you that gypsies have been known to cart children away?'

Dickie glared at Mrs Jackson. 'I'm not a blooming kid am I?'

'No, but sometimes you act like one.'

'Curiosity had got the better of me, so I did as he asked. Once inside the van, the gypsy pointed at the flasks in my hands. "This demonstration is so amazing you will probably think that it's some kind of trick. Out of the all the flasks on my stall, you chose those two. Which one would you like me to use?" he said with a smile, which showed two gold teeth. For sometime, I stood trying to make up my mind which one to part with, then, I handed him the one in my left hand. "For this demonstration," he unscrewed the stopper, "I'm going to use water. Once you've bought your own flask, you can use any beverage that you like." Then, he picked up a cup of water from a table poured it into the empty flask, and then he placed an empty bucket of water at my feet.'

Hugh tapped his gold capping. 'He must have been a rich devil if he could afford two gold teeth. I've only got one, and that cost an arm and a leg.'

Dickie sat back in his chair and crossed his arms. 'I didn't interrupt you when you was telling us about the gypsy fortune-teller, did I?'

Duckman looked at Hugh and shook his head. 'That lump of gold in your mouth didn't cost you a penny, you borrowed the money for it from your uncle Jack and he died before you could pay him back.'

Hugh looked embarrassed. 'I didn't say that it cost *me* an arm and a leg, did I?'

Mrs Jackson got unsteadily to her feet, walking an erratic path to the bar, she said. 'You two are like a couple of kids, bickering all of the time. When are you going to grow up?'

Hugh and Duckman winked at each other, and grinned. 'We're nice kids though aren't we?' Hugh shouted back.

Mrs Jackson made her way back to the table, with drinks for herself and Maggie. As she put them on the table, she whispered in Duckman's ear. 'We'll soon see how nice you are. I've just told Malcolm that you're going to pay for these drinks.'

Dickie shook his head and tutted impatiently. 'As I was saying, before Hugh butted in. The gypsy said. "The reason these flasks are a bargain at £ 50 pounds, is because they are never-ending. You saw me pour a cupful of water in that one, now let's see how much I can empty out." This is the same as the drinks in the kettle trick, I thought, as he held the flask over the bucket and began to pour. I've seen magicians do this on the stage. Soon there were two buckets of water standing at my feet, and he was pouring into a third.'

Hugh gave Dickie a sceptical frown. 'Did this gypsy have a hunched back, and was he wearing loose baggy clothes? If he was, then I reckon he had a tube running down his arm to his hand and he was filling the buckets from a rubber tank on his back.'

Dickie gave him a scathing look. 'You think I'm an idiot don't you? If he had been concealing that amount of water on his body, I would have noticed him getting thinner as he poured. But that didn't happen.' He pointed at the skeleton sitting at the bar. 'Besides, he was almost as thin as old Mr Bones when he started.'

'It had to be a trick,' said Maggie. 'If it wasn't, then it was pure magic, and everyone knows there's no such thing as that.'

Hugh shook his head and smiled at Dickie. 'I bet you thought I was stupid for buying that scratch card, but at least my outlay was only £1 and I did have a small chance of winning. I hope you're not going to tell me that you were daft enough to actually pay £ 50 for a so called never-ending flask.'

'I might have thought it, but I didn't say it, did I? And you've got no right calling me daft,' Dickie snapped indignantly. '£50 is nothing, compared to the £200 that you won on a scratch card and put on a dog.'

'With that bet, I came away a winner, but with a never-ending flask, you've got to be on a loser right from the start.'

'A few minutes ago, you said, gypsies have got strange powers. How do you know they can't use those powers to make never-ending flasks?'

Hugh raised his hands in defeat, and took refuge behind his glass.

'The gypsy took the flask he had used in the demonstration and put it to one side. "I wouldn't sell you that one even if you wanted it," he said. "It was used for the demonstration, so it will always only contain water. But if you would like to buy one, you can have the one you're holding in your hand." '

Maggie, and Mrs Jackson, looked at Duckman who was sitting with a look of incredulity on his face.

'After I paid for the flask, he folded the notes carefully and placed them in his pocket. "I said you would buy one of my flasks, when you knew what a bargain they are." I was about to walk out of the caravan with my purchase when he stopped me. "Before you carry it away, I must tell you the rules of purchase, and if they are ever broken, then, the flask will be endless no more. No one but the owner can drink any of the contents, nor are you allowed to sell as much as one single drop. Also, I must warn you to think carefully before you pour anything into it. The first liquid to enter the flask is how it will remain until it is broken, or you fail to obey the rules." '

Duckman picked up a small log threw it on the fire, then, he grinned at the others sitting at the table. 'You've got to admire the man's technique; Dickie must have been putty in his hands.'

'You wouldn't be saying that, if I still had the flask.'

Mrs Jackson moved back from the fire to dodge the shower of sparks heading in the direction of the hem of her dress. 'I suppose you threw it away in disgust when you found out you'd been conned,' she said. 'I know I would have, if it had been me.'

'It's a never-ending flask we're talking about here,' snapped Duckman. 'No one in Burnbury but Dickie, would fall for a trick like that.'

Mrs Jackson nodded at Hugh. 'He would have, as well.'

The look on Dickie's face, suggested that he was getting annoyed. 'I wasn't conned,' he snapped, 'I was unlucky. When I got back to Aunt Millie's I left my market purchases in the hall and went upstairs to pack. When I came down, I was still undecided what to put into the flask. I couldn't make up my mind if it would be whiskey, or brandy. Then, I noticed that the flask had gone. I was just about to ask Aunt Millie if she had seen it, when she came walking from the kitchen with it in her hand.

"You've got a long way to drive home," she said with a sweet smile. "So I thought I'd make you a nice hot flask of tea." '

'It might not have been as good as whiskey or brandy, but over the years it could save you a small fortune,' Mrs Jackson said with a grin. 'These days, tea bags aren't cheap.'

Dickie gave her a look that could have curdled custard. 'The last thing on earth I would ever want, would be a never-ending supply of my Aunt Millie's tea.'

'Where's the flask now?' asked Maggie.

'When I got back to Burnbury, I saw the little fat squatter who lives at Number 11 Piddle Close walking along towards their squat, so I pulled up and gave it to him. As I drove slowly away, I looked in my rear view mirror and saw him pour some of the tea into the cup. He took a mouthful, shuddered, and spat it out, then, he waved his fist at me menacingly and threw the cup and flask at the back of my car. I didn't bother calling in at my aunt Millie's, when I went back next market day to see if I could buy another flask.'

'You didn't really go back to buy another flask, did you?' Mrs Jackson gasped incredulously.

'The gypsy wasn't there was he?' said Duckman. 'And do you know why he wasn't there? I'd bet you £1 to a crate of rotten tomatoes, that he was at another market looking for more suckers.'

'Talking of gypsies, the ones who invaded our football pitch have left.'

All eyes turned to the speaker who was standing at the bar with a drink in his hand .

'Where have they gone?' asked Hugh, thinking of his wife's lost knickers.

'How should I know, I saw them moving off the playing field when I was on my way here.'

'How long have you been standing there Jimmy?' asked Maggie?

'About five minutes.'

'You came in so quiet, I reckon you could give lessons to ghosts.'

Dickie shook his head. 'Ghosts aren't quiet, and I should know. Did I ever tell any of you about the night I spent in a haunted house?'

Hugh picked up his coat looked at his watch and walked towards the door. 'It's always the same whenever I come in here for a quick one, I end up staying for hours.'

'Would you like another before you go?' Malcolm asked temptingly.

Hugh twisted his face into seemingly impossible shapes, as he went through the ritual of making up his mind.

Duckman answered for him. 'Of course he doesn't, he's hardly touched the one I bought him yet.

'That's because I didn't really want it,' grunted Hugh, as he pulled the door open.

'If you didn't want it, then why did you make me buy it?'

Hugh winked at Malcolm, then turned and looked at Duckman. 'So that you can honestly say that you once bought me a drink.'

Malcolm held out a hand and pointed it at Duckman. 'And when you've paid for Maggie's and Mrs Jackson's, you'll be able to say that you've bought them one as well.'

'By the way Hugh,' said Jimmy, as Duckman fished in his pocket for some money to pay for the drinks. 'I met your wife when I was on my way here, she asked if I had seen you on my travels, I haven't got a clue what she was going on about, but she said something about you being out for hours searching for the person who had stolen her fancy knickers.'

'Hugh looked alarmed. 'God knows how I'm going to get out of this one.' he mumbled as he walked out of the door.

###CHAPTER TWENTY-SIX###

April 1st

'Don't believe anything that any of the houses in the close tell you this morning,' Dunfoaming whispered to Eighteen. 'If you do, the chances are that they will be trying to make you an April fool.'

Eighteen hadn't been awake very long; in fact, it had been Dunfoaming talking that had woke him. Sleepily, he said. 'What's an April fool?'

'An April fool is the victim of a practical joke performed on the first of April, which is today. No doubt, when he gets up Damien will be trying to make April fools out of everyone that he meets.'

'Will it be anything worth watching?' asked Eighteen tiredly.

'It depends how clever the practical jokes are, but knowing Damien they will be more silly than clever.'

'I think he's already started,' said One. 'He's just come out of Three's back garden with a pile of washing in his arms.'

'If he has stolen the washing from Three's line, then why is he bringing it into my back garden?' asked Four.

'Maybe he really was the one who stole Mrs Wyatt Jones' fancy knickers last month,' Eighteen said accusingly.

'Hang on a minute,' said Four loud enough for all of the houses in the close to hear. 'You won't believe what he's doing now. He's taken all of the washing off of my line, and he's replacing it with the clothes that he took from Three.'

'Are there any fancy knickers amongst them?' Dunfoaming asked enquiringly.

'You must be joking,' said Three with a laugh. 'Percy's mum hasn't got anything fancy like that. Her drawers are long and thick, and they take days to dry, her husband calls them passion killers. But he did take four pairs of Percy's boxers.'

When Damien came out of Four with his arms full of washing, he tiptoed down the side of Five took the washing off the line and replaced it with the clothes he had taken from Four.

'You know what he's up to don't you?' screamed Five. 'He isn't stealing the washing, he's swapping it around.'

'I was right,' said One. 'Damien is working on an April fools joke, and it looks like he's going to play it on everyone in the close.'

'He won't be able to do it to my tenants,' Seven said smugly. 'They never leave any washing out overnight. They tried it once, and it was covered in Speedwell's pigeon droppings the next morning.'

'If Damien is swapping the washing,' said One. 'Then he isn't stealing it, is he Dunfoaming? So maybe he wasn't the one who stole Mrs Wyatt Jones' fancies.'

'You're right!' said Fifteen. 'I know who took them and it wasn't Damien.'

'If it wasn't Damien, then, who was it, and why haven't you told us before?'

'I was ashamed,' Fifteen mumbled softly. 'I saw Mrs Braithwaite take them, and having a knicker nicking thief as a tenant isn't something that I'm particularly proud of.'

'How did Mrs Braithwaite know that Mrs Wyatt Jones had two pairs of expensive fancy knickers?' asked Eighteen, in a puzzled voice.

'I can answer that question,' said Dunfoaming. 'I saw Mrs Wyatt Jones show them to her, when they were having a coffee together on the day after she got back from her second honeymoon. Mrs Braithwaite said at the time that she had never seen a pair of knickers that cost £60 before, and I knew from the sound of her voice that she was envious.'

'That woman has never seen a pair of knickers that cost 60 pence let alone £60,' mumbled Three sarcastically.

'I wouldn't say that,' said Fifteen. 'She's got a drawer full of them in her bedroom, but she only puts them on occasionally.'

'It takes some believing, doesn't it?' Three mumbled again. 'If Mrs Braithwaite has a drawer full of knickers and she hardly ever wears any, then, why did she steal the fancies?'

'I suppose she wanted to impress her toy boy Percy,' said Fifteen.

'Was he impressed when he saw her wearing them?'

'He might have been, his eyes certainly lit up when she took her dressing gown off.'

'What happened then?' asked Two lustfully.

'I don't know I didn't look anymore. I knew what was coming next, and as I've mentioned before, I'm sick and fed up with their abnormal sexual behaviour sessions.'

It took Damien almost an hour to complete his April fool joke. With a satisfied smile on his face, he strolled back into his house walked up the stairs took off his clothes and climbed back into bed.

###CHAPTER TWENTY-SEVEN###

Eighteen had been sniffing for about five minutes.

'It sounds like you've got a cold developing?' Seventeen sounded concerned. 'If you are about to sneeze, will you please not to do it in my direction. There's a lot of that swine flu going around and I don't fancy catching a dose of that.'

'I doubt if houses can catch swine flu, besides I'm not sniffing because I've got a cold. I'm inhaling the lovely spicy smell of hot cross buns.'

'I've noticed that there's been a nice aroma around here lately,' said Four. 'It certainly makes a change from the wet knickers in the tumble dryer smell that we usually get from One.'

The lace curtains hanging in the open front windows moved noticeably, when one sniffed several times in quick succession. 'I wish I could smell a sweet aroma,' she said. 'And it doesn't have to be spicy hot cross buns either; anything would make a change from Priscilla's knickers.'

'I feel sorry for you; if you can't you smell the spice.' Fifteen had joined the sniffing game. 'On and off, it's been around for weeks. I'll never be able to understand people. I've always thought hot cross buns are meant to be eaten on Good Friday, but someone around here has been buying them since Christmas.'

'It's my tenant Mrs Speedwell,' Six said guiltily. 'She has a passion for spicy hot cross buns.'

'I really like Easter,' Dunfoaming sounded as if she was in a good mood. 'I think it's my favourite time of the year. What I like about it, are the lovely smells. Like marzipan on simnel cakes, spice on hot cross buns, and chocolate, I go all weak at my foundations when I smell chocolate Easter eggs.' As if trying to recall the aromas Dunfoaming sniffed in really deeply.

'Have you left the front door open?' Mr Wyatt Jones shouted to his wife from the bathroom. 'I felt a terrible draft as I got out of the bath.'

Robert Jenkins the gravedigger's son could hardly believe his eyes when he first saw it on display in the shop window. Surely, he thought, this must be the biggest Easter egg in the world. I wonder how long it would take to eat. For almost five minutes, he stood rooted to the spot mentally weighing and measuring it with his eyes.

When he finally managed to drag himself away, he opened the shop door and walked in. 'Please could you tell me the price of that Easter egg in the window.' he asked the woman behind the counter. I would like to buy it for my mum.'

'It's not for sale son,' she replied with a friendly smile. 'We are giving it away.'

Robert returned her smile with a puzzled frown. 'If you are really giving it away, could I have it please?'

'I'm sorry dear, when I said we are giving it away, what I really meant was, it's the prize in the free Easter draw we are running this year for our customers.' She picked up a book of raffle tickets. 'As you can see there are two tickets with identical numbers on each page, every time a customer buys something in the shop I tear off one of the tickets and give it to them. The other half I leave in the book until it's time for the draw. On the Monday morning before Easter, I will tear all of the tickets out of the books and fold them in half, and then I will put them in a big box and shake them up. The next customer who walks into the shop will be asked to pick a ticket out of the box, the ticket the customer picks will be displayed on the egg in the window, and whoever holds the same colour ticket with the same numbers will be the lucky winner,'

Robert looked at her thoughtfully, then, taking some money from his pocket, he said. 'If I buy a Mars bar, will I get a ticket?'

During the following weeks, Robert became a regular customer in the sweet shop, spending most of his pocket money purchasing bars of chocolate. On the Monday before Good Friday, he had a collection of twenty-five tickets.

Five times during the day, he ran to the shop to see if the winning ticket had been stuck to the egg. When he made the journey the sixth time, he was delighted to see that it had. The ticket was blue with the number 202.

Robert's hands shook excitedly as he pulled the wad of tickets from his pocket. He was certain one of his tickets had that number. Eagerly he shuffled through them discarding all but the blue. Then, he laid his seven blue tickets across the palm of his hand and checked the numbers of each one. The excitement that showed on his face when he saw the number 208 quickly turned to a look of disappointment when he realized he had missed the prize by six.

Screwing the once cherished pieces of paper into a small ball, Robert threw them angrily into the rubbish bin outside the shop. Fumbling in his pockets, he pulled out a small handful of coins. With disappointment still showing on his face, he entered the shop and laid the coins on the counter. 'How much is your cheapest Easter Egg?' He asked.

The shop assistant picked up the coins and counted them. 'You've just got enough for a small cream egg.'

As he walked out of the shop holding the egg. He heard the woman behind the counter say. 'I'm sorry that you didn't win the draw, maybe you'll be lucky one next year.'

Easter Day

Robert placed the colourful foil wrapped egg in an eggcup and handed it to his mother. 'Happy Easter Mum,' he said. 'I'm sorry it's only small, but I didn't have enough money for a bigger one.'

'Thank you Robert! You are kind, what a lovely surprise.' Then, planting a loving kiss on his cheek, she said. 'Things don't have to be expensive, it's the thought that counts, and then, she walked from the room.

Moments later, she returned carrying the giant Easter egg.

Robert's mouth and eyes opened wide in amazement when he saw the blue 202 ticket. 'Things don't have to be expensive,' she said with a smile, as she handed him the egg. 'I got this, in exchange for a small piece of blue paper.'

###CHAPTER TWENTY-EIGHT###

April 6ᵗʰ

'They're coming today.' **Twelve shouted excitedly.** 'I heard them talking on the phone yesterday, and the House Doctor promised that he would be here today without fail.'

'Why are the doctor's coming to you?' **Thirteen asked in surprise.** 'Are you ill or something?'

'No, I'm not ill, not in a sickly way. They are coming to fix that little bit of woodworm they found in my loft last October.'

'Those house doctors don't believe in rushing do they? October was six months ago, the contamination could have spread all over you by now.

'Your tenants will have to move out for a week or two you know,' **said Fourteen.** 'The chemicals they will be using are too dangerous for humans to inhale.'

'Mr Jenkins my tenant isn't bothered about being locked out of his house for a couple of weeks, he says he's going to treat it like a holiday. His wife Florrie and their son Robert are going to stay with Florrie's mum and dad. Bernie says he will be quite happy sleeping in his shed at work. He reckons he'll able to have a lie in every morning and still be early for work.'

'What about you?' asked Fourteen. 'You're the one I'm concerned about.'

Twelve gave a sigh. 'It's me that they will be operating on, so I shall have to put up with it, won't I?'

'It isn't going to be something that you are going to enjoy you know.' Although Fourteen had said that he was concerned, it didn't sound like he really meant it. 'I told you last October that once they have finished working, your loft is going to look vile, smell vile, and you are going to feel violently sick. And you'll have a hacking cough and such a throbbing headache you won't feel like talking to any of us for a couple of weeks.'

Twelve suddenly seemed to brighten up. 'If that's going to be the case, maybe I should tell my story now.'

Before any the other houses had time to object, Twelve said. 'I got the idea for my story from Mr Jenkins my tenant; he is always complaining that his wife is the world's worse cook. I've called it. A recipe for Love.'

'I can't stand love stories,' Dunfoaming whispered to Eighteen. 'Shall we talk about something else?'

'You can if you want to,' Eighteen replied, 'but do it softly won't you, so that I can't hear, 'cos I want to listen to Twelve's story.'

'Recipe for Love,' Twelve said again, then, after breathing in deeply, he started the story.

'Pamela paused uncertainly outside the entrance to the fairground fortune-tellers tent and read some of the framed newspaper cuttings proclaiming Gypsy Rose Lee's past suc-

246

cesses. Despite what she read, she couldn't bring herself to believe that anyone could predict the future.

She was about to walk away, when a voice within the tent said. "I can see that the problem you are carrying has become a heavy load fort for you to bear. If you care to step inside, I will be able to relieve you of the bulk of that burden before you leave."

Dressed gypsy style, the fortune-teller sat at a small circular table in the centre of the tent. The old woman looked up from her crystal ball when Pamela entered and gave her a toothless smile. Pamela returned her smile with a frown. 'How did you know I was outside?' she asked.

Gypsy Rose Lee lifted her hand from the orb. "The crystal ball reveals all." Pointing at a chair in front of the table, she said. "Please take a seat."

Pamela looked at the woman suspiciously. 'I have never had my fortune told before. How much will it cost?

The gypsy shook her head. "Bless you dear, I'm not going to tell your fortune, I'm going to help you sort out your cooking problems."

Pamela frowned again. 'How do you know that I'm a really bad cook, I thought my husband was the only one who knew that.'

"I'm a seer," the gypsy replied. "Everything about you is written in my crystal ball."

Pamela's frown became a look of alarm. 'Not everything I hope, surely there are bits of my life that are shrouded from your view.'

As if to change the subject, the gypsy said. "With the amount of cookery programs on the television these days, I cannot understand how there can be so many bad cooks."

'I hardly ever watch television,' Pamela said defensively. 'And when I do, I never watch cookery programs. I find them boring.'

The fortune teller got up from her seat and walked to a bookcase at the far side of the tent. "It's a pity that modern girls aren't interested in cooking," she said, as she pulled a book out of the case. "It helps to hold a marriage together."

Returning to her seat, she thrust the book into Pamela's hand. "The problem with your marriage is, your husband married you, but he is in love with his mother's cooking. The book that you are now holding has saved countless marriages, it will do the same for yours, if you are willing to buy it for £10."

Pamela looked down at the book, titled, Gypsy Rose Lee's Magical Recipes.

"Your marriage will be saved, if you start with the recipe on the first page and work your way daily through the book. I guarantee that his mother's cooking will be a thing of the past before you reach the end."

Outside the tent, Pamela looked down at the book she had just purchased. 'How could I have been so stupid?' she mumbled softly to herself. 'I've just paid £10 to a fortune telling gypsy who also writes paperback, cookery books.'

With the book in her hand, she walked towards the supermarket. 'I might as well use it now that I've bought it,' she said, with a shrug of her shoulders. 'And if Steve isn't happy with the result, he can give it to the dog, like he usually does.'

Shaking her head in a gesture of self condemnation Pamela laid out her shopping on the table. I must be stark raving mad she thought, as she checked the items she had purchased against the list of ingredients needed for the recipe on the first page. They don't look very appetizing to me. I have a feeling that neither Steve, nor the dog, will be enjoying dinner tonight.

Pamela covered the contents of the saucepan with water, then, placed it on the cooker. Her eyes followed her travelling finger across the page, as she recited. 'Diddy cum piddy cum poo, this pot contains the ingredients for a magnificent magical stew. Stir eight times to the left and ten to the right, then, whoever eats this wonderful meal, will be happy, and loving, all through the night.' With a doubtful smile, Pamela closed the book.

Steve's keen nostrils detected the smell of cooking long before he opened the front door, once inside he closed his eyes and sniffed appreciatively at the air. "What a marvellous smell," he said, as Pamela came to meet him. 'I was really hungry when I opened the door, now I'm absolutely starving."

Pamela took hold of his hand and led him into the kitchen. 'I'm glad you said that.' With a smile, she lifted the lid off the saucepan. 'I've been standing at the cooker for hours trying to conjure up a meal that is better than anything you've ever tasted before.'

Whilst he sat eating his meal, Steve seemed lost for words. Pamela however was content to sit watching the changing expressions on his face. She knew the spell had worked, when he looked down at the waiting dog, then, pushing his empty plate towards the centre of the table, he said. "I'm sorry old boy, but tonight you will be eating dog food."

With a contented sigh, he leaned back in his chair and smiled at Pamela. "My mother is a brilliant cook, but she has never served up a meal that comes close to that. It was pure magic." Then, snaking his arm around Pamela's waist, he kissed her ear and whispered. "Shall we have an early night?"

'What about the washing up?'

Steve's lips moved down to her neck. "That can wait until tomorrow."

As they walked from the room, Pamela glanced at the bookcase smiled and said. 'Thank's to my new book, I have finally got the hang of cooking. I'm sure that from now on, you are going to enjoy every meal.'

'It's a good job you told it when you did,' Dunfoaming said excitedly. 'In an hour or two from now you won't feel like talking at all, the house doctors van has just turned into the close.'

Six hours later, as the van drove away. Thirteen whispered sympathetically to Twelve. 'Your operation lasted longer than I thought it would, were they gentle with you?'

'That doctor and his assistant are sadists,' Twelve replied hoarsely, 'they don't even know the meaning of the word gentle.'

'What did they do?'

'They cut out seven of my rafters and replaced them with new ones.'

'I didn't know you were as ill as that!' Eleven gasped in surprise. Seven new rafters is a serious operation.'

'I've been suffering in silence, for six months.' Twelve replied with a soft groan of pain. 'Although I was often in agony, I didn't want to beggar sympathy from the other houses in the close.'

'I bet you're going to make up for it now though,' said Dunfoaming coldly. 'I reckon you'll be moaning and groaning for the next couple of weeks.'

'Oh no I won't,' rasped Twelve. 'From today I'm going to be a listener, I'm so choked up with fumes and pain, I don't intend to say another word until I'm feeling better.'

###CHAPTER TWENTY-NINE###

April 20th

During the course of the morning for sale, boards had been erected in the front gardens of two houses in Piddle Close.

'I knew your owners were going to buy a holiday home in Benidorm, Dunfoaming,' said One, 'but I didn't know that they were going to sell up and move out there for good.'

'That isn't the reason they are selling,' Dunfoaming answered sadly. 'They've decided to split up and go their separate ways.'

'Are they going to get a divorce?'

'Not yet. They've decided to have a six month trial separation first, and then they will decide after that.'

'Why are they selling if they're not divorcing? Surely the best thing would have been for one of them to stay living in you, and in six months time if they decide that they are going for a divorce, then, they could sell up.'

'I think they both know that it's over really, but they don't like admitting it, that's why they decided on a trial separation. And even if they do stay together, they have made up their minds to sell me.'

'I wonder why they want to do that. You're quite good looking. And they don't know that you're the most unpopular house in the close because of your lousy temperament.'

'Mrs Wyatt Jones can't stand living around here any more, she reckons that if she doesn't move soon, Damien will drive her nuts, he's one of the reasons why their marriage has broken up.'

'Have you any idea why you have been put up for sale Two?' Asked One. 'Do you think Damien has driven your owner out as well?'

'I don't think he's been too happy about the smells that come from you when that spin dryer is working,' **Two answered in reply.** 'But he hasn't been driven out. He's buying a house in Cornwall with the lottery money that he won, so that he can be closer to his grandchildren.'

'I can't understand adults,' **Dunfoaming said under her breath,** 'especially old adults. Why on earth would they want to move to be near their grandchildren?   I could understand it if they wanted to move further away.'

'I think he's fed up with being lonely.' **Two answered in reply.**

'How could he possibly have been lonely living next door to Damien? I should have thought an experience like that would have put him off of children for life.'

###CHAPTER THIRTY###

May

'Wasn't it in December last year that the health inspector gave your tenant, the inventor, one week to clean you up or face eviction?' One shouted up the close to Ten.

'There's nothing wrong with your memory, is there One?' Ten shouted back. 'However, your hearing can't be too good if you didn't hear me cheering, when the inventor packed up and left exactly a week after the Inspector called.'

'You've surprise me there, I certainly didn't hear you cheering, if I had I would have joined in. Nor did I see him move any of his furniture. It must have happened at night when I was asleep.'

'You didn't see him move any of his furniture because he didn't have any, he only had rubbish. What little furniture there was scattered around the rooms belonged to his partner. He didn't even say goodbye to her when he sneaked out of my front door at three o'clock in the morning, and all he took with him were the clothes he was wearing, and a pack on his back.'

'Does anyone know where he's gone?'

'His partner doesn't, and she's as pleased as punch about that. I heard her telling Mrs Ledger at Nine that she is going to call the police if he ever tries to come back.'

'What about all of the rubbish that he's left in you, I thought the health inspector told him to clean it up.'

'That's probably why he left. It's going to be a Herculean task cleaning me up. I've probably got more rubbish than there is at the council tip.'

One was about to ask what a Herculean task was, when Dunfoaming beat her to it.

'What's a Herculean task?' she said. 'Is Herculean the name of a cleaning company?'

'You really don't know much do you?' said Ten. 'Everyone knows that Hercules is a hero of classical myth, who possesses tremendous strength and courage. A Herculean task means it will take a gigantic effort to achieve a successful outcome; it will also take four or five workers and about six skips. '

Dunfoaming then tried to prove that Ten had been wrong saying that she didn't know much. '*I know what a skip is.* It's a large open container used for transporting building materials, but in your case it will be nothing more than loads of rubbish.'

As if, One shouting up at Ten had fired the health inspector's memory. A lorry carrying a skip arrived in the close the next day.

'It looks like the Herculean task is about to begin,' Dunfoaming shouted sarcastically as the lorry drove away from Ten, leaving the heavy metal skip standing in the road.

'I'm going to feel so embarrassed when they start loading,' Ten whispered to Eleven. 'All of the people in the close, and the houses as well, will know just how much junk I've been hoarding.'

'You've got nothing to be embarrassed about.' Eleven replied comfortingly. 'It isn't your fault. I'm sure the houses will understand that you were abused by that idiot inventor.'

Two weeks and seven skips later, Ten breathed a long happy sigh of relief. 'I've been given the all clear by the health inspector,' He said happily. 'I am now officially clean.'

Dunfoaming however wasn't at all happy. 'I think there's every chance that I might end up with a family like yours living in me One.' She said downheartedly; when an estate agent opened her front door and held it open for three children and two adults to walk enter.

'Cheer up,' said One. 'They haven't seen around you yet, you never know maybe they won't like you. Anyway I'm sure that they won't be as bad as the Kreamer's.'

'What makes you think that?'

'They've got three girls and no boys.'

Four started to laugh.

'What are you laughing at?' **Snapped Dunfoaming.**

'I just thought that if they decide to buy you, and those three girls are as bad as Damien, then, you are going to end up with three little female monsters living in you.'

'And it will serve you right,' said One. 'I've had to put up with a lot from you since the Kreamer's moved in, now perhaps you'll be getting a taste of your own medicine.'

'That's right,' said Two, siding with One. 'What goes around comes around. That's what they say.'

'I don't think I'm going to bother making up a story,' **Seventeen** shouted at the top of her voice.

'Why not?' **Eighteen sounded disappointed. He had enjoyed all of the stories so far.**

'It would only be a waste of time, there's more going on in this close, than you'll ever find in any story.'

###CHAPTER THIRTY-ONE###

June

It had been a quiet evening in the close. Most of the houses were in darkness by eleven o'clock.

Mr and Mrs Grant had retired to bed in a very high state at half past ten. After checking that the eight one hundred watt electric light bulbs were still burning in the attic, their son Percy followed them fifteen minutes later.

At Five o'clock, Samuel Sprocket opened Dunfoaming's gate, with two bottles of semi-skimmed clanking in his hand, running up the path, he stood them on the doorstep. He was about to return to his van when five police cars drove slowly into the close.

Awakened by the noisy milkman, Dunfoaming was the first house to see the police cars. 'Wake up everyone,' she shouted as loud as she could. 'You won't want to miss this; I think it's the police raid that we've all been waiting for.' Then, when she noticed that two of the cars had stopped outside One, she added. 'And it looks like they intend to arrest Dennis Kreamer as well as the Grant's.'

Walking swiftly back to his van, Samuel Sprocket climbed in and made himself comfortable. He had no idea what was going on, but whatever it was, he intended to sit tight and enjoy it. The nearest thing to excitement he had ever had to on his round before, had happened a few months ago. *He was driving past Number 15 when he noticed that the front door was wide open. Suspecting burglars, he had armed himself with a bottle of milk and walked to the door. Holding it like a club, he was about to ring the bell when he heard a noise behind him. Turning quickly around he was surprised to find Mrs Braithwaite walking down the path towards him in a very short flimsy nightdress. Although he was standing directly in front of her, she didn't seem to notice him. She must be sleepwalking he thought, otherwise she would have seen me. Stepping to one side, he allowed her to walk into the house. She was about to close the door, when she looked at him. 'Good morning milkman,' she said. 'What are you doing on my doorstep? You don't deliver here.' Then, she slammed the door in his face.*

Awakened by Dunfoaming, most of the houses in the close began to talk excitedly amongst themselves.

'Has anyone been arrested yet?' asked Two.

'Give the police a chance to get out of their cars,' said Four. 'Dunfoaming only screamed for us to wake up a couple of seconds ago.'

'Isn't this exciting Dunfoaming?' said Eighteen. 'Do you think they will arrest young Damien as well?'

'I doubt it, but I hope they do. In my opinion he's every bit as bad as his dad.'

'Here you go picking on Damien again,' One shouted hysterically. With two police cars outside and several coppers, climbing out she was nervously wondering what was going to happen next. 'He may be a bit of a handful, but he's never done anything as bad as his dad.'

'A bit of a handful, he's much worse than that,' countered Dunfoaming. 'You wait and see, when they get round to searching his bedroom, I wouldn't be surprised if they find it's an Aladdin's cave of stolen goods.'

'Why should they search his bedroom if he hasn't done anything wrong?'

'He hasn't done anything wrong? What are you talking about; didn't he send begging letters to the Queen, the Prime Minister, and the Leader of The opposition?'

Eighteen seemed to be taking Dunfoaming's side when he said. 'I wouldn't want to be standing on your foundations, or Three's for that matter. Once the police have smashed down your doors and arrested who they came for, they're going to spend days going through your rooms with fine tooth combs searching for evidence, and if they find anything incriminating in Damien's room, then, they will have to arrest him as well.'

'It's a good job he put your name plaque back on the wall then isn't it Dunfoaming?' said One, as the police smashed down her front door and stormed into the house shouting— 'Police raid, stay where you are, this is a police raid.'

Dennis Creamer, normally a heavy sleeper, *Percy's mums biscuits had that effect on him,* was suddenly wide-awake. The front door crashing to the floor wasn't a sound he heard every night, in fact, he had never heard it before and he hoped he would never hear it again. The shouted words 'Police raid, stay where you are, this is a police raid,' brought him instantly to a sitting position. The sound of heavy footsteps pounding up the stairs, were enough to lift him out of his bed.

Standing stark naked with a tin in his hand, Dennis was ramming biscuits into his mouth like someone who hadn't eaten for months. 'Get some of these inside you,' he pleaded, spraying the air with biscuit crumbs, he handed several to his wife.

'Are you mad?' she shouted looking at the clock. 'It's five in the morning. You know that I don't like biscuits, they make me put on weight, and even if I did like them, I wouldn't eat them at this time of the day.'

'I'm not asking you to like them,' said Dennis in a panicky voice. 'If you don't want me to be arrested, then you'd better start getting some of them down you as quick as you can.'

'Haven't you got any romance left in you,' she screamed, 'waking me up from a beautiful dream at five o'clock, just to offer me biscuits.'

Then she hit him.

A heavy boot opened their bedroom door from the outside. The two police officers who entered the room, found Dennis sitting on his wife's chest stark naked ramming biscuits into her mouth as fast as he could. With his own cheeks ballooned like a greedy hamster, he was shouting, 'Just swallow them as quick as you can you silly cow, there's only three left, and then I'll be in the clear. They won't be able to charge me with possession with intent to supply, if we've eaten the evidence.'

'Why do you always have to be different,' his wife snarled up at him splattering his face with masticated biscuit. 'Why do we have to eat them, wouldn't it be easier to flush them down the toilet?'

'We haven't got time for that,' Dennis shouted spraying the arresting officer's boots with biscuit crumbs as he rammed the last three biscuits into his wife's mouth and clamped his hand over her lips. 'Besides that would be terrible waste.'

'Have they been arrested as well?' Two asked Three, when Percy's mum and dad came out of the house with their hands behind their backs.

'Of course they have,' said Dunfoaming. 'They wouldn't be wearing handcuffs if they hadn't.'

'Why have they put handcuffs on Percy's mum?' asked Two. 'Surely a frail looking old lady like her is harmless.'

'You wouldn't be saying that if you had seen the fight she put up in her bedroom.' Three said proudly. 'It only took her about half a minute to put three police officers on their backs after they entered her room. It was fantastic to watch. As soon as they stepped into the room, she crawled out from under her bed and started throwing them about. Luckily one of the officers had the presence of mind to spray mace or something like that into her eyes, but that didn't stop her, even though she couldn't see what she was doing she still went on fighting.'

Two sounded puzzled. 'If she continued to fight after mace had been sprayed in her eyes, how did they manage to get the handcuffs on?'

'They didn't put them on; her husband did it for them.'

'Why on earth did he do that?'

'When he attempted to get out of the bed, she threw him over her shoulder to the floor and when he got up, she did it again, unfortunately he fell against the side of the wardrobe and cut the back of his head.'

Two sounded more puzzled than before. 'Why did she keep attacking her husband?'

'I don't think she knew it was him. She probably thought he was one of the police officers, remember, one of them had sprayed her face with mace, so she was fighting blind. Naturally, Mr Grant didn't appreciate being thrown around the room like a rag doll in front of the police officers, especially when he hadn't done anything wrong, besides he felt embarrassed, his wife is a lot smaller than he is. While she was putting a hold on another officer, he pulled the duvet off the bed crept up behind her and threw it over her head, then, he pulled her down and laid on top of her until a grateful policeman handed him a set of handcuffs which he slipped on her wrists.'

'When they come up for trial, I wonder if the judge will take into consideration the part that he played in her arrest.'

'Look at her now,' **said One.** 'She's kicking the police officer who's trying to get her into the car. I don't suppose she's going to be too happy when she finds out that it was her husband who put her in handcuffs and helped the police.'

'None of us houses really know our tenants, do we?' **said Three.** 'The Grant's have been living in me for nearly six years, and in all that time I didn't believe Mrs Grant would say 'boo to a goose.' But this morning she has singlehandedly beaten up three coppers and her husband.'

As the bruised police officer closed the car door on Mrs Grant, she looked up at him and grinned. Then, she said. 'That will teach you not to go messing with a little old lady who's got a black belt in karate.'

'She doesn't look big enough to be able to throw three police officers and her husband about, does she?' **said Two.**

'You don't have to be big to use karate,' **said Three authoritatively.**

'There are millions of Japanese and most of them are small, but nearly all of them have black belts in Karate.'

'What about Percy?' asked Two. 'Has he got a black belt in Karate, and did he put up a fight as well?'

'No he didn't.' **Three sounded disappointed.** 'When the police went into his room he was as high as a kite and when they led him out of his bedroom with his hands behind his back, he was singing. He'll be coming out in a minute, then, you'll be able to hear for yourself.'

Dressed only in boxer shorts, with a police officer gripping his shoulder, Percy stepped out of the door. As soon as the air hit him, he collapsed to his knees. He was still singing when they carried him to the car.

'Look at him,' **said Three.** 'He's a disgrace to his mother.' He didn't even try to hit a copper.'

'At least he's happy,' **said Two.** 'And judging from the state of him, it will be about a fortnight before he knows he's been arrested.'

Spouting biscuits crumbs out of her mouth like a harpooned whale Mrs Kreamer stopped in the doorway of the house. 'What about my children?' she cried. 'Who's gong to take care of them, my little Priscilla hasn't been potty trained yet.'

'How old is she,' asked the officer sharing her handcuffs.

Mrs Kreamer, sprayed him with the last of the biscuits crumbs. 'She's three and three quarters,' she said.

The police officer looked at her in disbelief. 'How old did you say she is?'

'Are you deaf or something, I said, she's three and three quarters.'

'And she hasn't been potty trained yet?'

'She's nearly there,' said Mrs Kreamer proudly. 'She only wets her knickers occasionally now, and they soon dry in the tumbler.'

The police officer pointed with his free hand at Stuart who was standing with his back resting against one of the police cars drawing in a sketchpad. 'Who's that?' he asked.

Mrs Kreamer dragged the police officer's hand up into the air and waved at Stuart. Beaming with pride, she said. 'He's the middle one of my three children. He's going to be a great artist one day.'

'How old is he?'

'Nearly ten, but he draws and paints like a genius. Didn't you notice his paintings of sunflowers when you broke in, they're on nearly every wall in the house?'

'He must be a really cool character,' the police officer replied. 'Most children his age would be crying and screaming their heads off, if they were witnessing their parents being taken away, but he's casually leaning against a police car sketching the arrest.'

Mrs Kreamer shook her head. 'I don't think he's doing that, more likely he's drawing your face.'

The police officer seemed impressed, 'I've never had my portrait drawn before.'

'I doubt if you'll like it,' she replied with a grin. 'If he's drawing you as he see's you, it will probably be a grotesque caricature, and it will probably end up as the centre of a giant sunflower.'

'Standing in a close like this, we don't get to see very much in the way of entertainment.' said Five, But when we do, it can nearly always be placed in the top class category.'

'I wish I could wave and shout goodbye when they move off,' said Three, 'I really hated Percy Grant and his mum and dad living inside me. It would be nice to let them know that I'm glad to see the back of them.'

'You can shout goodbye, if you want to,' said Four. 'But they're not going to hear you, so you'll just have to be satisfied that they've gone.'

'Now that the Kreamer's have been arrested,' Dunfoaming said without any emotion. 'I wonder what will happen to the children.' Then, before any of the houses could answer, she said. 'If the police keep Mrs Kreamer inside, I suppose they will be taken into care.'

'I'm more worried about what's going to happen to me if they end up doing a stretch inside,' said One. 'Will they evict them and smarten me up for a new family? Or will they board me up like they did Eleven, and leave me empty until they've done their time?'

'I doubt if they will board you up, it will mean you standing empty for too long and there's a shortage of good accommodation around these parts.' **Dunfoaming paused as if she was thinking. Then, she said.** 'But I'm forgetting, you're not good accommodation are you? So in your case I should think they will board you up until they've done their time.'

'This is going to be fun,' **said One.** 'Damien is trying to stop the police taking their prisoners away.'

'What can he do?' **said Two.** 'He's only a small boy, and there are fifteen policemen.'

'Don't underestimate him.'

'But, Mr Kreamer and Mrs Kreamer and the Grant's, have already been handcuffed and arrested.'

'It isn't the end of the story,' **said One.** 'They won't be going anywhere just yet.'

'How do you know that?' **asked a puzzled Two.'**

'Whilst they were inside arresting his mum and dad, I saw Damien sneak out of the house with five bananas, then, he stuck one up each of the police cars exhausts.'

UKUnpublished
.CO.UK

Are you an Author?

Do you want to see your book in print?

Please look at the UKUnpublished website:
www.ukunpublished.co.uk

Let the World Share Your Imagination

Lightning Source UK Ltd.
Milton Keynes UK
177313UK00002BA/1/P